"Where's Brittany?"

"She has ballet practice after school twice a week. She really misses her troupe in San Francisco."

Michael stood and moved around the bar, his gaze on hers. "When does she get home?"

Liana tilted her chin to keep the connection. "About six."

Michael glanced at the microwave clock. "Hmm. I have thirty-five minutes."

"For?"

Her mouth softened and her breasts rose and fell at an accelerated rate.

Very good. He excited her as much as she did him.

Michael slid his hands around her waist and pulled her against him. "For something I've wanted to do since I met you. Crazy huh?"

"Very crazy and not too wise."

"Um." He moaned when she pressed her body close and drove all reasonable thought from his head. "What if I don't want to be wise?"

"A quick kiss could erase the mystique and let us get our minds back on our lives." She leaned closer and wrapped her arms around his waist.

"Quit talking and we'll see what happens."

Just Plain Lucky

by

Tesa Devlyn

Just Plain Lucky

Cover Art by *Tina Lynn Stout*

The Wild Rose Press, Inc.
PO Box 708
Adams Basin, NY 14410-0708
Visit us at www.thewildrosepress.com

Publishing History
First Champagne Rose Edition, 2013
Print ISBN 978-1-61217-659-8
Digital ISBN 978-1-61217-660-4

Published in the United States of America

Dedication

To Don, my knight in shining armor for 40 years...
To my local RWA group who understands
the voices in my head...
and to my dear friend, Mary,
who on a manual typewriter painstakingly typed
much of the first manuscript I wrote
many years ago.
It won't ever see the light of day,
but it was a labor of true friendship.
And always,
thank you The Wild Rose Press,
for believing in my work!

Chapter One

"Frank, cut the crap, would you? Let's discuss why you really called." Liana clenched the cell phone and her teeth. "Are you tortured with the idea I might have a happy birthday?"

"Are you sure you can handle the truth?"

Liana glanced toward her daughter's bedroom. Thank goodness Brittany was involved tweeting, posting, or updating. She didn't need to hear this conversation. "The truth? What's that supposed to mean?"

"You've never apologized for what you did." His voice raised an octave. Worse than the day she and Brittany left San Francisco, a U-Haul trailer in tow.

She stared at the textured ceiling and groaned. "I've apologized multiple times for what happened. I'm not nor will I ever be happy with the way I handled myself, but the blame isn't entirely mine. How many times did I ask for a divorce? You knew our marriage couldn't work."

"Brittany's my concern. She needs a stable home. Who knows when you'll take off with some other guy?"

The room tilted. Liana weaved on her feet. She backed toward the couch, gripped the upholstered arm and sank to the cushion. "How dare you! I..." She lowered her voice. "Neglect of Brittany had nothing to do with what happened. We should have ended our marriage when we just mildly hated each other." Liana punched the red disconnect button with her thumb and blinked through a haze of anger and shock.

"What's wrong with Dad?" Brittany sailed out of her room, her full lips tight.

Liana struggled to control the anger Frank stirred up like a master chef. "I'm sorry for whatever you heard, but your dad pushes my buttons."

"I know, Mom." Brittany sat beside Liana and folded her hands. "He called me last night all upset about Molly moving out. He wants me to visit over Thanksgiving."

Liana stared at her daughter for a long moment. Brittany had transformed into a beautiful young woman—a clear blend of her mother and father. Her deep auburn hair and mahogany eyes a stamp of the Nash genetics. Liana longed to tell her daughter the truth, but the confession could irreparably harm their relationship.

"You're already visiting your dad over the Christmas holidays. Thanksgiving is my favorite time of year. My entire family will be here."

"I know, but Dad sounds so down. I might cheer him up."

Liana clamped her back teeth. "He plays us against each other and I'm tired of it."

"I wish he'd marry Molly. I really like her; she's so good for Dad."

Liana wrapped her arms around Brittany and hugged her close. "Don't get caught up in the stupidities of the adult world." She gazed into her daughter's sad eyes. "I'm going for a run. When I get back, I'll shower and change so we can meet Shari and Meagan."

"Are you sure you still want to go shopping on your birthday? We could do something else."

"Any time with you is my idea of a perfect day."

Brittany hugged her and skipped back to her bedroom.

Liana's shoulders sagged. For four years she'd walked on eggshells to keep the ugly truth behind her marriage and divorce from Brittany. There were things no child should know about their parents. If she could turn back time, she'd handle her unhappy marriage and divorce in a completely different manner. She gripped her head and closed her eyes. The past couldn't be changed, just used as a measuring rod for what never to do again.

"If you need me, I have my cell."

Brittany stuck her head around the archway into the hall. "Will do. I'll finish my math homework. See you when you get back."

Liana detoured on her way to the back door and smacked a big kiss on her daughter's smooth cheek. "How did I get such a fabulous daughter?"

"Oh, I don't know, just lucky I guess." Brittany smiled wide.

Liana held her close and breathed in the familiar floral scent of Brittany's shampoo. "I've never put much stock in luck. Things happen for a reason, even if we don't understand them." She tucked Brittany's hair behind her ears. "I'd go crazy without you, Brittany Nash. I'm eternally grateful you're my daughter. Now, I'll leave before I get really sappy."

"Watch out for ice!"

Liana stepped out the back door and gasped. Would she ever adjust to the different climate? She'd grown up in the desert of Southern California. When she moved to San Francisco, she'd thought she'd freeze to death, but Montana was even colder.

She stretched and inhaled the unique scents of fall, the crisp air tinged with damp, pungent earth, dying leaves and the hint of smoke from the chimney. She paused to drink in the positive results of her move, not the least of which the distance from Frank.

His obsession and control over her life had reached new heights. The latest threat to take her back to court for full custody of Brittany could destroy both his and her relationship with their daughter. Frank would use Liana's indiscretion and she'd be forced to tell all. Then what?

Liana rounded the corner of the house she'd bought shortly after their move to Kalispell, and cringed at the huge sheet of plastic over what had been the west wall of her living room. It crackled and rustled in the breeze. Frank wasn't her only problem. She needed a new contractor, and fast. Winter would wait for no one. Without the new wall and insulation, they'd have to move—abandon their new house until spring.

She jogged out of the tree-lined lot and into view of town. The vista opened up with the mountains as the backdrop, the bustling town to her right and ahead a few miles, Flathead Lake. On occasion, she'd run as far as the shoreline and, if time and the weather allowed, she'd take a quick swim.

Her close friend Shari had been right to persuade Liana to relocate. In only six months, Liana had signed on as an agent with Flathead Realty, bought a new house, and maybe someday, she'd open an interior design business. Someday. For now, she had to make money and settle things with Frank.

Determined to shrug off her frustration and anger, Liana focused on planting one foot in front of the other, breathe in and puff out to keep her heart rate at a safe level.

House after house, block after block, she ran for the sense of satisfaction and well-being running gave her. Out here, she could control her pace—her breathing—and offset the results from stress and her love for good food and wine.

Liana glanced at her watch. Wow, she'd covered a mile in ten minutes. Not bad. She slowed a bit and wound through an older neighborhood toward the highway leading to Flathead Lake.

Brittany had giggled over the name of the lake until she read the history of the Native Americans who occupied the area. San Francisco had tons of culture, but something about being on the edge of the vast Glacier Park, and in a less inhabited area, fascinated her daughter into reading the history of Western Montana.

What a relief Brittany had settled in and accepted Kalispell as her new home. Of course it helped that Shari's daughter, Meagan, who had been Brittany's best friend from childhood, lived here too.

A chill wind blew off the high snow-capped mountains. She rubbed her upper arms through the thermal jacket she'd thrown on. She'd been so upset over Frank's call, she hadn't thought to wear more layers.

Pausing to glance both ways at an intersection, she placed one foot on the blacktop. Pain shot through her other ankle. She shrieked and spun around. A thin, mangy Border Collie mix sat on the curb, his sad brown eyes pleading for attention.

"You nipped me!" She examined her ankle for blood, but didn't find more than a red spot.

The dog whined and wagged his tail. Liana's heart melted. She slowly moved toward the animal, her hand out to give the dog a chance to stay or run. She'd grown up around her brother's dogs and always thought she'd like to have one.

"Do you want my attention? You've got a collar and a tag too. Can I look at it?" She turned the tag. "Lucky. Your name's Lucky." Goosebumps scattered up the back of her neck. Weird. She'd just told Brittany she didn't hold much value in luck. Of course, she'd referred to random, off-chance events, not to the name of a dog. Nevertheless...

A truck rounded the corner of the housing development and roared toward them. Lucky whined, yelped and ran into the street.

"Lucky, no!" Liana waved her arms at the driver, invisible through the tinted windshield. She could only hope it wasn't some sadistic bastard who enjoyed hurting small creatures. "Lucky, come back!"

Lucky ran smack dab in front of the truck. Brakes squealed and rubber burned. Lucky scurried back a few feet, planted his butt, and stared up at the shiny grill.

Liana hurried into the street and patted the dog. "You silly thing!"

"Silly? Is that all you can say?" a very irritated male voice demanded as he towered over her and the dog.

Liana straightened and squinted against the

morning sky at the broad shouldered man. "What would you like for me say?"

The man shifted to one side and blocked the sun. His features became clear. Damn. Wow. He looked like he'd stepped off a movie set. Of course he'd be the leading man, hands down.

"How about, Sorry you almost hit my dog?"

Liana shook her head to clear it. "What?" He might be absolutely delicious to look at, but his attitude stunk.

"There are leash laws in the city limits. I could have killed your dog."

Liana planted her hands on her hips, the chilly air forgotten. "What about loud trucks? Are there laws about those? Lucky might not have run into the street if you hadn't scared him."

The man blinked his dark amber eyes and slowly shook his head. "Are you for real? My truck is not loud. It's a truck. You scared the hell out of me." He squatted on the heels of his black western boots and patted Lucky's head. "Are you all right, girl?"

Liana took a step back and stared in disbelief as the man baby-talked to the dog. Was he for real? He came off like a jerk to her, but putty for the dog!

"How long have you had Lucky?" He glanced at her under the brim of his black cowboy hat.

"I don't have Lucky. We just met. Poor thing needs to eat and bathe. He has a tag, but he looks too neglected to have an owner."

The man nodded and stood back to his full height, his shoulder eye level to Liana. Just the right height to bury her face in—to lay her head on. She mentally slapped herself. Had she lost her mind?

"In that case, sorry I yelled at you." He scrubbed at

his whisker-roughened face with both hands and looked her up and down. "You must live around here."

Liana tried not to be affected by the sweep of interest. "A couple miles away." Not smart to be too specific.

"Look"—he lifted his hat and forked his fingers through jet black, thick, wavy hair—"it's probably not realistic to expect the dog to follow you home. I can give you a lift."

Her stomach flip-flopped. "I'm not keen about jumping into a stranger's truck. How about we put Lucky in the back and I'll run alongside?"

"You're probably a wise woman." He cracked a smile and held out his hand. "Michael Saxon."

She accepted his gesture. "Liana Campbell." His large, calloused hand wrapped around hers a little longer than she'd like. Heat flared up her arm, and goosebumps skittered over her neck. She glanced around, anywhere but the dark gaze threatening to penetrate her soul.

"You have a lumber rack. Do you build houses?"

"Yeah, I build houses."

Her mind traveled a million miles a minute. A builder. A hunk who built houses and helped rescue stray dogs. "Mr. Saxon, if you have time when you reach my house, I'd like to talk to you about my remodel." Hello? She'd just met the guy was she so desperate to finish her living room? Uh yes, as a matter of fact.

He bumped his hat to the back of his head and raised a dark brow. "Oh yeah?"

"I know it sounds bazaar, but I'm in a bind. I don't expect a bid today."

One corner of his mouth turned up. "Good, because I don't have much time. I'll take a look and get back to you."

"Thank you." She glanced at her watch. "I have to get home before my daughter starts to worry. I'll put Lucky in the back."

"I'll put her in the back." With little effort, he swooped the dog into his arms and set him in the bed of the truck. "Sorry, girl. If you weren't so dirty, I'd put you in the front."

"Oh, I think it's a male."

He glanced at her. "Why?"

Liana shrugged. "I don't know, I just assumed."

Michael grinned and Liana's world tilted. "I checked her out. She's a girl."

Her face warmed. "Well, I'd better get home. I'm sure you'll keep up with me, but I live on Evergreen Road."

Michael's grin widened and his dark brows rose. "Sure you don't want to ride?"

"I'm sure." She moved from one foot to the other to loosen up her joints for the run home. "I'll start out slow so you have time to catch up before I leave this street."

"I think I can keep up." He touched the brim of his hat with two fingers and opened the driver's door.

Liana ran in place until he made a U-turn in the intersection. Acutely aware of Michael Saxon cruising behind her, she built her pace to a full run. Sensations she hadn't experienced for a very long time made her want to move faster. How did she look from behind? Why hadn't she worn warm-up pants instead of leggings? Did her behind jiggle with each step? Did her thighs slosh all over the place? She'd been working out more lately...had it paid off?

Many times before she reached her driveway, she wished she'd taken him up on the ride, fear be damned. Something about Mr. Saxon spoke of trustworthiness and safety. He was no serial killer or a wacko.

Frank's hurtful words from their early morning conversation hurtled back at her. *Who knows when you'll take off with some other guy?* "Go fly a kite, Frank!"

Liana adjusted her breath to slow her heart rate and turned into her drive.

Michael crept behind her in his big truck. Lucky barked and raced around in the bed in excitement. The moment he stopped and killed the engine, Michael hopped out of the truck. Before he or Liana could stop her, Lucky leaped over the tailgate and hit the ground with a yelp. "You poor thing. She's so hungry she aches." Liana cooed to the dog.

"You're probably right." Michael examined the dog. "No to mention her paws are in bad shape."

Brittany rounded the house, her young forehead creased with worry. "Mom? Are you all right?"

Liana brushed dog hair and dust off her hands. "Yes, honey, I'm fine. This is Mr. Saxon. He happened along right after I found Lucky. The poor thing's in desperate need of food and a bath."

Michael shook Brittany's hand. "Good to meet you. You look like you might be my son Leif's age."

"Leif Saxon is your son?" Brittany blinked at Michael, awe in her expression.

"You know Michael's son?" Liana hadn't heard her mention him.

"Everyone knows Leif." She glanced at her mother and grinned. "He's cool and a very talented musician."

"Leif does love to play his guitar." Michael looked toward the house. "Ouch. Looks like you're one step away from camping."

Liana gestured toward the aborted remodel. "More than one step away. We keep a constant fire in the fireplace, but the furnace runs full tilt."

Michael lifted the plastic to expose the framing beneath. "Do you have a set of plans I can borrow?" He assessed the destruction. "I'll need them to work up my bid."

"So, you'll give me a bid?"

Michael glanced at her and his dark eyes did something wild and crazy to her body. "I can't leave two beautiful ladies in distress. What happened to your contractor?"

"He had an emergency and left the state."

"Uh-huh. It's unconscionable to leave a job like this. He should have lined out another contractor. Honestly, I have a full schedule, but I'll do what I can."

"I appreciate whatever you can do. I'll get the plans."

"Might help if I see the inside too. Do you mind?"

Liana's thoughts jumbled. Handsome he might be, but Michael was still a virtual stranger. Yet, something about him said she could trust he wouldn't case her house for theft or assault. If she wanted her house finished, she'd have to trust someone.

"Of course, it only makes sense. We use the back door right now."

"I can see why." Michael anchored the end of the plastic with the front door, just as he'd found it.

Liana led the way around the house to the back door, and into the laundry room. Thank goodness she'd cleaned yesterday, including the cat litter box.

Hurrying into the den, her heart fluttered and her hands trembled as she sorted through her house plans. She picked out the one showing all phases of the remodel. If he could just finish the living room, she'd be very grateful.

She returned to the living room in time to catch Oscar, Brittany's cat, slap Lucky. "It looks like we'll have a problem with Oscar. Maybe I should load Lucky up right now and take her to the shelter." As much as she pitied the dog, she didn't need one more thing on her plate.

"Mom! What if they don't find a home and have to put her down?" Brittany's eyes filled with tears.

Michael crouched between the animals and petted them both. "I'll take Lucky home. Leif's been wanting a dog. I'll run an advertisement. If nothing happens, we'll keep her."

The man grew larger in Liana's estimation by the minute. "Are you sure you don't mind?"

"Not at all." Michael glanced at the plans, rolled them up and tapped them against his leg. "Let's go, Lucky." He grinned at Brittany, and shook hands with Liana.

"Nice to meet you, Mr. Saxon." Brittany smiled back at him. "Please tell Leif hello for me. Mom, I still have to take a shower before we meet Meagan and Shari!" Brittany practically skipped to her bathroom.

"Okay, honey."

Liana trailed through the laundry room after Michael. "I hope we didn't disrupt your day too much.

You were on your way somewhere." She struggled to keep her demeanor professional and not give away the attraction she already had for him.

Michael shrugged. "To tell you the truth, it's been a welcome diversion. My former brother-in-law, who I still count as a brother, got married in Libby yesterday. My ex-wife flew in Thursday and since our children are with me, has stayed at my house. All she can do is grouse about how I didn't stock her favorite brands of booze." He stopped at the end of the house and folded his arms over his broad chest, the plans under one arm. "After a circus last night, I escaped this morning to check on a building project."

"Yes, ex-spouses can be a real joy."

"I take it Brittany's dad is your ex?"

"Yes, he is." Liana had an insane urge to correct that statement, but now wasn't the place or time. Strange how Michael instilled such trust after little more than thirty minutes of meeting him.

Brittany emerged from the house, an old blanket in her arms. "I'm glad I caught you. Can you use this for Lucky?"

"Good thinking." Michael took the blanket and continued to the truck where he folded it into a bed for the dog. He tapped the blanket. "Come on, girl. Curl up on this."

Lucky finally settled down and obeyed. Michael turned to Liana and Brittany with a smile. "How can I contact you about my bid?"

"Oh!" She chuckled. "You need my phone number." Liana dashed to her SUV and grabbed a business card. "Here's my information, both work and cell." Their fingers touched. Michael's gaze caught and held hers.

"I should give you my card too." He fished one from his wallet and handed it to her.

Liana tried not to look like the breathless teenager she'd become inside. "Thanks. I hope your day improves."

"It already has." Michael's sculpted mouth turned up in a sexy grin.

****

Today Liana turned thirty-five. Thirty-five and single. Not that age mattered, but lying alone in bed night after night, did matter.

Maybe Shari was right. She needed to get on with her life, and let Frank know he no longer controlled her. What Shari didn't know, was getting on with her life wouldn't break Frank's control. Only a sympathetic judge could do that.

Oh, but Michael could be worth the risk of stirring up Frank's jealous anger. He tempted her like no other man. If it worked out, and his bid fit her budget, he'd be around a lot. Whoa girl, she reminded herself, you just met him.

After several hours of relentless shopping, Liana chose Ciao Mambo in Whitefish for her birthday lunch. A remodeled and expanded house from the turn of the century, she loved the charm and atmosphere as much as the delicious Italian food.

Shari nudged her as they walked to a table in the dining room. "Okay, what's given you the new spring in your step, and the twinkle in your eyes?"

Liana shrugged. "I didn't realize I had a twinkle in my eyes."

"Okay, when will you tell me about him?"

Liana raised her brows. "What do you mean?"

"Come on, old friend. I know you. Something's changed."

"Your imagination's running wild, my dear friend." Shari and Liana had grown up together in San Diego. When Liana moved to San Francisco with Frank, they'd stayed in touch and visited each other often. Focusing on raising Brittany might have been her sanity, but Shari was the only person she could vent her frustrations to.

They were barely seated around an antique oak table when Brittany hit with both barrels. "Shari, did Mom tell you about Dad's call this morning? Molly moved out and he's really depressed. He wants me to visit over Thanksgiving."

Liana smiled at her daughter. "Sweetie, I really don't want to talk about Frank right now."

"I'm sorry, Mom. I know we're celebrating your birthday, but he sounds terrible."

"I agree, but it doesn't mean we have to change our plans." No matter how much he tries to ruin my day, Liana silently finished.

"Good heavens, when will Frank start acting like an adult?" Shari picked up the wine list and hid behind it.

Liana pursed her lips and resisted the urge to throw her fork at her friend. Shari was right. Frank did act like a spoiled child, but it didn't help to discuss it in front of Brittany.

Meagan darted her gaze from Liana to Brittany and back. Liana cringed. Ugly things could come out of this conversation. "The fact is, Brittany, you can't afford to miss school. Not even a couple days. When your math grade comes up, we'll consider another visit later this winter."

Shari lowered the wine list and laid her hand on Brittany's. "Listen to your Mom, Britt. She only wants what's best for you."

Liana appreciated Shari's support, but at the same time, jealousy reared its ugly head. Since the move to Kalispell, Liana had worked long hours to build her real estate business. Consequently, Brittany spent hours after school and some weekends at Shari's. Her friend had been there for Liana, but she couldn't stop the resentment when Brittany listened to Shari more than she did her own mother.

Liana rolled and unrolled her napkin. "Exactly. I'm being the adult, not Frank. We can't react every time your dad has a crisis. He misses you, and he's angry with me for moving away."

"I know." Brittany blew out a sigh. "I'm sorry I brought it up."

"That's okay, sweetie. Let's just enjoy our lunch, or is it dinner?" Liana snatched the wine list from Shari. "Hmm, since Brittany has her daytime driver's permit, we should order a bottle. You girls can have a virgin cocktail if you'd like."

"Cool." Brittany grinned at Meagan. "I'll have a virgin margarita, and I get to drive home."

Shari grabbed the wine list from Liana, and signaled to the server. She ordered a bottle of Chianti, and waited for the girls to order their drinks before she leaned toward Liana.

"Maybe you should call Frank tonight, and convince him he should propose to Molly."

"Humph!" Liana shook her head. "Are you loony?

Frank listen to me about his love life?" Shari had been with Liana through Jack's deployment, his death, her marriage to Frank, Brittany's birth and the list went on, but Shari didn't know half of what drove Frank.

"Maybe if you stress how good Molly is for him, and how much Brittany likes her, he'll let go of you, and start a new life." Shari shrugged. "It's worth a try."

Liana nibbled on her bottom lip. If Frank stopped his obsession over Liana and their failed marriage, he might fall in love with Molly. They could even have children. After the things he'd said to her this morning? Before he entered a new lasting relationship, he needed to learn how to have one.

The server returned with the girls' drinks and presented the wine.

Shari swirled the Chianti in her glass. "How goes the search for a new contractor?" The main restaurant door opened and several people stepped into the entry.

"Interesting you should ask. I met someone this morning and he promised me a bid. I'd like to look at his work." She pulled out his business card. "Maybe I should call and ask for the addresses of the houses he's built or remodeled. We could take a look after lunch."

"I'd love to see the homes and the builder." Shari raised her glass and clinked it with Liana's.

Liana raised her wine glass to her lips just as a group of people passed their table. The familiar scent of a man's cologne drifted by. She swallowed hard and glanced up.

The man she'd fantasized over for the past few hours stood two feet from her table. When their gazes met, his warmed.

"Michael."

17

"Hey there." He graced Shari and Meagan with his killer smile and greeted Brittany. Liana introduced them.

"Michael?" a feminine voice called. The stunning owner of the voice sashayed to his side and looped her arm through his.

Liana wanted to crawl under the table. Her perfectly styled hair was almost as dark as Michael's and her eyes a jewel-tone blue. Contacts? Her lips were full—no doubt from injections—and pouted to the extreme. "Are these friends of yours?"

Condescension filled her eyes and dimmed her beauty. Liana lived with an emotionally controlling man for ten years. This woman couldn't intimidate her, just made her realize how foolish she'd been to daydream about a delicious man like Michael.

Michael's eyes narrowed and he unhooked himself from the woman. "This is my ex-wife, Meredith."

"Meredith." Liana pushed her chair back and shook the glamorous woman's hand. Looks definitely hadn't been what ended their marriage. They could successfully grace a magazine cover.

"Liana." Meredith's full lips tightened.

"Michael's agreed to bid on my house remodel." Liana threw the verbal dart and it struck.

Meredith blinked and pulled back her shoulders. "Of course he has." She turned to Michael. "Darling, I think I'll join Leif and Greg."

The moment Meredith left Michael smiled and folded his arms. "Sorry about that. If you're interested, I'll give you the addresses of the houses I've either built or remodeled. Would you like to check them out?"

Liana didn't have to glance at Shari to read her

friend's mind. She'd think Liana should check out whatever Michael offered. Liana cleared her throat. "We just ordered, but we could look at them later."

Michael sent a quick glance over his shoulder. "If I didn't have obligations, I'd give you the tour."

"Thank you, but the addresses will be very helpful."

"How long have you lived in Kalispell, Michael?" Shari fingered the stem on her wine glass, her expression openly assessing.

"Two years. I built high-end houses in Oklahoma City, but got tired of the rat race."

"Impressive. I'm eager to see your work. I hope you're the knight in shining armor for Liana." She smiled at Liana, one brow cocked.

Liana could have choked her. "Michael, I don't want to keep you from your party. We'll be here for a while." She gestured to her table. "So don't worry about the addresses right now."

Michael stared at her for another moment. Liana flushed. Shari would have a heyday with her later.

His eyes were just as compelling as she remembered. From head to foot, Michael was the most handsome man she'd ever met. Not to mention, one of the nicest. Her jealousy of Meredith, turned to sympathy for Michael.

"I'll do that." One corner of his mouth turned up in his signature grin. Michael nodded at Shari and the girls before he turned to join his family.

Liana tore her attention from his backside and sat down. Good heavens, he'd changed into worn, form hugging Wranglers. Her heart would never be the same.

The food, the wine, and spending the day with her

best friend and their girls, made this one of her best birthdays. Liana hadn't relaxed so much for a very long time, and hadn't tingled with such awareness for even longer. Halfway through lunch, Michael presented her with a paper napkin he'd used to jot down the addresses.

He pulled out the chair between Liana and Brittany. "I suspect you'll favor the remodel here in Whitefish. It's very similar to your plans."

Liana glanced at the addresses, but was preoccupied with the long finger pointing at them. His nails were clean and cut short, and his fingers had tiny scars here and there. The hands of a working man.

She looked up.

Michael's gaze met hers.

Brittany reached across Michael and snatched the napkin from him. "Since Mom's having wine with lunch, I'm the driver."

Michael leaned back and smiled at Brittany. "Good idea. No drinking and driving."

"I had driver's education this fall and drove in Whitefish." Brittany straightened up in her chair and met Michael's glance, as if daring him to doubt her.

"Uh-huh. Good deal. In that case you should find the golf course and the house." He lifted his square chin at the napkin and winked at Brittany. She blushed.

Liana warmed with gratitude for the attention he paid her daughter.

"Well…" Michael pushed the chair back and stood. "I'd better return to my lunch before Leif finishes it off."

"I saw Leif was with you! Is he your son?" Meagan planted her chin on her palm and beamed up at

Michael.

"He is. Do you know him from school?"

"Everyone knows Leif, don't they, Brittany?" Meagan couldn't quite stifle a giggle.

"Yep." Brittany shrugged. "Michael and I talked about Leif this morning."

"Huh." Michael's dark brows arched. "He's so involved in school and basketball, I didn't think he had time to socialize."

Meagan nodded emphatically.

Liana thought it time to step in and let him gracefully escape the teens. "Thank you for the information. I'll call you after I see the houses."

"Sounds good." Michael held up two fingers as if to tip the western hat he must have stashed under his chair. "Pleased to meet all of you. Brittany, be sure you get everyone home safe, okay?"

Brittany smiled. "I will."

Liana hadn't been sure how her daughter would react if a man gave Liana more than casual attention; or had he? She was so aware of Michael, she could have misread his glances, and how the tone of his voice changed when he spoke to her.

"Yes, well,"—Shari cleared her throat when Michael left to rejoin his party—"I'd hire him on looks and charm alone." Liana nudged her under the table, and sent her a tight look.

Shari laughed. "I said I'd hire him. You do what you want."

The teens shook their heads at their mothers and resumed eating their lunch and discussing Leif Saxon.

Chapter Two

Liana floated on her stimulated senses through the rest of lunch.

Even when Shari insisted she pay the check, Liana didn't argue. She was too distracted with the table in the far corner of the dining room, right over Shari's left shoulder. She wondered how Michael handled his ex, but tried not to glance their way as she followed the girls to the door.

Brittany almost skipped with excitement as she climbed into the driver's seat. Meagan groused about having to sit in the back instead in front with her buddy. They all clamored into the SUV and fastened their seat belts before Brittany slowly backed out of the parking spot, and pulled onto the street. Liana's heart fluttered when they passed the big black truck bearing the Saxon Construction sign.

The house on the golf course looked exactly like what Liana had in mind. She called the listing agent for the entry code.

"Wow," Shari said, meandering through the living room and kitchen. The girls bounded off to check out the bedrooms.

"I agree." Liana crouched and ran her fingertips over the hardwood floor. "This is what I envision for my house."

"Perfect. All you have to do is snag, I mean hire,

Mr. Saxon."

"You're hilarious." Liana wandered to the bar for a closer look at the oil rubbed bronze pendant lights.

"I saw how you two looked at each other. It's magic. Love at first sight."

"Shhh." Liana held a finger to her lips and shook her head. "All I need is for Brittany to tell Frank." She moved closer to Shari. "Frank's call this morning was excessive, even for him." She sighed. "I want to tell him to buzz off, but not at the price of placing Brittany in an even more difficult situation."

The girls returned and cut off their conversation. Liana had a strong attraction for Michael, but if she acted on it, Frank might become more volatile. Pushed too far, he'd use his trump card and tell Brittany the divorce was due to Liana's affair. The one she didn't technically have, but that didn't matter to Frank.

"Okay, I like the flooring and the pendant lights. Let's move on to the next house. It's in Kalispell, not far from the airport."

The next house was occupied so they couldn't see the inside, but the outside showed the same high quality workmanship of the one in Whitefish.

"Thanks for tagging along, guys." Liana stashed the notebook in her purse and fastened her seat belt. "It's Sunday night. Back to school and work tomorrow."

"Speak for yourself." Shari stretched her legs and yawned. "If Richard has a job tomorrow, I'll watch some soaps and eat bonbons."

"Yeah, right." Liana chuckled. "You've never been idle in your life. The title company will call you back to work any day."

"Be real, Li. The real estate market's still stagnant. You're one of the handful of agents who are busy right now."

"Yes, but this trail of referrals will run out and I'll struggle like so many others."

"You could start your design business."

Liana twisted in her seat to face Shari. "In this market? How many people can afford a designer?"

"It's a great idea, Mom!" Brittany glanced from the corner of her eye, her attention on the road. "You've wanted to get back into interior design since I can remember."

"Yes, she has, Brittany, and don't let her forget it." Shari reached forward and patted Brittany's shoulder. "She never should have left the firm in San Diego, but Frank had to further his career."

Liana cringed. Would Shari never let up?

Brittany pulled into the Collin's driveway. Liana got out and hugged Shari. "Thank you for lunch and for being there. I didn't meant to snap at you, but I can't start my business right now. I need to find more clients and become better established."

"Hey, just think about it, all right? I'd never lead you down the wrong path." Shari looped her arm through Meagan's. "Ciao!"

Liana climbed back into the SUV and fastened her seat belt. "Homeward, James."

"Funny, Mom!" Brittany guided the vehicle out of Shari's driveway. "I really like Mr. Saxon. He talks directly to me instead of pretending to make you happy."

"Yes, he's very nice, and very talented. I'll call him tonight about the bid on the remodel."

"Cool! Can he remodel my bedroom too?"

Liana chuckled. "We'll see after the living room's finished. Thanksgiving will be here before we know it and Grandma would faint if she saw the hole in our house."

"So would Grandpa!"

Liana looked at the passing scenery. "I'm not sure Grandpa's coming. I haven't heard."

Brittany sighed in dramatic fashion. "I hope he does. I really miss both of them. It's so stupid when people get divorced."

"I know, honey. It's not fun for anyone."

"Why did Grandpa and Grandma split up? I mean, what's the point when you're that old?"

Liana chuckled. "They weren't this old when they divorced. I was twelve when they split up. Grandpa was gone most of the time with his Naval Career, and Grandma was lonely. She got tired of waiting for him and snapped."

She snapped when she learned he'd had an affair. Poor Mom. She'd had a rough life, practically raising Liana and her two older brothers on her own. Liana had barely spoken to her father since she found out what caused their divorce.

Brittany pulled into the driveway and cut the engine.

They hurried into the house and rubbed their arms against the chilly air. Liana immediately crumpled paper to revive the fire in the fireplace.

How long before she had to tell Brittany the details of her parent's breakup and hers?

Their problems had shaped some of her ideas about relationships. Her father's choices had scared her away from committing to Jack.

Jack's excitement over his Naval Air career might have swayed if he knew a baby was on the way, or he might have forged on and left her to raise their daughter while he traveled all over the world. She didn't have the courage to risk her heart, so she didn't tell Jack about her pregnancy and he died in the training mission without knowing about Brittany.

The familiar ache pinged her heart. She clutched her hair with both hands. It did no good to bring it all back; cry over what might have been. She had a daughter to raise, their daughter. She also had Frank to placate.

She picked up her phone. Michael might solve her house problem and at the same time bring things into perspective. She'd come back to earth and realize he might be the most handsome man she'd ever met, but he didn't reciprocate her attraction.

Her call went straight to voice mail. Was he with Meredith?

Forcing herself to stay calm and detached, she left him a message and stared into the fire. The seconds ticked by. Who was she kidding? She had to see more of Michael Saxon.

****

Monday morning, Liana drove to work determined to catch up on the stack of paperwork she'd made no progress with on Saturday. Today held a completely different distraction: Michael and the restless night she'd spent dreaming about him.

Michael Saxon, who hadn't returned her call.

The minute she sat at her desk, her clients the Cummings's, called to request she meet with them for lunch at their rented condo in Whitefish. If all went well, they'd make an offer on a house on Whitefish Lake. If the sale closed in thirty days, she'd have an advance for a contractor. Courtney Cummings also expressed an interest in a condo at Big Mountain Resort. Two sales to the same clients would bring some financial relief.

With lunch traffic to contend with, she left her office at eleven. Bundled in her long wool coat, she slipped and slid across the ice coated parking lot. Her Italian fashion boots weren't cut out for winter weather. She'd been so upset with Frank yesterday, she'd forgotten to buy sensible winter boots.

The hybrid SUV quickly warmed. She pushed out of her coat and set in on the heated passenger seat. If she hit the traffic just right, she'd stop to buy a bottle of Courtney's favorite wine to accompany lunch.

Her mind on the negotiations, she drove toward the gourmet shop. Three cars ahead, the traffic light turned red.

"Damn!"

She glanced in the rearview mirror and calculated the risk of making a sharp left turn into a side street. A car pulled up snug behind her. Too late now. Drat it, she'd be late if she took the time to get the wine.

Her phone rang. Liana fished it out of her oversized bag. Maybe the Cummings wanted to postpone the meeting. "Hello?"

"Liana, it's Frank."

"Frank, I'm in traffic at the moment, and running late for an appointment." At least she would be if she got tangled up in a conversation with him and had to pull over.

"I'll get to the point. I want Brittany to spend a long weekend here. Right away."

Her stomach roiled. "Frank, you've already hammered Brittany about Thanksgiving, which, as you well know, is my favorite holiday."

"If you lived in San Francisco, it wouldn't be an issue."

"No, there'd be plenty of other issues to deal with. We agreed she'll spend Christmas with you. I'll book our flights right away."

"Our flights? You're coming with her?"

"Only to meet you before I catch a connecting flight to San Diego."

"Liana, this separation isn't working."

"Separation from me or Brittany?" She drummed her fingertips on the steering wheel. The large pickup ahead of her inched forward. So did she.

The large, black pickup.

Her heart fluttered. She caught the driver's reflection in the side mirror. Square jaw peppered with dark whiskers, full bottom lip and a slightly crooked nose, shadowed by a dark cowboy hat.

Michael.

Her breath caught as he placed a travel mug to his mouth and took a drink. That mouth. Oh my, she'd thought of little else since she met him.

Transfixed, she ran her gaze over his broad shoulders and the glimpse of black hair brushing his collar just below the brim of his hat. From memory she pictured his eyes. Deep amber. Intense. Passionate.

"Liana, are you there?" Frank's irritated tone jerked her out of her fixation.

The light changed and the line of traffic flowed

through the intersection. Liana stayed on his trail and thought back to their meeting yesterday in Whitefish. He'd looked so good in Wranglers and a white shirt, and he'd been so sweet to Shari and the girls.

"Liana!"

"I'm here, Frank. For heaven's sake, I told you this isn't a good time."

Brake lights flashed. Liana hit her brakes—a second too late.

The front end of her SUV connected with Michael's tailgate.

Mortification vanquished lust.

"Damn!"

"What is it? What happened? Is Brittany with you?" Frank's tone jangled across her nerves like a saw over metal.

"Frank, this is why I don't like to discuss things while I'm driving. I just bumped into someone so I have to go. I'll call you later." She disconnected the call in the middle of Frank's objections.

The driver's door of the pickup flew open. Michael's long legs, covered in soft washed blue jeans, swung out of the truck followed by the rest of his gorgeous body. Liana rested her head against the seat and resigned herself to a lecture.

His delicious mouth was set, his jaw tense, and just as she thought she could handle an angry man, he tipped his hat back and furious amber eyes met hers. Nothing like his smoldering expression when their fingers touched as he handed her the napkin with the addresses of the houses he'd contracted.

Before she could vacate her vehicle, he stood at her door, his arms crossed over his broad chest, one hip angled as if braced for an attack. Well, she'd like to attack him, but not from anger. She hit the button to roll down the window.

"If you wanted my attention, you could have called instead of whoever you had on the phone when you hit me."

Liana opened her door and slid from the seat. She brushed past him to survey the front of her vehicle. Luckily, both rigs were built tough, and she hadn't been going very fast.

"Yes, well, I generally don't use the phone while driving, and I did call you last night." Liana glanced back at Michael.

He was not happy with her.

She pulled her cell phone from the clip on her belt and glanced at the screen. Eleven-twenty. "Hey, I'm sorry I hit your truck. I'll give you my insurance information, and we'll be on our way. I'll call you after my appointment."

A city police officer pulled up, his lights flashing.

Michael followed her back to her car door. "Are you always distracted behind the wheel?"

Her proof of her insurance in hand, Liana slid back out. "Excuse me?"

He propped his hands on his hips. "You just rear ended my truck."

Liana had been prepared to accommodate him in every way possible. Well, yes maybe too much, but now sex was the farthest thing from her mind and so was being nice!

"Morning folks, everybody okay?" The officer approached them and glanced back and forth, no doubt aware of the sparks between them.

"I'm just dandy, officer." Michael lifted the chin Liana had admired before the accident. His eyes narrowed. "I'll be late for a job bid and probably lose it. Other than that and a repair bill, I'm a-okay."

Liana's jaw dropped. The nerve of him! Never mind her part in the accident. Did he have to be so callous? So rude? Nothing worse than a hot looking guy who turned out to be a smart-ass jerk.

Liana propped her hands on her hips. A gust of cold wind blew through her linen slacks. She fought against a shiver, but lost.

"Officer, I'll take responsibility. I hit this man's truck and I'll be happy to give him my insurance information so he can be on his way."

"Well," the officer drawled and tugged up his uniform pants, "there is the matter of inattentive driving."

Liana's mouth gaped. "I will take care of Mr. Saxon's truck."

"The law is the law, little lady." The officer puffed out his chest, more than Liana would have thought possible.

"I don't believe this!" She folded her arms and rubbed them against the chill. Her cashmere sweater didn't protect her against the early winter weather.

Michael shook his head and slipped by her to reach into the SUV. He grabbed her coat and placed it on her shoulders. "Here, you're freezing." His tone had marginally softened.

She could understand his distress over the inconvenience of having a damaged truck, but really!

"Officer, I don't want to press charges against Ms. Campbell. She'll cover my expenses and that's all I ask.

Can we go now?"

The officer ran his tongue around in his mouth and pushed it against one cheek. "I suppose if you're satisfied Ms. Campbell will compensate you, we'll wrap this up with a warning ticket. Ma'am, I want you to pay attention while driving."

"Yes, Officer. I'll be more careful. Thank you for not adding a ticket to my other considerable expenses."

The officer ripped the ticket off the pad he'd scribbled on and handed it to Liana. "I want to see this truck when it's repaired, Mr. Saxon. Bring the paid in full receipt from Ms. Campbell's insurance company. If all is in order, we'll drop the matter."

Michael thanked the officer and waited for him to climb into his patrol car before he turned to Liana. "Hell of a way to meet up again."

Liana's heart refused to behave no matter how irritated she'd been with him moments ago. "I called you last night to discuss the remodel. Didn't you get my voice mail?"

He stepped closer and blocked the sharp wind. His spicy scent mingled with fresh cut wood swept around her and reawakened the excitement she experienced every time they were close.

Her love life had been far from perfect. She'd spent ten unhappy years in a loveless marriage with Brittany her only bright star. She'd given up on ever meeting a man who could fulfill her expectations of a relationship.

"No, I didn't get it." He glanced at his phone and frowned. "I do have a voice mail. Sorry, I was probably busy fielding Meredith's nonsense. By the way, I placed the ad for Lucky this morning. I hope no one responds because Leif wants to keep her."

He slipped his phone back in the holster at his hip and placed his hand on the roof of her car. She couldn't tear her gaze from his. Deep amber eyes fringed with dark lashes assessed her and gave her a glimpse of the man inside.

He scrubbed at his face with his free hand. "Look. I'm sorry I yelled at you. I haven't slept well for two nights. When you hit me, I lost it."

"I'm sorry I hit you. You're not the only one with stress. Would it be possible to connect on the remodel later today? I saw the house in Whitefish and I really like your work."

"You saw the inside?"

"Yes, I'm a realtor and I called the listing agent for the lock box code."

Michael slowly nodded, appreciation in his eyes. "How about over dinner?"

A car stopped behind them. Michael waved it around, but the driver wasn't happy at the moments delay. He shook his head and emphatically pointed his index finger.

"Uh, I have to meet with clients in Whitefish right away. I'll file a claim with my insurance agent when I return to the office."

She didn't want to leave him, but they were in a bad spot on the street. The lunch rush had started and soon there'd be oodles of traffic.

He wrung at the back of his neck with one hand. "Is that a no to dinner?"

The image of a crackling fire, a glass of wine and Michael, flashed through her mind. "Not if it includes our children." She didn't trust herself alone with him.

"Not a problem. I'll bring Leif."

Liana tingled from head to toe. Michael had experienced two weird encounters with her and still wanted to spend time together. He didn't mind having the teens with them. As a single parent, he was the answer to a prayer and it scared her.

"Six o'clock okay?" She just hoped she wasn't rushing into disaster.

****

Michael stepped out of the shower and toweled his hair.

Damn. If he meant to impress Liana, chewing her out wasn't the way to go. She made him crazy with an awareness he hadn't felt in—he didn't remember when. He wanted to hold her. Kiss her. Hell, she threatened his resolve not to get intimately involved with a woman until Leif was out of the house. To complicate things, she clearly had ex-husband issues. Did he really want to disrupt the peace he'd found for him and his son?

Michael pulled on a pair of jeans and a new chamois shirt before he headed toward the kitchen for a cold beer. The clatter of Lucky's toenails on the wood floor signaled the pooch was on his heels. Michael patted the dog's head. "You are a lucky dog, and if I'm not careful, I might be too."

He sucked in a deep breath. Liana Campbell had to be the most complex and sexy woman he'd ever met.

"Dad, do I have to go with you?" Leif ambled out of his room, his hair standing on end, his mouth drawn down on one side.

"Wouldn't you rather go than stay home alone? I thought you liked Brittany Campbell."

"Her last name's Nash, Dad. Yeah, she's all right."

Michael frowned. "Her mom's last name is

Campbell. I just figured they'd be the same."

Leif raised a brow in a very adult way. "A lot of women keep their original name. Until Mom moved to California, I hoped she would. My friends razzed me every time her name popped up in the police blotter for DUI."

"Humph." Michael drained the bottle of beer and set it in the recycle box under the sink. "Regardless whether she deserves it or not, you need to respect your mother."

"Isn't respect earned, Dad? She needs to get her act together."

"Okay, back to the dinner plans. It's important to me that you go."

"Oh, all right." Leif ran a hand through his messy hair making it spike even more. "I'm worn out from arguing with Mom all weekend. She just doesn't get that I'm happy here."

Michael's heart broke from the misery on his son's face. "It isn't easy, is it? She's determined to lay the guilt on until you move to California. Don't let her get to you. If she needs a handyman, she can hire one. I'm proud of how you've turned around since you moved to Kalispell."

"Thanks, Dad. Sometimes I feel sorry for her and other times…she's made her life hard all on her own." He finger combed his hair. "I'll be ready to leave in ten."

"Thanks, Leif. I want to help Liana with this remodel. You'll understand when you see the house."

Leif paused in the doorway. "I'm sure I'll understand when I see her."

"Get going, buddy." Michael tried to sound stern,

but chuckled.

He'd do whatever he had to, to make his bid on Liana's remodel work. It'd give him time to explore this crazy attraction. She evoked a protectiveness in him that made him want to be the knight in shining armor her friend Shari had mentioned. He couldn't wait to see her again—her short, messy blonde hair and mossy green eyes.

He couldn't fault her urgency to make real estate deals. He'd spent plenty of his life chasing the almighty dollar. Maybe he could teach her to slow down and enjoy life.

A tiny tune cut through his thoughts. He snapped up his cell phone. "Saxon Construction."

"Hello, Michael?"

His blood instantly heated. "Liana? Is everything all right?"

"Yes, we're fine. It just occurred to me that we should look at the plans during business hours."

The heat in his midsection cooled. "Evenings are when I work on plans. I have two other projects in the works. The sooner we settle on a bid, the sooner the subcontractors will start on your house."

Silence stretched over the phone connection.

"Liana?"

"Okay. Why don't we meet after dinner? About seven?"

Was she afraid dinner looked like a date? They'd have two teenagers with them. He could hardly take advantage of her.

"If that's what you want." He forked his hand through his damp hair. "See you at seven."

Michael snapped his phone shut and glared at it.

Damn.

Frustrating didn't begin to express his feelings for Liana. She stirred him up then jerked him around.

He'd better start working out at the gym.

Chapter Three

"Wow, Dad. This looks serious." Leif slid out of the truck the moment Michael brought it to a stop in front of Liana's sorry looking house.

He lifted the plastic. "Gosh, there's nothing there!"

"Tell me about it." Liana appeared in the living room, rubbing her arms from the chill. "However, we do still use the door."

Leif flinched and dropped the plastic. Michael chuckled and patted his son's shoulder. "Startled you, didn't she? Let's go in."

Michael led the way to the back door. His stomach churned with anticipation like a kid on his first date.

Liana opened the door as they rounded the house.

Michael grinned at her. "Sorry about that. Leif is too much like his old man."

"There's nothing wrong with curiosity." Liana ruffled her hair and stepped back to let them enter. "It's good to see you again, Leif. We didn't formally meet yesterday at Ciao Mambo. I'm Liana, and I think you know my daughter, Brittany?"

Leif gave his dad a side glance. "Nice to meet you, Ms. Campbell."

"Please call me, Liana."

A fire blazed in the fireplace, but the forced air furnace blew full force. Her electric bill must be steep.

Liana led the way to the dining room and gestured

toward the table, positioned in front of double-sided fireplace. "Please have a seat. I have to apologize, Leif. I forgot about Brittany's school play rehearsal tonight. She has to leave right away so you'll be stuck with your dad and me."

Leif shoved his fingers into the front pockets of his jeans and rocked back on his heels. "Brittany, do you have a ride to the school?"

"Jennie's mom. She'll be here soon."

"Why don't I drive you?" Leif turned to his dad. "Can I borrow the truck?"

"Sure," Michael said, impressed with his son's intuition. "As long as it's okay with Liana."

"It's very considerate of you, Leif. Brittany, does Jennie have a cell phone so you can save her mom a trip?"

Michael clamped his hand on his son's shoulder and looked around the house. While Liana made sure Brittany was lined up for the evening, he pretended to explore the exposed studs he'd already checked out on Sunday.

Liana joined him in the living room, shook her head and smiled as the kids bantered their way out the door. "Oh, to be so lighthearted again."

Michael's chest tightened with emotion. She was so damned beautiful. He wanted to pull her into his arms and make use of the thirty minutes it'd take Leif to drive to the high school and back.

"What do you think?" Liana folded her arms under her breasts and glanced around the room.

She didn't want to know what he thought. Michael cleared his throat. "The roof will have to be jacked up while the rotted studs are replaced. There'll be some

39

drywall damage."

"Whatever it takes to get the job done." She sighed. "I just want it finished by Thanksgiving. My entire family will be here."

Michael fought the urge to promise her the world. Her perfume wafted around him and drove him crazy along with her snug blue jeans and fuzzy sweater. Get a grip, Saxon.

He'd done fine before they met yesterday morning. He didn't really want a woman in his life…did he? The past two days with Meredith should have reminded him what could happen.

Liana gave him the grand tour of the rest of the house and pointed out plans for future remodels. When they stepped into her bedroom, the sight of her big bed and female trappings sent a flame of desire through him.

"Oops!" She grabbed a black lace nightie off her pillow and stuffed it under the comforter. "Guess I didn't pick up before you arrived."

Her face pink, she hurried out of the bedroom. "How about I open a bottle of wine? We can have a glass while we go over the plans."

"Sounds good." Michael followed her to the kitchen and unrolled the plans on the granite counter top. "Looks like your kitchen had a remodel."

Liana nodded as she worked the cork from a bottle of merlot. "It's what sold me on the house. That, and the secluded lot. I like everything about the kitchen, and it's the most difficult room to live without."

"For sure. You can rough it as long as the kitchen and at least one bathroom works."

She poured the dark red wine. "After I left the

scene of the crime this morning, I not only made it to my meeting, but I also wrote up an offer for a condo on Big Mountain. How did your day go? Do I owe you damages for job loss?"

Michael thanked her when she set a glass next to his hand. "I made the meeting and got the job, so you're off the hook."

"Whew! Glad to hear that. Did my voice mail ever arrive?"

"It did." Michael nodded. "You loved the house in Whitefish and want to talk about it. It's one of my favorites too."

Liana climbed onto the wrought iron barstool next to his and crossed her legs. "My favorite aspects are the high ceilings and how the light streams in from so many directions. The flooring is exactly what I had in mind, and I love the pendant lights over the bar."

Michael grinned as he fingered the stem of his glass. "We can sketch those ideas into your drawing."

"Wonderful. I have a lot of ideas, but mainly the living room has to be finished by Thanksgiving."

"So you said. We'll cut it close, but it can happen. I'll provide you with references before I leave tonight. One thing's for sure, whether you hire me or someone else, the work needs to be done right away. Another month and we'll see some serious snow." He held up his wineglass. "Here's to snug houses and pregnant dogs."

Liana blinked. "Pregnant? I guess that officially ends the gender debate!"

"Yeah. Sad the way people dump their pets like they're garbage instead of a commitment. Typical of our society to take the easy way out." Ouch. He hadn't meant to sound so bitter, but even after three years of single fatherhood, his teeth set on edge at how Meredith left Leif only to want him back at her convenience.

Thankfully, Trinity left for college the year before the divorce and got away from her mother's drunken tirades. Meredith swore Michael cared more about his business than his family. "I took her in for a checkup and the vet confirmed she's about three weeks along."

"What should we do with her?"

"Huh?"

"With Lucky, the not so lucky Border Collie? What should we do with her? If no one responds to the advertisement? I certainly didn't mean to burden you with more than a temporary situation."

"Lucky's not a burden. We still want to keep her. Once the pups come, we can find homes for them and have her fixed."

Liana stared at him like he had two heads. "Wow. Maybe Lucky is aptly named after all. My ex would have thrown a fit if I'd brought home a dog, let alone a pregnant one."

Michael's heart squeezed at the thought of Liana's life with an unfeeling jerk. He tried to decide if he should say something or let it go. No matter how angry and disillusioned he became over Meredith's affairs and how she handled the end of their marriage, he didn't air his frustrations, or wallow in self-pity.

"Do you ski?"

The expression of amazement on Michael's face when she commented about Frank's aversion to pets impressed her. At the same time, she couldn't blame Frank for not taking in more strays when he already had her.

"You're good at changing the subject. When I take the time, I love to ski. Brittany and I spent weekends at Tahoe and Big Bear. She signed up for the ski team this year, so I'll have to dig out my equipment." She sipped her merlot. "Do you?"

Michael nodded and his expression softened. She could look at him all night. His dark eyes twinkled with humor. Uh-oh, she'd been caught staring. Again.

Liana gazed at him for another long moment. "Brittany's into snowboarding. I'm not very good at it."

"You probably haven't taken the time to learn."

"So, are you game for the job?"

Michael drained his wineglass and narrowed one eye. "You're very good at changing the subject too. The remodel? Is that what you mean? Hey, I wouldn't miss it for the world."

Liana laughed. Having Michael work on her house meant she'd see him a little bit each day. He'd be here when Brittany came home from school. Possibly when she came home from work. The prospect filled her with pleasure and pain.

Michael made her head spin and her body ache with need. She'd cancelled dinner with him tonight to limit their time together, the intimacy of eating together. When Leif offered to drive Brittany to ballet, she swore father and son had conspired against her, but at the same time, she could have hugged the young man for the thirty minutes of alone time she and Michael shared.

****

Over the next three days, Michael went over the bid with Liana. With her approval, he called in his subcontractors to start the demolition work.

The rest of the front and side walls of the living room would have to be removed, along with part of the roofing to allow for a new gable. The gable would connect the old part of the house with the addition.

The place was a mess.

Original shingles had worked loose and water ran between the tarpaper and plywood. When spring rolled around, he'd be back to investigate the rest of the house. Right now, the focus had to be closing in the new living room.

Liana kept stressing Thanksgiving as the deadline.

Not that he'd seen her. She'd called a couple of times to go over costs and the finishing materials she'd chosen. Michael learned another facet of Liana Campbell; she was an expert in design. She was also ambitious, smart, beautiful and sexy as hell. He wanted to see her, get to know her and test the attraction on his mind night and day. Especially at night.

When his cell phone rang at the end of the day, Michael figured Liana called to check up on progress. "Saxon Construction."

"Where's your son?"

He switched the phone to his other ear, and turned away from the crew. He'd just suggested they load up and call it a day. "Meredith, he's home doing chores."

"He's changed since he moved to that godforsaken place."

"If you mean he has good friends, good grades and isn't in trouble, yeah you're right, he has changed."

"You're still impossible."

Michael sighed at the slur in her voice. He glanced at his watch. Five o'clock and she was already sloshed. "Why did you call?"

"Leif doesn't want to come home for Thanksgiving."

"This is his home. If you want to see him, come here."

"You're suggesting I go back to Montana to see my son?"

Michael drew a deep breath and waved as the crew left. "Leif has adjusted to the new town and school. He's not drinking and goes to school everyday without incident. He's turning himself around, Meredith. Work with him."

A car door slammed. Michael turned toward the parking area. Liana walked around the dumpster he'd ordered a couple of days ago. Her jaw went slack with the shock of more destruction to her house.

Lucky bounded toward her, tail wagging. Liana leaned down and massaged the dog's back with her slender fingers. Michael barely heard Meredith's tirade. His full focus had switched to the fashionable hardworking woman who'd lived in his thoughts since he first laid eyes on her.

Liana straightened and glanced at him. He held up an index finger while he ended his conversation with a protesting Meredith, and snapped his phone shut.

"Hi there."

"Hello." Liana stared at the new prospective of her living room. "I didn't think it'd be so traumatic."

"It'll get better from here on out. The footings will be poured by the end of the week. We'll add chemicals so the concrete will set up faster. Weather dependent, the new gable will take a week. After that the stem wall goes up and so on. It takes a while, but my crew's fast." He smiled. "Imagine how it'll look when it's done."

"I'm trying to. Do you have time for coffee? I found some hammered copper ceiling tiles I'd love to show you." Liana turned away and started around the house before he had the chance to make an excuse.

He didn't want to turn down her invitation, but he was a little hurt over her lack of communication over the past few days. "I have to get home. Leif's ravenous after basketball practice."

Liana faced him, her beautiful mouth in a pout. "Of course. He's a growing boy. How about we call him and promise you'll be home in forty-five minutes? If you agree to the tiles, I'll need to order them."

Michael shrugged and followed her. Hell, he acted like a trained dog just waiting for her to throw him a morsel. He stared at her backside, her trim waist and tousled hair. He remembered the tight stretchy things she'd worn the day they met, and how she looked from behind.

Right now, she wore those ridiculous high heel boots, and had to carefully pick her way over the stone path. Her perfume drifted back on the cool air like an invisible leash pulling him along.

Liana set her purse and briefcase on the kitchen counter and hurried to the coffeemaker. "I'm sorry I haven't been more available. Two counter offers came in on Wednesday and another one today. If I drop the ball, I could lose the sales."

"I'm surprised you're home this early." Heck, he'd thought he was dreaming when he saw her in the yard.

Michael slid onto a bar stool while she poured water into the coffee maker. Her blouse hiked up and exposed a strip of creamy skin. His mouth watered. She lowered her arm and the blouse hid the skin he wanted to touch.

Liana set mugs next to the coffeemaker before she turned to face him. "I decided to leave early so I could catch you." She leaned against the counter. "You're not an easy man to connect with. I stopped by yesterday, but you were off on another job. Didn't your helpers tell you?"

Michael laughed. "I don't think my crew would like that title." He glanced around. "Where's Brittany?"

"She has ballet practice after school twice a week. She really misses her troupe in San Francisco."

Michael stood and moved around the bar, his gaze on hers. "When does she get home?"

Liana tilted her chin to keep the connection. "About six."

Michael glanced at the microwave clock. "Hmm. I have thirty-five minutes."

"For?"

Her mouth softened and her breasts rose and fell at an accelerated rate.

Very good. He excited her as much as she did him.

Michael slid his hands around her waist and pulled her against him. "For something I've wanted to do since I met you. Crazy huh?"

"Very crazy and not too wise."

"Um." He moaned when she pressed her body close and drove all reasonable thought from his head. "What if I don't want to be wise?"

"A quick kiss could erase the mystique and let us get our minds back on our lives." She leaned closer and wrapped her arms around his waist.

"Quit talking and we'll see what happens."

She huffed and he chuckled. The moment his lips

connected with hers all doubts fled. Over the past three years, he'd simplified his life; the past three days had complicated it. He should pack up his male hormones and leave right now.

He couldn't leave. She tasted like heaven and felt like a dream. He ran his hands up and down her back and pressed her against the edge of the bar.

Liana slid her hands up his chest and over his jaw. She touched his cheekbones and slid her fingertips up to fork through his hair.

Goosebumps scattered down his neck and a fog blocked every reason why he should stop. He slipped his hands under her blouse, touching the creamy skin at her waist. She was as soft as she looked. Soft with toned muscles; a mind blowing combination.

A ringing started in his ears. Must be his blood pressure going through the roof.

"Michael? Michael?"

"Hmm?"

"Your phone's ringing."

He groaned and pulled away to take his phone from the holster on his belt. "Leif, hey buddy, what's up?" He hoped he didn't sound like he'd just been kissing the most amazing woman he'd ever met.

"Dad, I'm famished and there's nothing quick to make. Could you stop at the store?"

"Yeah, sure. I'm about done for the day. Have some popcorn in the meantime."

Michael said goodbye and disconnected. "Wow. A needed wake up call."

"I think we established our physical attraction." Liana brushed back her hair and clasped her head with both hands.

"There's chemistry all right. Now, how do we handle it? We have two very impressionable teenagers."

"Yes, and I have an ex-husband who'd love to have a viable reason to take Brittany from me."

Michael frowned. "Could he do that? You're divorced. You have the right to start a new life."

Liana met his gaze. "Frank's still bitter over the divorce. He won't hesitate to use Brittany to punish me."

"Punish you? Wasn't the divorce a mutual decision?"

"At the end it was." She looked away.

He brushed her cheek with the back of his hand. "Hey, sorry I pried. Let's take a look at those copper tiles."

"I don't mean to shut you out, Michael, but we just met. We've agreed our children have to come first and we both have complicated relationships with our former spouses." Liana dumped their coffee in the sink, and refilled the cups with hot brew. She added cream and sugar to hers, slid his across the bar, and climbed onto the stool next to him. "I can't believe we've moved this far so fast."

"Hey, when it's right, it's right. I want to see you, Liana. More than chance meetings while I remodel your living room. I've experienced a divorce. Tell me about your ex."

Liana signed and ran her finger around the rim of her mug. "Let's just say Frank suffers from bouts of jealousy. I couldn't live with his volatile moods."

He gripped the edge of the granite countertop with both hands. "Did he hurt you?"

"Not physically." She twisted on the stool until her

knees touched his. "You have to go home. Maybe we'll talk about this later. Do you have time to glance at the tiles, or should I email you the link?"

He leaned toward her and nuzzled her neck. "Better email the link so I can get out of here and feed Leif. The kid's probably gone through a bag of popcorn and a peanut butter and jelly sandwich by now."

Liana laughed and pulled him off the stool. "Go home before we get sidetracked. Let me know what you think of the tiles."

****

Liana had barely settled into her chair at the café for an overdue lunch with Shari, when her friend launched a barrage of questions. "How are things with that hunk contractor of yours?"

Liana smiled at the waiter and thanked him for the water and menus. "You never mince words, do you? Well, he's up to his ears with my remodel and has several other projects in various stages. Tuesday we settled on a price, and Wednesday morning the crew arrived to destroy what was left of my living room."

"Oh, my gosh! I have to come by and see it." Shari propped her elbows on the table, something her mother would have firmly objected to. "Have you spent any time with Mr. Saxon?"

Liana straightened her silverware. The memory of kissing Michael the night before sent heat through her body. "I have. He stayed for coffee after work last night."

"That's the first time since Monday night?"

"Yes, first time since Monday night. He's gone when I get home from work and arrives after I leave in the mornings. I thought he might be avoiding me, but I don't think so now."

"Uh-huh." Shari raised a brow and twisted her smile to one side. "Let's see, Brittany came home about six."

"Would you get your head out of the bedroom?" Liana shook her head. "We talked." She stared at Shari and tried to look convincing. "All right, so we kissed too. There's a chemistry between us. We've both been divorced for a number of years and have been busy raising kids, so neither of us have gotten involved in a relationship."

"Involved? My girl, you haven't even gone out to dinner since you left Frank. I'm thrilled you've met Michael. The man's handsome, charming and Brittany already likes him."

"Did she tell you about Monday morning when I rear-ended him?"

"Ouch!" Shari covered her mouth and laughed. "I mean, it sounds rather provocative."

"Believe me, things were tense for a while. The police officer tried to charge me with inattentive driving, but Michael talked him out of it. Oh, my gosh, what a fiasco."

"What were you doing? I swear, Li, you've been so distracted lately."

"Lately? This has been years in the making. Last Friday night I drove the wrong way and ended up two hours from home."

"Now you've scared me. Why didn't you call?"

"Because I felt like a fool."

"And Monday?"

"Just like Friday night. Frank called and expected me to talk when I should have concentrated on traffic. I lost focus and didn't stop when Michael did."

"Interesting how you ended up behind him."

Liana covered her face with both hands. "Pure coincidence and luck. Someone else might have sued me. Oh, Shari, I'm in a huge dilemma."

Shari pulled one of Liana's hands from her face. "A dilemma? Good heavens, I don't think you've slept with him yet so you can't be pregnant."

"Of course I haven't slept with him," Liana hissed, glancing around to make sure no one overheard her confession. "My dilemma is, I want to!"

The waiter arrived with their Caesar salads. Shari waited until he'd added course ground pepper, refilled their ice tea and left before she commented.

"Maybe you should just relax and have sex with the man."

Liana smiled and patted Shari's hand. "Thank you for always getting right to the heart of the matter. Are you insane? I have no idea how Brittany would react to another man in my life. At the very least, she might tell Frank and I'd have a court order at my door."

Shari set down her fork. "Liana, you can't continue to live in fear of Frank Nash. What kind of power does that man have over you?"

Liana pushed her salad away. "I can't eat now. I'll take it for later."

"I'm sorry. I didn't mean to upset you, but we always get to this point in a conversation and you back off. I get the feeling I'm out of the loop on what's really happening."

Liana shook her head when the server offered more ice tea. "May I have my check and a box for my salad?"

"What are you doing? Eat your salad and I'll drop

it." Shari took another bite, set down her fork and pressed her palms together. "Look, to have a relationship with Michael or anyone, you have to settle things with Frank. Ex-husband indicates he's no longer your husband."

Liana's eyes burned with tears. She swallowed against the lump in her throat. She couldn't answer Shari, not here. "I have to get back to work and you need to go home. Can we talk later?"

Shari glanced at her watch. "We have plenty of time. Fine, if you don't want to talk here let's go somewhere else."

"My car?"

"You got it."

They signed their card receipts and left the cafe.

Liana unlocked her SUV and slid onto the driver's seat. Shari settled in on the passenger side. They both shivered and moaned when Liana started the engine and the fan hit them with cold air.

"I'm not ready for winter!" Shari rubbed her hands together.

Liana didn't know where to start. The small amount of salad she'd eaten sat in her stomach like a lump of lead. "Me either. Especially with my house torn apart. Oh, Shari, I want to give this thing with Michael a chance. I've known him for less than a week, but I can't think of anything else." She leaned her head on the headrest and folded her arms over her middle.

"So what's the problem?" Shari laid her hand on Liana's shoulder. "We've always confided in each other. We have a trust many friends don't. You can tell me whatever it is, Liana, and I'll never judge you."

"We do have a relationship many friends don't

have. I've been too ashamed to tell you something that happened right before Frank agreed to the divorce. I almost cheated on Frank."

Shari gasped. "You cheated on him? I always suspected the opposite."

"I didn't cheat on him. I almost did. Of course Frank thinks I slept with the guy so he's used it as a weapon."

"Tell me what happened."

Tears welled and spilled down Liana's cheeks. She sniffed and swiped at them. "I was so lonely for excitement and passion—being in the arms of a man who made my blood run hot. Frank and I never had that. You already know we married out of convenience to give Brittany the Nash name and a stable home with two parents. Few people our age would have married because of pregnancy alone."

"Honestly, Li, Frank always wanted you. I saw his expression on more than one occasion when Jack was alive and with you. He was eaten up with jealousy. He'd do anything—even accept his brother's child as his own—to have you."

Liana shifted in her seat and faced Shari. "He paid a big price because I could never be what he wanted. After several failed episodes in bed, we gave up. Ten years is a long time to live without intimacy and love."

She took a deep breath. "When I met Ryan through a client of mine, I got caught up in his looks and charm. His willingness to have an affair tempted me to test if I was the failure in the marriage, or was it the combination of me and Frank?

"Twice, I met Ryan at the downtown Sheridan for dinner and drinks. He went from touching me with his eyes to touching my hand, my arm, my shoulder. He made me feel feminine and wanted. The third time we met, I went with him to his room. We kissed, and he started to unzip my dress. Somehow reality crashed in, and I snapped out of the passion zone."

"So nothing happened."

"If you can call kissing and caressing a man not my husband in a hotel room nothing, I guess nothing happened."

"Liana, Frank pushed you over the edge. Your reaction was normal, but you stopped in time."

Liana groaned. "The fireworks really fizzled when I left the hotel and saw Frank with Brittany walk up the sidewalk. They'd attended the ballet that night. He saw me leave the hotel. Our eyes met. He turned and walked across the street before Brittany saw me. I am very grateful for that gesture. Later that night, he agreed to the divorce. Before I made an appointment with an attorney, he filed on the grounds of adultery."

"Oh, Li. How terrible for you." Shari gripped Liana's hand and rubbed it between hers.

"If Brittany finds out, she may never talk to me again. I don't like what I did. Just because I didn't take it to the bed, doesn't excuse my actions."

"So you think if Michael finds out about Ryan, he won't want to see you again?"

"Exactly. Michael and Brittany are at stake here. Especially Brittany. I'm the mother, I'm supposed to set an example. How can a teenager process the knowledge that her mother made out with some guy while she went to the ballet with her father? Frank has been very good to Brittany. This news could crush her world."

"I agree you don't want Brittany to find out, but,

Li, what you had with Frank—which was nothing by the way—is completely different from what you could have with Michael. You and Michael have a chemistry you never had with Frank. There's no comparison. This is much closer to what you had with Jack. Jack set you on fire and if I don't miss my guess, Michael could burn you up. The man is hot."

Her nerves ragged, Liana giggled and shook her head. "You are so good for me. Why didn't I unload all this on you sooner?"

"Hell if I know." Shari puckered her lips. "I want you to be happy, like Richard and I are happy. This guy could be the one. Look, we all have skeletons in the closet. Go with your gut. If it starts to progress, tell him. Get it out in the open and let him make the decision."

Liana took a tissue from her purse, wiped her eyes and blew her nose. "How about I host a cocktail party and invite you and Richard and Michael?"

"You'd have a party with your house torn apart? I'm proud of you!"

"You are a smart-aleck. I can make the dining room cozy and since it's just us, no biggy."

"Good idea. How about tonight? It's Friday."

"What about Richard's Elk Unlimited meeting?"

"It starts at five. He can meet me at your house by seven."

Liana sniffed, and suddenly felt a weight lift off her shoulders. "What can I tell Michael? I have to have a reason for the party."

"Tell him you've had the party planned for a couple of weeks. But honestly, it sounds like you've moved past the point of having to conjure up a reason to get together."

"You're right. Last night took us over a hurdle. We want to spend time together. I'd better get back to the office and order hors d'oeuvres. How about Chinese BBQ pork and a platter of spring rolls?"

"Sounds good. I'll make tortilla pinwheels. Brittany can stay with Meagan just in case you and Michael want privacy after the party. See you at seven?"

Liana pressed her fingers against her chest. "I'm scared, Shari. I'm getting into something that might break my heart and take another sixteen years to get over."

"I think you've paid your dues, my friend. It's time for some happiness."

****

Before Liana drove back to her office, she called Michael's cell phone. It went straight to voice mail.

"Hi, Michael. Liana Campbell calling." Her heart sped up. "I know it's short notice, but I'm hosting a small cocktail party tonight and would love for you to join us. When you get this message, please give me a quick call and let me know if you can make it." She severed the connection and stared at the phone for a moment. Her beach and palm trees spread over the screen.

She glanced out the windshield and shifted into Drive. Light snowflakes fluttered through the air. According to the locals, winter was coming early.

Wow. The front of her house was torn off and she had strong thoughts of sleeping with the contractor. Maybe she should list the house, pack up and move to Hawaii before taking another step.

She returned to the office and called the Chinese take-out before attacking the ever-present paperwork on her desk. The next time she surfaced, it was five. She checked her messages; nothing from Michael. Had he overlooked her voicemail like he had Sunday night?

Determined not to slip into a blue funk, she left the office to pick up the hors d'oeuvres. At the last minute, she detoured into the market and bought a few needed groceries.

What if he ignored her message?

She couldn't ignore the pain that possibility caused. She wanted to spend time with him, get closer to him. All the insecurities of her teen years rolled back and in her mind, she was sitting by the phone waiting for Jack to call.

No! She had no desire to revert to the clingy girl she'd been. She was a woman now, a mother, and she'd lived through ten unhappy years with Frank. Hadn't she learned anything?

Chapter Four

The house was dark and quiet when Liana pulled into the drive. No sign of the workers, Michael or Brittany. Of course Brittany had ballet tonight and Jennie's mom had agreed to take Brittany and Meagan to Shari's after practice.

Now, if only Michael would call and accept the invitation to her last minute, engineered cocktail party!

By some weird fluke, the snow had turned to rain and came down at a steady pace. The perfect night to spend with friends in front of the fire.

Until that moment, she hadn't realized how much she missed a social life. She loved time with Brittany, but everyone needed time with other adults.

She flipped the hood of her raincoat over her hair, and slid from the SUV to retrieve the groceries from the back. Arms loaded, she trudged to the door through the rain and mud. The construction project had taken a toll on what little lawn she'd had to begin with.

Why had she bought so many groceries, and why paper instead of plastic?

The bags soaked up the steady downpour of rainwater. On the back step, Liana juggled her burden to fish the keys out of her coat pocket. The bag of fruit and fresh veggies began to tear.

She aimed the key for the lock, connected and turned. Her cell phone rang. Her fingers cramped.

Slipping and sliding over the tile floor in her wet boots, she almost made it to the counter when the bag gave out. Oranges and apples hit the floor rolling. A head of cabbage thumped against the cabinet door.

"Damn!"

Her phone silenced. She set the other bags on the island and pulled out her cell phone. Michael's number.

"Double damn!"

The landline rang. Liana stepped over her produce and raced to the den to snap up the cordless receiver. "Hello?"

"Hi there."

"Michael." Her heart pounding from exertion, she pressed her hand to her chest.

"You sound out of breath. I was afraid you drove off and I wasn't there to find you."

Liana smiled against the phone, amazed at how fast he could smooth out the kinks in her life. "Okay, who told you about last Friday night?"

"Brittany of course. She worries about you. Hey, I got your message. I'd love to attend your cocktail party." Michael's voice sounded warm and sexy.

"She has no reason to worry. Did I mention the party is at seven?" Liana hoped she didn't sound too eager. She'd thought of him way too much and, despite Shari's support and reassurance, she feared heartbreak.

He chuckled. "That's what your message said. Can I bring anything?"

Liana bit her lip to keep from saying, just you. "I think we have everything. What's Leif up to? He's welcome to come over."

"Leif's studying with a friend tonight. Will Brittany be home?"

60

"After ballet practice, she's staying over with Meagan."

Michael's chuckle warmed her to her toes. "I hope Leif's not studying girl's ballet practice."

Liana laughed. "I think you'll like Shari and Richard."

"I'm sure I will, but what I really look forward to is more time with the beautiful, sexy woman who hired me to remodel her house."

Liana wandered toward the bedroom, unbuttoning her damp blouse on the way. Anticipation bubbled inside her until she thought she'd giggle. "I want to spend time with you too."

"In that case, I'll see you at seven?"

****

At seven o'clock sharp, Michael stood on Liana's back step, amazed she wanted him to join her party when she'd cancelled their dinner Monday night. Little by little, he learned more about her and what pushed her buttons. He didn't intend to push a sensitive one tonight.

Tomorrow would make one week since he'd met her. She excited him and at the same time scared the hell out of him.

His life had been simple and uncomplicated since he and Leif moved to Montana. He didn't want to disrupt it with a relationship that could go south.

Liana opened the door and his midsection clenched. A short black dress hugged her curves. Black tights conformed to her long legs and stopped at her shapely ankles. Damn, how'd she do it? She turned him on from the top of her artfully messy blonde hair, to the tips of her bronze polished toenails. A fire curled through his midsection. Good Lord, had he lost his mind when he turned forty?

"You look great." He struggled to sound unaffected.

"Thank you. Come on in. Shari and Richard are here." She stepped out of the way and gestured for him to go into the dining room.

Since a heavy sheet of plastic was still the only barrier between the great outdoors and the living room, she'd set up a seating area in the dining room in front of the fireplace.

"Michael, you've met Shari. This is her handsome and charming husband, Richard."

"Keep that up and I'll never be able to live with him." Shari smiled and shook Michael's hand before she stepped back for Richard to do the same.

Richard impressed him with a firm handshake and direct look. The Collins's were important to Liana; he was grateful he could honestly like them.

He stepped toward Liana, at war with his inclination to pull her into his arms. Slow down, Saxon.

"Michael, what would you like to drink? I have wine, of course."

"Of course." Michael grinned.

"I also have the makings for martinis. I even picked up Richard's favorite scotch."

"Wow, I can't refuse a good scotch. On the rocks, please."

"Better taste it before you dilute it with ice, Michael." Richard lifted his own glass. "This vintage is extra smoky and mighty fine."

"All right. No ice, please." He stared at Liana's backside as she walked to the bar.

Richard cleared his throat.

Michael tore his attention from the way the little black dress slightly cupped Liana's behind and snapped his focus back to the other guests.

"Richard, what brought you and your family to Kalispell? I assume you came from California."

Richard grinned at Michael, a glint in his eyes. "I retired from the San Diego Police Department a year ago. Several of my fellow SDPD moved here over the years to hunt, fish and enjoy retirement. Seemed like a good plan for us."

"Smart man. How do you like Montana, Shari?"

"I was skeptical when Richard caved into the persuasion of his friends. I thought I'd miss the shops and my job, but it's really beautiful here and there's plenty of shopping."

"It's a good thing Kalispell is so beautiful because once they decided to move here, they started to work on me." Liana returned with a crystal rocks glass Michael estimated held at least three fingers of scotch. He hoped the hors d'oeuvres were substantial enough to cut the alcohol before he drove home.

He accepted the glass and slid his hand over hers. This party had little to do with the remodel in progress. Her friends were here to check out the man she'd hired. Judging from the glances from Richard and Shari, they suspected more transpired than a remodel.

"Liana wasn't as easy to convince. She had a very successful real estate business in San Francisco," Richard said, a brow raised.

Michael appreciated the way Liana's friends protected her. He'd be under tough scrutiny, but hey, he could handle it. "I'm sure she's a success at whatever she chooses to do." He met Richard's gaze with assurance, and turned to Liana. His heart squeezed at the moisture in her mossy green eyes.

"Liana's excellent with real estate, but it isn't your dream job, is it?" Richard lifted his glass toward her. "I'm sure you'd like nothing more than to delve back into design work."

Liana glanced around the room, her bottom lip held captive by her teeth. Damn. Michael wanted to wrap his arms around her, hug her into his side and kiss her fragrant hair.

"Liana told me about her degree in Design. I'm impressed." He moved a bit closer. Her friends meant well, but they needed to back off and let her enjoy the evening. "She has great plans for this house."

Liana sipped her Martini and gazed at him over the rim of the glass. "I'm sure what Richard and Shari are dying to tell you, is that before Frank was hired in the Silicon Valley, I worked for a large firm in San Diego."

Michael slowly shook his head. "You gave up your career to move with him?"

"I had to. Brittany was little. I didn't want to upset her life."

"Liana has always been an unselfish person. Sometimes too much so." Shari did what Michael ached to do and wrapped an arm around Liana. "Okay, enough seriousness. Let's get those appetizers set out. I'm famished."

Richard moved to one of the wing-backed chairs in front of the fire. "Let's sit and chat, Michael. I'd like to hear about your business."

Michael appreciated the change in conversation.

He'd lived through so many emotional ups and

downs with Meredith, he didn't relish the thought of another relationship full of issues. He respected Liana even more after hearing what she'd done for her daughter, and to make her marriage work. So what had finally happened to end it?

Trays of hors d'oeuvres appeared on the table, along with colorful plates and napkins. Candles were artfully placed to enhance the spread, but not cause a hazard to the diners.

Michael loved what Liana did to everything she touched. She was a professional designer, but she kept things pure and natural.

"This is a feast." Michael pushed out of the wing-backed chair and led the charge to the table. Food always smoothed the tension of meeting new people. He dished up a little of everything and exchanged his empty glass for a glass of merlot.

"Help yourself to more scotch, Michael," Richard said, refreshing his own glass.

"I might after we eat. I'm curious about the native Californian with northwest wine." He tasted the Washington State vintage and rolled his lips in and out. "Very good."

Liana smiled. "I tried it shortly after I moved here. I was pleasantly surprised." She clinked her glass to his and took a sip.

Settling into one of the four chairs in front of the fire, she set her glass on a small table between her and Richard.

"Michael, we've never discussed your family back home."

"Yes." Shari leaned forward in her chair. "Please tell us."

"Not much to tell. My maternal grandmother's half Cherokee. They were part of the relocation in the eighteen hundreds. She met and married my grandfather, a full-blooded Irishman. My father's family came from England in the early nineteen hundreds."

"The mix was a success." Liana bit into a slice of pork and licked her lips.

Michael stifled a moan and struggled to keep the conversation going instead of kissing Liana mindless in front of her friends. He had to stay on track and not make a fool of himself.

"Liana, what's your family background?"

Liana wiped her hands on a burgundy napkin. "The usual, English, Irish, Scot. You know the Heinz mix."

"There's nothing generic about you, Liana Campbell." Michael fingered the stem of his glass. What would happen when the party ended and the Collins left? Would she ask him to stay?

"Well, thank you, sir. Can I refresh your wine?"

She stood and moved toward the bar before he could respond. She struck him speechless. With every word, every move, she sent his senses into overdrive. His reaction to her made him feel like an over-sexed, middle-aged leach.

The evening wore on with him and Richard in a rapt discussion about bow versus rifle hunting. Michael agreed to join Richard's hunting group for cat season later in the winter.

A few minutes past ten, Shari yawned and stretched her legs. "I have to get home to bed."

"Wow." Liana tried to hide a yawn, but failed. "You used to be the life of the party."

"Not any more. Anyway, Richard's driving to Missoula early in the morning to look at some hunting supplies."

"Arrows, dearest." Richard turned to Michael. "My favorite sporting goods store has a sale on bows and arrows. Want to come along?"

"I would, but I have a house to finish and winter won't wait."

Liana shifted in her chair, and glanced from Michael to Richard and back. "If you mean my house, I don't want to spoil your weekend. I don't expect you to work seven days a week."

"Good." Michael walked toward the kitchen and set his wine glass on the counter. "Because I never work on Sundays."

Liana moved beside him at the sink and her perfume wafted its way into his air space and kick-started his testosterone levels. "I don't want to prevent you from going with Richard."

Michael itched to kiss her adorable pouty mouth. "There'll be another time when your house is snug and warm."

"Michael's right." Richard gave Liana a hug. "I'll keep you posted if I see another big sale. Good to meet you, Saxon." He shook Michael's hand. "Plan on cat hunting later when we have a good layer of snow."

Shari sidestepped her husband and gave Michael a hug. "Be good to her," she whispered in his ear.

"Bet on it."

Michael truly liked the Collins and appreciated their loyal friendship with Liana.

Anticipation built while Liana saw them out the door. When she returned to the kitchen, she acted withdrawn. Huh, what had he done?

"It's late."

Michael chuckled. "Is that your way of saying it's time for me to leave?"

"I'm just saying, it's late. You're working tomorrow so you should get some sleep."

"I'm a big boy, Liana." He stepped toward her and grinned when she blushed. "Aren't you working tomorrow?"

"Only for a while in the morning. The new office schedule came out this afternoon, but I didn't have time to look at it." He stepped closer. She didn't move away.

"Can't you access it online?"

Liana gripped the edge of the granite countertop. "I guess I can."

Michael stopped a hair's breath in front of her and braced his hands on either side of hers. His belt buckle brushed the front of her dress and turned to molten metal. Here came the lovesick teenager with the appetites of a man.

She tilted her chin and gazed into his eyes. "You'll be here early in the morning? I can make breakfast."

"Sounds great. Bacon and eggs?"

She nodded and her breasts pressed against him. "With pancakes?"

"Um, really good." He took a shaky breath. "One of these days I'll be here long before breakfast."

Her tongue darted out to moisten her lips. Michael moaned and slanted his mouth over hers, tasting wine and spices.

She leaned into him and responded to his every move. His head swam and a haze settled behind his eyes. He should stop right now and leave.

She slid her hands up the front of his shirt, bunching the fabric in her fingers.

Michael pulled her against his aching body. "I don't want to leave. Brittany's gone for the night. I think your friends approve."

"What happens then, Michael?"

The lady knew how to cool him off. He rested his chin on the top of her head. "I don't have any answers about later, Liana. I can't make any commitments until I know you better."

"Exactly." She slid her hands up and down his shirtfront then brought them back to her sides. "That's why I can't let you stay. My body wants you, but my heart couldn't handle it if you don't feel the same way."

He cupped her face and kissed the tip of her nose. "I'll always be honest with you. I don't make love casually. I'd still be married if my ex hadn't cheated on me. I could've probably handled her alcohol problem, as rough as it was. Fidelity is everything to me. I won't break your heart."

****

"No, but I'll break yours." Liana mumbled as she stared her computer. The words had tumbled through her mind over and over since Michael left last night.

Another sleepless night.

Restless, she'd gotten up at four and went online to review the current office schedule at work. Way too many hours of floor time. She didn't need the walk-in business right now and would rather pass the opportunity to her fellow agents.

She composed a very professional, grateful, but no thank you, email to her broker and hit send.

What she needed was more time with Brittany.

With Frank's daily phone calls and his looming presence in the background, her daughter needed to be her main focus.

Weary with exhaustion, Liana curled up on the couch with her down comforter and closed her eyes. What would Michael say when he learned she'd almost cheated on Frank?

"That which I feared the most," she muttered, and burrowed down to sleep.

A truck door slammed.

Liana groaned and covered her head with the comforter. She'd floated in a dream where Michael understood her and didn't hate her for the past.

"Go away." Maybe it was UPS and they'd leave her package and go.

Knuckles firmly rapped on the back door.

Liana sat up and swung her feet to the floor in one move. Michael. Oh, my gosh. She'd promised him an early breakfast since he planned to give up his Saturday to work on her house. Tightening her robe, she hurried to the back door finger combing her hair as she went. She glanced out the kitchen window. His black truck sat in her drive.

She caught her reflection in the stainless steel front of the microwave. "Nothing like removing the mystery in a new relationship."

He rapped again. Liana unlocked the back door and opened it.

Freshly showered and groomed, Michael looked as handsome and brawny as ever. Only a close glance into his amber eyes revealed a hint of tiredness. Fine lines fanned out from the corners of his amazing eyes and verified her suspicions. He hadn't slept well either.

"Good morning." He lifted his dark brows and glanced past her to the dimly lit kitchen. "Did I wake you?"

Liana took a deep breath and let it slowly escape. "I haven't cooked breakfast yet."

"No problem." He reached out and tugged on her robe ties. "Got any coffee?"

"I can make some." She stepped back. "Come on in."

Michael stepped around her and into the utility room. The scent of spicy soap and clean male almost knocked her off her feet. She took a deep breath again, but this time to savor the scent and presence of Michael Saxon.

She shook off the groggy weirdness she always felt when she napped and hurried into the kitchen to start a pot of coffee. She glanced at the clock.

"Wow, it's only six."

"Yeah, sorry I'm so early. I couldn't sleep so I gave up and started my day."

Liana pushed the button to start the brew cycle. "Sounds like my night."

He sat on one of the bar stools and planted his elbows on the granite. She stared at his bronzed forearms, left bare by the rolled sleeves of his chambray shirt. His intense eyes caught her gaze and held it.

"Maybe we would've slept better together."

"Maybe." Her body tingled, her stomach fluttered. She held out her hands and fanned them down the front of her robe. "Well, here's what I look like in the morning. The mystery is over."

Michael laughed, his teeth white against his dark skin. "Honey, you're beautiful any time of the day or night. No makeup and messy hair won't scare me off."

"I don't want to scare you off." She took several measured breaths and moved around the bar, walking her fingers on the granite countertop as she went.

Michael swiveled the bar stool and pulled her between his thighs. "Good, 'cause I don't plan on going anywhere." He touched his lips to hers, drew back and gazed into her eyes for a moment before kissing her again, this time deeper—soul shattering deep.

Liana wrapped her arms around his neck and the movement pulled her robe apart. For some insane reason, she'd worn her black lace teddy to bed. Now, she was glad she had.

Michael slid his hands under her robe and over the whisper of lace. The warmth and strength of his hands sent sensations through her body and fire through her veins. His calluses caught on the lace.

He pulled his lips from hers. "Guess I shouldn't do that. I don't want to ruin that work of art."

Liana giggled. "It's an extravagance I indulged myself in after you left last night."

"You should have put it on before I left." He moved his hands down her hips and gripped her thighs.

"I had it on under my dress."

"Wow. Don't tell me that." Michael moaned, and buried his face in the fluffy collar of her chenille robe.

She should step out of his arms and get dressed. She'd promised him breakfast. He had work to do and Brittany might come home early.

With every bit of restraint, she pulled away and put the island between them. "Black coffee?"

"Yes, ma'am. There you go again—changing the subject."

He moved around the bar and placed one hand on either side of her just like he had last night. This time his front pressed to her back. Even through the thick fabric of her robe she detected his heat and hardness. She leaned against him and nuzzled her face into the side of his neck.

Oh, how she wanted to stay here, maintain the contact with his masculine body, but after what he'd said last night…she couldn't deceive him by giving into what they both wanted before he knew the full truth.

"I have no doubt making love with you would be incredible." She turned in his arms and handed him a mug. "Nor do I doubt how complicated life would become."

A half smile tilted Michael's delicious mouth. He took the mug, but didn't move away. "Liana, meeting you has already complicated my life. Making love could make it all simple again."

Liana sipped her coffee. "Think so?"

"Yep. I haven't had a decent night's sleep in over a week. I'm so distracted, my crew had a heyday razzing me." He took a drink of coffee and rolled his lips together. "Think we could discuss what keeps us apart?"

His proximity wouldn't let her form the words to explain anything, let alone the deep subjects of her past. He completely fogged the logical side of her mind.

She cupped her mug and gazed into his eyes. "I-I'm not prepared for such a serious conversation right now."

He tilted his head and feathered his fingers over her cheek. "All right, so where does that put us? It sounds crazy since I've only known you a week, but more than my body needs to be close to you, Liana."

He set his mug on the counter, grasped her wrists and pulled her against him.

"This isn't casual for me. I have an impressionable teenager I rescued from his promiscuous mother. I refuse to expose him to the same thing. What I want with you isn't short termed."

"How can you know? It hasn't been a week, it's less than a week."

"There are no guarantees, but I know how I feel." He cupped her bottom and buried his face in the side of her neck. "What time does Brittany get home?"

Liana could hardly think with his hard body planted against hers. He left no doubt about what he wanted. "Probably late morning. I should call her and check in." Oh, how she wanted to finish this. Take him to her room and do all the things she'd dreamed of since they met at Ciao Mambo. If only it were that simple.

She pressed her hands against his chest. "Please put me down."

Michael rested his forehead against hers for a moment before he slowly let her feet touch the floor. He shoved his fingers through his hair and exhaled a frustrated breath. "I need to get to work."

"What about breakfast?"

He shook his head and scrubbed his face with both hands. "Maybe later." He turned and left the house.

Chapter Five

Liana braced her arms on the sill of the kitchen window while Michael unloaded the tools for his day's work. She released a tension-filled sigh. Maybe making love would simplify things for Michael, but for her? No. Not with Frank waiting in the wings for her to slip-up; display a behavior he could use to drag her to court and take Brittany away.

Panic coursed through her. She couldn't let that happen. She'd make Michael a hearty breakfast, but she wouldn't stick around. She had to leave before she gave in to her heart's desire.

Liana built the fire in the fireplace. Why had she worn a lace teddy to bed? She didn't have anyone to impress. In her bedroom, she stripped out of the indulgence and tossed it in the laundry basket.

"Am I kidding myself?" She stomped to the shower. "I deluded myself into thinking I could have a love life."

The lace had felt good against her skin. The fantasy of sleeping in something Michael would like added to the delicious sensation. Had she subconsciously hoped he'd see it this morning and go crazy?

The hot spray of the shower eased away some of the tension and exhaustion. She had to sleep or she'd get sick.

After a vigorous toweling, she performed her usual

skin care routine. Outside, Michael banged and sawed. His closeness made her breasts tingle. She stomped into her room, tossed the damp towel in the laundry basket and pulled on some underwear. "Get a grip. He's off limits!"

Michael wasn't the only one with an impressionable teenager. Brittany liked Michael, but friendship didn't compare to discovering her mother had almost jumped into bed with him. Dammit. Why couldn't she have met Michael after Brittany turned eighteen and moved off to college? At that point Frank's power would end.

Liana slipped her feet into a pair of clogs and headed for the kitchen, prepared to face the day and her resolution to stay out of Michael's bed.

An hour later, with a plate loaded with hash browns, an omelet and crisp bacon in the warming oven, Liana headed out the door to let Michael know his breakfast was ready.

Shovel in hand and up to his knees in mud, he dug away at the trench for the footings he planned to pour next week.

She hesitated before calling out to him, but stood there, drinking in the sight of his strong, muscled body at battle with the frozen earth. Her heart pinged with sorrow. She may never know the thrill of making love with him or the sweetness of waking in his arms.

"Michael, time to eat."

He barely looked at her. He had to be frustrated over their close encounter. She certainly was. He stabbed the shovel into the pile of muddy earth and wiped his forehead with his shirt sleeve.

"Liana, I can't go into your house, I'm covered

with mud."

"I'll set it on the picnic table. Are you warm enough to eat outside?"

He looked up at the sky. "Yeah, it's warming up. I'm glad it cleared off."

Liana tightened her hold on her sweater and shivered. "If you say so."

Michael climbed out of the trench and walked toward her. Dear heavens, even covered with mud and sweat the man turned her into a puddle of molten liquid.

"I'll get a pan of warm wash water."

"What about you? Did you eat?"

"I need to get some work done before Brittany comes home. She's going to shop with Meagan most of the morning. If you need anything, please call."

Michael's mouth tightened. "You don't have to run away. I won't tear off your clothes."

"Don't be ridiculous! I'm the one who wants to tear off my clothes. I trust you implicitly. It won't work, Michael. You won't be happy when you learn more about me."

Michael tilted his head back and laughed. "I wouldn't be happy if you tore off your clothes and made love with me? Are you crazy? I'd be ecstatic!"

Liana blinked against the pesky tears she'd experienced a lot lately. "I don't have an answer right now. Please just eat your breakfast and go home early. I'm sure Leif wants to spend time with you."

"I'll get the footings dug and the forms set." He continued toward her, his amber gaze drilling her for the truth. "Never doubt it, Liana. I want you. All of you."

Liana hurried into the house for a pan of hot water,

a bar of soap and paper towels. When she returned, Michael waited next to the picnic table.

He washed while she took his plate from the oven and carried it outside. At least she'd covered the patio chairs so the upholstery was dry.

Michael laid paper towels over the taupe brocade seat before he sat down. "This looks great. Thank you."

Before she stepped away, he grabbed her arm and pulled her toward him. He kissed the back of her hand, his gaze conveying a wealth of feeling.

Pain thrummed in Liana's heart. She wanted more from Michael than his beautiful body. She wanted the dream, but the nightmare from her past may never let it happen.

"I'll see you later." On impulse, she kissed his lips, tugged from his hold and hurried into the house.

****

"Your numbers are great, Liana. You're a real asset to the brokerage."

"Thank you, Stan." Liana gave her broker a quick smile. "I appreciate your understanding on the office schedule."

"You have enough out of state referrals to keep you busy. I respect your need to spend more time with your daughter, so consider it done. I'll revamp the schedule to reflect two office days and the rest from home. Just let me know if the referrals dry up and you need more walk-in business."

"I will. Thanks again." Liana swiveled her office chair, and handed Stan her client schedule for the next week. "Two more couples from Canada plus the final counter offers on five properties."

Stan gave a low whistle and smacked his lips. "Just

don't burn yourself out. I'd hate to lose you."

Liana reached across her desk and patted his hand. "Never fear. You treat me very well." She glanced at her cell phone. The message light blinked.

"I heard through the grapevine Michael Saxon's remodeling your house. Good choice. He did some work for me last summer. I was impressed with his speed and quality."

"That's good to hear. Since I'm relatively new to town, I had to make my best judgment call."

Liana glanced at her computer. Michael had emailed about an idea. Could she be home by four? Intrigued, she confirmed the appointment. A shiver of emotion made her wiggle in her chair. The past week had been a crazy rollercoaster and she bordered on exhaustion.

One challenge at a time. That's all she could do.

With the revised buy and sell agreement for the Cummings completed, she faxed it to them for review and signatures.

Her second home and vacation home clients had saved her from the real estate slump. Thanks to her contacts in the San Francisco business world. It didn't hurt that Kalispell and Whitefish were beautiful resort areas.

If only she could compartmentalize Michael this easily.

Most women would think her crazy for not jumping into bed with him. He'd saved her on the house remodel disaster, he liked Brittany and she liked him. He was handsome, charming, sexy, and she feared her heart would break when he finished her house project, accepted her payment and walked away.

He'd move on. Start a new job; maybe meet someone else.

She fiddled with her paperclip holder. Their relationship was doomed no matter how she looked at it. When he learned how she'd almost succumbed to an affair, an affair that finally made Frank agree to the divorce, Michael's warm gaze would go cold and he'd leave.

Why did her life have to be so complicated! People made mistakes and bad choices, but those mistakes didn't haunt them for sixteen years, did they?

At least her finances were secure at the moment. As long as the stream of referrals came her way, she'd earn the money to complete the remodel, pay Frank's alimony check and take care of Brittany's needs without touching her savings. But experience had taught her to be realistic. The referrals would inevitably slow down.

Even more to the point, Frank had no right to receive the alimony! Blackmail money better described what she'd been paying every month for the past four years. It went against all fairness and it had to stop.

When Brittany turned eighteen, Liana would confess all to her daughter and stop the payments. Frank could take her to court or take a flying leap—she didn't care. With the threat gone, she could open her design business. Everything would fall into place.

Shutting down her computer, she hurried out to meet with the new couple who'd left the message on her cell phone. They were interested in a vacation home close to the golf course in Whitefish. She'd agreed to meet them at a popular wine bar downtown.

They'd also mentioned rental property, so she had

to strike while the proverbial iron was hot.

"I like what I see," Jackie Bishop said an hour later as she looked over the assortment of properties Liana had picked for them to consider. "I had no idea we'd find a bonus like this one."

Liana sipped from her glass of Syrah, and nodded. "It's a buyers market and when you don't have to depend on financing, you have it made. I'll write up the offer tomorrow morning and fax it to the listing agent. I'm sure she'll call me by Monday."

"Very good." Pete waved to the server to order another round.

"Oh, not for me thank you. I have to drive home." Her cell phone vibrated and skittered across the table. She grabbed it just before it pitched over the side. "Liana Campbell."

"Hello."

The sound of his voice usually sent tingles over her body. Tonight, his tone startled her. "Michael, is there a problem?"

"Yeah, it's four-thirty and you're not here."

Liana glanced at the clock on the wall. "Oh, no! I lost track of time."

"Ouch. Well, I'm at your house right now. With Brittany."

"Oh no! Michael, I'm so sorry. I did call Brittany with my schedule today." Why did she need to explain herself to him? Brittany was fine.

Liana covered her phone with her free hand, and smiled at Pete and Jackie. "I'm sorry guys. I forgot about another appointment. I have to take off."

"No problem." Pete leaned forward and patted her knee. "We understand. Go ahead and take your call.

We'll touch bases on Monday."

"Thank you." Liana mouthed the response and gathered up her purse, briefcase and coat with one hand while she juggled her phone with the other. "Michael, I'm on my way out the door and should be there in fifteen if you can stick around. If not, we can reschedule."

"We don't have time to reschedule. This meeting affects the structure of the addition. Don't worry about dinner. I brought pizza."

"Oh." Liana fumbled with her lock gadget, opened the door and set her stuff on the back seat. "How considerate. I'll be right home. You can add the pizza to my bill."

Silence.

"Michael?"

"I refuse to bill you for a lousy pizza. I'll see you when you get here." He disconnected.

Liana leaned back in her seat. Heaviness squashed the pleasant affects of the wine she'd had with her clients. "Here we go again. My work isn't as important as his and I neglected my daughter. Grrrr."

She had enough stress in her life without Michael overstepping the boundary. She was a big girl and Brittany did fine at home alone sometimes.

Sometimes?

Liana started the SUV and flipped on her seat heater. "Okay, so she's spent quite a few evenings alone while I work. She's almost sixteen. It's not like she's a little girl anymore." She tapped her palm against the steering wheel, turned to look both ways and backed out of the parking space.

Night began to wrap itself around the Northwest

Montana day. Snow fluttered through the sky and gathered in patches on the parking lot.

"Face it, he's right about Brittany being home alone, or at Shari's far too much." She navigated the weekend traffic and arrived at her house within the time she'd promised Michael.

She shifted into Park and sat in the car for a moment, hoping the best approach to the evening would appear. She couldn't blame Michael for being irritated. She'd agreed to the time and had spaced it. She rotated her head from side to side, stretching out the kinks in her neck. She needed a moment to decompress, prepare herself to meet with an irritated Michael.

The house was well lit and smoke curled from the chimney, creating a warm and cozy image. Far from what she usually came home to at the end of the day.

She sighed. Despite her attraction to Michael, they had a business agreement for the remodel. Exactly why she'd canceled that first dinner. Mixing business with pleasure wasn't a good idea. But, it was too late to go back.

"Thanks to my black teddy and a weak moment."

Besides, the kids were involved and they didn't need to hear their parents arguing over whose time was more valuable. She needed to keep her cool and get through the evening.

Cutting the engine, she grabbed her briefcase and left her warm vehicle. The constant drizzle chilled her to the bone before she reached the back door. Inside the utility room, she shook the droplets out of her hair and brushed at the sleeves of her cashmere jacket.

A multiply array of impressions hit her senses. A warm glow spilled from the kitchen, the yeasty scent of baking pizza, the clink of glassware, harmonized with low masculine humming. The irritation mellowed and left her body more relaxed, but her mind in a turmoil. Maybe he was concerned, not angry.

Until Michael started working on her house, Brittany often went home with Megan after school. Liana would pick her up about six and they'd come home to a chilly, dark house and eat a late dinner. She'd never liked the routine, but being a single parent didn't allow her the luxury of permanently changing things anytime soon.

Liana stepped into the light, afraid the surreal sights and smells would evaporate when Michael looked at her with the disappointment he'd displayed earlier.

A glass of wine sat on the kitchen island. The fire crackled in the fireplace and reflected off the plates and glasses on the table. The burgundy candle centerpiece was lit and rivaled the aroma of pizza with the scent of cranberries and cinnamon.

Michael took the pizza from the oven. He jerked his hand back as he set the pan on the stovetop. "Damn." He stuck his thumb in his mouth.

Liana's breath caught. How could the man look domestic and oh so ruggedly masculine at the same time? He turned toward him and his eyes widened. "I didn't hear you come in. You're soaked."

Liana absently touched her hair and glanced down at her rain dappled olive green jacket. "I look like Lucky dragged me in."

"As usual, you look beautiful." His voice was low and gravely. "I don't know how you do it."

"Dress wrong for the weather?"

"No. Be wet and cold and still look so damned good." He turned back to the pizza. "Now go change and hurry back for a sip of wine before I set dinner on the table and call the kids."

The warmth and comfort she'd perceived when she walked into the house mystified her. She'd been ready to defend herself and instead, he treated her like a queen.

She'd lived on her own for four years and it went against her grain to accept his suggestion without protest. She bit back a retort and headed for her room to change. Shedding crumpled wet clothes, Liana slipped into a chocolate brown, velveteen jogging suit. After she blow-dried and fluffed her hair she took a minute to freshen her makeup and apply a coat of lipstick. The tin of sparkly scented powder she splurged on beckoned her. She glided the puff over her throat and chest above her zippered jacket.

She returned to the kitchen just as Michael set a large bowl of tossed salad on the table. He ran his gaze from the top of her head, to the tips of her polished toenails. "Dinner's almost ready. The kids are playing some game on the computer."

"Thank you, Michael." Liana didn't want to resurrect their recent disagreement, but, despite his consideration with dinner and making sure she was comfortable, tension hung in the air like a heavy rain cloud. Her marriage had taught her that give and take relationships were make believe. She wasn't quite sure where to go from here.

Michael rested the salad tongs on the edge of the bowl. "Hey, our canine is gaining weight and glossing up."

"Wonderful." She moved next to him and luxuriated in his warmth. Warning bells went off in her head. Had she forgotten the internal dialogue she'd had on her trip home? They had to slow down and stick to business. Things could get too complicated and she had enough complication in her life.

"Yeah. I'm glad you found her. She's really a good dog." He cupped her upper arms and rubbed up and down to warm her.

Tears pricked Liana's eyes. "We've hit some bumps today, haven't we?"

"Everyday can't be perfect, Liana. It's all part of getting to know each other."

She smiled through her tears and sniffed. She shook her head and glanced around the fragrant kitchen. "Is there anything you can't do?"

"You'd find out if you gave me a chance," he murmured close to her ear.

The perpetual goosebumps traveled down her neck and back. "I should say hello to the kids."

"Let's leave them to the computer game for another minute." He nuzzled her ear and tightened his arms around her, skimming the sides of her breasts. "I'm as puzzled by this whole thing as you are, Liana. Let's stop getting upset about it and go out. On a real date."

"Oh, Michael," she said on a sigh. "You don't know how tempting that sounds, but it won't change anything. We're both old enough to face the facts. We have teenagers to finish raising and very different life styles."

He stepped back and picked up the salad bowl. "One of these days, you'll wake up and realize some great opportunities passed while you had your head down and your nose to the grindstone."

"You're quite the philosopher." She set the salad dressing on the table, refusing to become irritated with yet another reminder of how he disagreed with her work schedule.

"Not at all." He transferred the pizza pan to a trivet on the table. "I believe if you want something, you'd better go after it before it moves on."

"Are we talking about my work schedule or do I only have one chance to go out with you?" Disappointment hit her. Maybe she should end this now. She didn't have the energy to play emotional games. Frank had exhausted her in that arena.

He shrugged. "I won't ask again if that's what you mean."

Her stomach sank. She'd only known Michael for a short time, but the thought of never knowing what could have been hit her almost as hard as the news of Jack's death.

This thing with him was already too deep.

Rooted next to the island, she gripped the edge of the counter top and tried to shake off the pain deep in her heart. "I'll get the kids."

Liana stepped into the den to find Brittany and Leif bantering about the treasure hunt game. "Dinner's ready."

"Hi, Mom. I didn't hear you come home." Brittany stood and propped her hands on her hips to stretch her back. Had Liana ever possessed such a naturalness?

"I've been home for a few minutes. Michael has dinner ready. You guys hungry?"

"Starving." Leif grinned. "I'm sure Brit is tired of

losing." He fiddled with the computer another moment and closed out each window.

Liana looped her arm through Brittany's and headed for the dining room. "I met with Stan today. I've decided to cut my office hours back to two days a week. That means I'll work from home three days a week plus weekends."

"That's great, Mom, but please don't do it for me. I'm fine as long as Michael's working on the house. He's here when I get home, or I go to Meagan's."

The pain in Liana's heart intensified. She'd failed as a wife *and* a mother. "Only time will tell how long this new schedule will last, but I want to do this for us, Brit. Shari has been a godsend, and so has Michael, but I want my life back, and you're the most important part of it."

"Thanks, Mom." Brittany hugged her and blinked back tears. She pulled away from Liana and stuck her tongue out at Leif. "After dinner we're on for a rematch, Saxon."

"Bring it on, sister." Leif punched her in the arm and bee-lined to the table. "Are you guys through with all the sappy stuff so we can eat?"

Liana laughed and her heart lifted.

Michael pulled out a chair and gestured for Liana to be seated. "He's a master at levity, isn't he?"

The pizza and salad were delicious, but Liana couldn't shake her misgivings over spending so much personal time with the Saxons. Later, when the house was finished and Michael moved on, she wouldn't be the only one hurt. Brittany had taken to Michael and Leif and would be heartbroken when it all ended.

Despite the risk to her heart, Liana wanted to say

yes to his date and test their strong attraction. Maybe in private, away from the kids, they'd discover they weren't compatible and the attraction would dissipate.

Her appetite dimmed, she gave up on eating and sat back to sip her wine and study her dinner companions.

Leif and Brittany acted like old buddies. Even if in jest, she loved how he'd called Brittany, sister. His youthful good looks promised to transform into his father's rugged handsomeness. For now at least, her daughter seemed unaffected.

She gazed at Michael. He glanced at her over the rim of his wine glass. Her breath caught in her chest. Damn, the man did things to her she hadn't thought possible. Even Jack hadn't affected her with such intensity. They'd been young. Would their relationship have turned into what she felt every time Michael looked at her?

The kids sparred over the debate teams in Leif's speech class and which would win.

"Are you okay, Mom?"

Liana tore her gaze from Michael's. "I'm fine. Just lost in my thoughts. Michael, dinner was great. Thank you again for your thoughtfulness."

He wiped his mouth with the green linen napkin Brittany had dug out of their dining room linen drawer. The things they used for company. "Not a problem. You made breakfast."

"Michael ate breakfast here?" Brittany asked, pizza halfway to her mouth. She glanced from her Mom to Michael and back.

Liana could throttle him. Why had he brought it up? It made it sound like he'd stayed the night. "Michael came to work early this morning, so I cooked him a hearty breakfast before I left for work."

Apparently satisfied with the answer, Brittany shrugged and continued to eat.

Her nerves jangling, Liana shoved her plate back and stood. "I'll put on some coffee."

"It won't take long to go over my plans." Michael gathered up his plate and Liana's. "Like I said in my email, I have an idea that needs a decision before we go any farther." He joined her at the sink and rinsed the plates before he stacked them in the dishwasher.

"I can't wait to hear about it." Liana pushed away her earlier fears and doubts. Liana loved Michael's presence in the kitchen, how he helped with dishes while they discussed the building plans. It almost seemed as if they had a life together.

"Mom, go over the plans with Michael. Leif and I can finish the cleanup," Brittany called from the dining room. She gathered up the pizza pan and salad bowl.

"Thank you, sweetie." Liana poured water into the coffeemaker and added grounds to the basket. She pushed the brew button and wiped her hands with the tea towel hanging on the refrigerator handle. "Okay, I'm ready. Let's look at your idea before the night gets away from us."

"It's Saturday night." Michael leaned one hip against the counter, his amber gaze shuttered and his usually mobile mouth firm.

Liana blinked. "It is, isn't it? Regardless, I'm sure you have things you'd rather be doing."

"I'm doing what I want to do." He folded his arms over his chest. "What happened?"

Brittany and Leif arrived with the leftovers and dishes.

Liana wove through the hubbub and started for the living room. "Let's move out of the way. I'll never discourage Brittany from cleaning up after a meal."

"Hilarious, Mom." Brittany laughed when Leif got tangled in the plastic wrap.

Michael followed her to the living room. "I'd like to finish the conversation."

"I refuse to discuss us in front of the kids. Now what's your idea? I can't wait to finish this remodel so I can think about something besides cost and the fact that Thanksgiving is looming." She rubbed her upper arms. She didn't want to be so abrupt, but she had to protect herself from the spell Michael cast on her every time he was near.

Michel propped his hands on his hips and huffed. "I won't force you into a personal conversation." He picked up the plans and unrolled them on the coffee table. "Since we have to patch into the roof line anyway, why not add an upstairs? You could use it as a guest room, or an office."

"I could do that?"

A design studio flashed through her mind, complete with fabric swatches and paint samples. Large windows and a work-table in the center of the room. "Could it have an outside entrance?"

"A separate entrance?"

"Yes, a separate entrance."

Michael's stance eased and his eyes warmed. "If we came out a few more feet we could run a balcony over the front door and a set of stairs down the front of the building at an angle. I sketched some of it on the plans. Let's pencil in your idea and see what you think."

Liana glanced around the corner toward the dining room. Brittany and Leif were still in the kitchen engrossed in their banter. She turned back to Michael. "This sounds intriguing."

He smoothed the large paper out on the table. "Here's the original plan with scissor trusses to support the new peaked roof over the addition. We can replace them with regular trusses and add the second story, with stairs running up from the living room." He stroked his pencil across the plans like an artist.

Fascinated with his talent, Liana edged closer and almost moaned when his warmth and spicy scent wrapped around her.

As much as she tried to fight it, Michael Saxon decimated her better judgment. Seventeen years had passed since she'd felt even close to this degree of excitement and passion. If she didn't go out with him, she could miss out on a once in a lifetime chance for true love.

"What do you think?" Michael glanced at her and caught her stare.

"About what?"

"The new plan." His mouth softened and twitched into the shadow of a smile. His eyes heated a few degrees, the disappointment from moments ago gone.

"I really like it."

He slid from the couch to the floor next to her and propped his hand on the carpet between them. "Don't be afraid to take a chance, Liana." He leaned close enough to bring their mouths a breath apart.

Her heart fluttered. "I can't help it. I have a lot to lose."

"There's always a price, sweetheart. Stop this

dance with Frank. The song ended four years ago." He brushed her hair back from her face.

"He has an endless supply of quarters for the jukebox."

Michael laughed. "You've caught onto my parables."

"Parables?" She tilted her head to one side.

"That's what Trinity calls them. Over her teen years, I started to compare her issues with something to help her make sense of them."

Liana's heart lightened. "Trinity sounds like quite the young lady."

"I want you to meet her." His voice lowered and rasped with the passion she clearly saw in his face.

He placed his hand on her thigh. They were wedged between the couch and the coffee table, but Liana stayed on guard in case the kids popped into the room. She heard a thread of conversation and frowned.

"Frank."

"What about him?"

"Brittany's talking to him on her phone. I didn't hear it ring. She must have called him."

"What're you worried about? It's natural for her to call him."

"It's what he pries out of her that worries me. He tries to fill her head with crap."

"Are there things Brittany doesn't know?"

Liana slowly nodded. "Adult things she wouldn't understand, possibly not forgive. Things you might not be able to handle either."

"Let me get close enough to find out. I'm a good judge of character, and I learned the hard way with Meredith. Whatever you're hiding won't chase me away." He treaded his fingers through her hair. "Give us a chance."

Maybe if they dated, and she told him about Ryan, the matter would be settled. He'd either turn his back on her, or declare his love regardless of her poor choices. Before sanity returned, Liana took the leap.

"When do you want to go out?"

His delicious mouth tilted into a full, blown smile. "Sooner the better as far as I'm concerned."

"Well, this is Saturday night and it's about gone. Let's plan on next Friday night."

He leaned in for a quick kiss. "You've got it. What do you think? Ready for the design studio you've dreamed of?" He tapped the plans on the table.

Liana leaned back, her eyes wide. "How do you know I'm thinking about a design studio?"

"When you asked about the outside entrance. Follow your dreams, Liana. Let's do it."

"Mom!" Brittany came into the living room, her phone still at her ear. "Dad wants to talk to you."

Liana glanced at Michael before she smiled at her daughter. "Please tell your dad I'm busy with the contractor and will call him back later. Probably tomorrow."

Brittany hesitated, uncertainty etched on her face. "O-kay." She turned and relayed Liana's message.

"Good move. I'll bet he's digging for quarters right now."

He pushed off the floor and rolled up the plans.

Liana chuckled and joined him on the couch. "He can look all night as far as I'm concerned." A new lightness and confidence flowed through her. She'd taken control of her situation with Frank and it felt good. At least for now.

Liana walked with Michael to the back door. For now, Brittany's conversation with Frank hadn't diminished her good mood. She wouldn't quit joking with Leif until he said goodbye and hopped down the back steps, then she thanked Michael for dinner and went to her bedroom.

Michael lingered in the doorway with Liana. He started to say something until Leif backtracked from the parking area. "Can I have the truck keys, Dad?"

"Sure, son. Warm it up and you can drive us home." Michael tossed them through the air and Leif caught them with one hand.

Michael pressed his lips against Liana's forehead. "Get a good night's sleep. I'll be around early Monday morning. I promise the living room will be completed by Thanksgiving."

"I appreciate that. It means a lot to me." She wanted to tug his face down to hers and kiss him until he moaned in that gravelly way of his. But, Leif waited in the truck and Brittany could pop out of her bedroom anytime.

She folded her arms to keep from touching him. "What should we do on our date?"

He grinned. "Uh, dinner? Dancing? Whatever you want."

Damn, the man tempted her.

"I'll let you know."

Michael did his typical two-finger salute to the brim of his hat and rounded the corner of the house.

Back in the warmth of the laundry room, Liana locked the door and wandered into the kitchen. She made a cup of chamomile tea and settled into a chair in front of the fire.

Stalling Frank might seem like a victory right now, but he'd retaliate. An angry Frank had never been a good thing.

Chapter Six

Liana found new excitement in the remodel.

She loved to design and change, but when the original contractor left, she'd lost her zest for the plan. Michael had restored her enthusiasm on every level.

True to his word, he showed up at seven Monday morning looking so deliciously handsome Liana leaned against the doorjamb and drank up the sight of him.

The anticipation of their date made her nervous and giddy. She wasn't ready to have her heart broken again, but oh, she wanted to experience complete passion.

Now to figure out how to tell Brittany she planned to date the contractor.

Her daughter rushed from room to room getting ready for school. She called out a hello to Michael as she left to catch the bus.

Liana lingered at the kitchen window, and observed the dynamics between her daughter and the man Liana fell harder for every day.

Brittany seemed to really like him, but there'd been a couple of times when Michael and Liana talked, that she'd looked unsettled and not completely happy when her mother showed interest in someone other than Frank. Liana determined she had to keep Brittany involved in the things she loved to do, and include her when Michael was around.

When Michael's crew arrived, Liana went to her

bedroom to dress for the office. She decided on chocolate brown leggings and a thigh-length, curve-hugging beige cashmere sweater. Okay, so her goal was to wow Michael. She fastened a wide, dark brown belt at her waist, and finished the look with tall boots, hoop earrings and a jangle of bracelets. Completing her hairstyle and makeup, she grabbed her purse, a long raincoat and left the house.

The moment she rounded the corner, every man on the crew stopped and watched her. Liana's head swelled. She smiled and waved at them. Nothing like male appreciation to confirm she'd picked out the right clothes.

Like the head cock of the walk, Michael met her at the Hybrid SUV and opened her door. "Want to quit distracting my crew? We'll never get finished if you look like this every day." His sexy mouth curled up in a smile.

"Jealous?" The word popped out before Liana could stop it.

"Damn right." He ran his hand up and down her arm and brushed his lips across hers. "Now they know I found you first."

The egotistical male routine would normally have turned Liana off, but not with Michael. Instead of inflated ego, he radiated raw sexual male confidence.

"Yes, you did find me first."

She climbed onto the cold leather seat, turned on the engine, and leaned out to press her lips to his. "Now, they know for sure," she murmured against his mouth. She smiled and leaned in while he closed the door. He backed a few steps, waved and turned toward his gawking crew and the disaster zone that was her house.

****

The week progressed better than Michael would have predicted.

With the new plans of a second story, he hired two more men to help with the concrete work and demo the roof to the ridge beam.

He and Liana met to discuss paint choices and confirm the hardwood floor she'd liked in the Whitefish house. He quickly became impressed with her professionalism and choices. With her expertise, he had no need to do more than agree. The kitchen, laundry room and guest bath were remodeled right before Liana bought the house, but she didn't care for the paint colors. Since the house was in a mess anyway, she chose new colors and added a bid to paint the additional rooms to Michael's bill. He'd never turn down more money, so he called Harvey Smith, the best painter in town to do the job.

Harvey stopped by on Wednesday. "Saxon, I can pick up the paint and start on the kitchen tomorrow, but it's gonna to be hard for the family to live here while I work."

Michael nodded. "You're right. It's one thing to have the living room out of commission, but people don't function well without a kitchen. I'll call the owner right now and warn her."

Damn, he didn't want Liana and Brittany to move out even for a short time, but at the very least they have to eat out for a couple of days. Then there were the paint fumes to contend with. He'd miss them every morning, and Brittany when she came home after school.

Liana answered his call on the third ring. "Hi, Michael."

"You recognize my number now, huh?" His chest expanded a little with the knowledge.

"Of course. What's up?"

"I've got some good news and some not so good news. Harvey can start right away and get it done in a few days. The problem is, your kitchen will be out of commission."

"Eek. I should have thought about that. I guess we'd better find a place to stay."

"What about Shari's? Does she have room? I can feed Oscar and water the plants." Liana's cat had taken a liking to Michael.

"Oh." Liana drew out the word. "Shari's mom arrives this weekend and plans to stay through Thanksgiving, so she'll use the guest suite." She groaned. "I suppose we'll have to check into a hotel."

"I'll do everything I can to help Harvey expedite the job."

"You do so much more than the standard contractor, Michael. I don't mean to sound ungrateful. I'll adjust and go with the flow."

Michael was impressed. She'd been so resistant to change since he'd met her. He shouldn't delude himself though. The complication she kept referring to hadn't been resolved. It could tip her over at any time.

"I'll call the Outlaw Inn and make a reservation. Can I move back by Monday?"

"That should work." Later that night, he'd just put some steaks under the broiler when Liana called to confirm she'd made reservations at the Outlaw Inn, and would be out of the house early Thursday morning.

"Brittany will stay with me Thursday night, but she insists she should stay with Meagan Friday night. I'd like to know how she found out about our date since I haven't worked up the courage to tell her."

Michael's head spun. Dinner with Liana where she'd booked a private hotel room. "Uh, I'm not sure. Maybe Leif told her?" He couldn't think straight. "Are you okay?"

"Yes, I'm fine." Her sigh carried through the connection. "I'm just have to prepare myself for a call from Frank."

"Relax, sweetheart. I'm here for you, whatever happens."

A pause stretched out.

"Thank you. I'll see you soon."

Michael disconnected the call and glanced around his kitchen. Damn, she tied him in knots!

"Leif! Why is your homework spread out on the table and you're not here?"

****

Early Friday morning, Michael lined out the exterior crew before he wheeled a hand truck into the house to move appliances away from the walls and throw a tarp over them. He had the utility room cleared out and a good start on the kitchen when Harvey arrived.

"Saxon, since when do I need your help?" Harvey joked, while Michael draped the counters with heavy paint fabric.

"You don't, my friend. I'm eager to get the kitchen done by Monday so the family can move back."

"Just don't mess up my walls." Harvey laid out his tools of the trade and pried open a can of paint. "Mick, I

101

get the feeling this is more than a job to you. The lady must really be something."

Michael chucked at the nickname his subs had given him right after he moved to Kalispell and started his contractor business.

"She is something. Her family arrives the day before Thanksgiving so I want to make sure the house shines for her."

"Can't blame you." Harvey poured the paint into a pan. "Look at this, will you? Hal at the paint store said she's a designer."

Michael looked at the bold paint color Liana had chosen for the utility room. "What do they call that?"

"Goldenrod, with a touch of Adobe," Harvey said in the hoity-toity tone of voice he liked to use when they worked on an upscale home.

Michael grinned. "It'll look great."

At noon, he checked in with Harvey to find the older man tapping the lid back on the paint can.

"Done with this room, Mick. Lunch time." He wiped his hands on a paint spattered rag and cracked open a small red cooler. "If I don't stop and eat, my wife will have my backside tonight. She gets mad when I don't eat all day and come home starving."

"No problem. I'll check on the new construction project, and grab something at the taco place." Michael started for his truck, relieved Liana and Brittany had moved out until the fumes settled.

Fumes. Oscar.

The poor cat had been confused when Liana and Brittany carried their bags out last night. Now, strangers worked in the house and filled it with what might be toxic fumes for an animal.

He jumped out of the truck and went into the house.

"Back already?" Harvey sat at the table eating his sandwich.

"Guilty conscience. The daughter has a house cat she adores. He must be hiding out somewhere. I think I'll take him home."

"Yep, you got it bad, Mick." Harvey shook his head, a big smile on his face.

Yeah, he did have it bad. In ten short days, his life had become intertwined with Liana and her daughter. He caught himself scrambling for excuses to see them. Judging by the way she drew back when things heated up, he might need to slow down. He was crazy to get intimate with a woman with so much baggage.

Oscar was under Brittany's bed amidst a million pairs of shoes. He pulled the terrified cat out and held him close. "It's all right, old man. I'll take care of you. Just have to find your carrier."

Michael opened the closet door. Damn the thing was bulging with clothes, scarves, hats and everything else a girl would want.

Frank? Had to be. He must pay a healthy child support payment.

Michael took the cat carrier from the top shelf, careful not to upset the stacks of folded clothes. An overstuffed photo album started to fall. With Oscar under his arm, he had to let it fall. Photos fluttered to the carpet.

"First things first." He put the spooked cat in the carrier. As he picked up the photos, he couldn't help but glance at them. Liana in front of what must have been their new house in San Francisco. The house was upscale and much larger than this one.

A photo of Brittany in front of the house with Oscar in her arms.

The last photo made him pause. A man, early twenties, who bore a striking resemblance to Brittany. Frank? He turned the photo over and froze. *Uncle Jack* was scrawled across the back.

Uncle Jack? Whose brother was he? Liana's or Franks? No last name on the photo. He flipped it back over and studied the broad smile and dark cherry brown eyes, just like Brittany's. Was it possible for her to look so much like an uncle?

He slipped the photo into the album, put it back on the shelf and picked up Oscar's carrier.

"Enough snooping, old man. Time to hit the road."

Chapter Seven

Michael checked on the new construction project, and dropped Oscar off at his house. He left the cat in his bedroom with the carrier open, so Oscar didn't freak out, or tangle with Lucky.

Back at Liana's house, he was surprised to see her SUV in the driveway. He found her in the kitchen, a pleased smile on her face.

"You're here." His body stirred from the sight of her.

"I couldn't wait to see the wall color." She seemed so innocent of her effect on him.

"Like it?" He could barely restrain himself from kissing her. The woman tore him up without the blink of an eye.

"Like it? I love it!"

"Harvey will be glad to hear it. He contracts all my painting jobs."

Liana went from the kitchen to the utility room and back. "It's gorgeous!"

Michael leaned against the granite countertop and waited for her to finish soaking up the new look. He had to admit she'd made excellent choices. The tonal theme of the utility room bled into the kitchen with bolder strokes. Adobe dominated the kitchen walls and picked up on the flicks of red brown in the granite countertop. "You did well, Liana. Your house will be a great example of your design and color abilities."

She smiled at him. "You came up with the new second story and the outside entrance. I can't take credit for those ideas."

"Maybe we make a good team." He moved toward her, admiring her shapely figure in the fitted black pantsuit and low heeled leather boots. She looked every inch the fashionable businesswoman.

"That's a possibility." She tilted her head to one side. "I like your work and now you've seen a hint of mine. It'd be fun to work together on a project, and see how it goes."

Back to work, Saxon, he coached himself. Don't blow the date she'd agreed to by jumping the gun. "Once the kitchen dries and the house airs out, you can move back in for a while."

"A while?" She glanced around the house.

"The flooring you chose comes unfinished. I have to apply three coats of sealant once it's down to create the look you liked."

"It can't be done before installation?"

"It can, but it won't look as good. I prefer to finish once it's down, and seal the cracks between the planks." He scratched the back of his head and squinted one eye. "We talked about the floor the other night. Sorry, I didn't detail that step."

"Hmm." Liana walked around the room, turning her head from side to side. "My choices are: move out of my house again for up to a week, or take the chance of an unfinished floor when my Mom arrives."

"That sums it up."

"So." Liana whirled to face him. "I should have rented a condo for a few weeks instead of hotel hopping."

"Liana, I'm sorry about this. If I didn't mention the process, I sure meant to."

She propped her hands on her hips. The black suit jacket pulled tight over her breasts and widened the gap between the buttons. Her silver locket glistened against her skin. "It's not your fault. I should have thought about it. I also should have thought about Oscar. Poor guy was shook up from all the commotion."

"I agree. That's why I moved him to my house." And snooped in your daughter's photos while I was at it.

"How is he? Is he scared?" Liana's eyes glistened with tears.

"He's fine. I left him in my room with food and water and a cat box. His carrier is open in case he feels insecure."

"I can't thank you enough. Poor Oscar. At least he'll be healthy. I should have taken him to an animal hotel." She looked so guilty and upset that Michael stepped toward her to take her in his arms.

Liana's phone rang. She dug it out of her cavernous purse. "Hello?"

Michael turned away. Maybe he should be thankful her phone interrupted him. Time for a reality check to cool off his impulse to jump into the sack with her.

While she talked to what sounded like a client, he wandered outside and waited until she joined him. The excitement had disappeared from her expression.

"I have to go."

"Back to the Outlaw?"

She madly jotted something down on a little notepad. "No, the Cummings's sent a couple to the office to meet with me."

"Tonight?"

"They leave Sunday and want to make an offer. If I hurry, I can be ready to go out by eight."

"Eight? For dinner?" He was tired, hungry and disappointed that she'd put a pair of demanding clients ahead of him. They'd had all day to look at their blasted houses.

"That's not so late. Meet me at the hotel?"

"I don't know. Maybe we should cancel." He'd busted his butt all week and didn't like to play second fiddle. If the plans they'd made were so easy to change, maybe they should change them completely.

"Michael, I have to take advantage of business while it's here." She stepped toward him, her eyes reflecting her hurt. "We can still have a great evening."

"Hey, the clients are waiting." Michael considered himself a calm and mature man, but right now, he wanted to put his fist through the newly painted walls. Something he'd never in his life stooped to doing.

The woman drove him crazy.

Heat suffused his face. Michael struggled to steady his temper. He had no right to stop her, or even criticize her. They had no agreement, no commitment. They'd kissed. So what if they'd been the most mind-blowing kisses he'd ever experienced?

"See you later."

Michael strode to his truck and shut the door, not waiting for Liana's reaction. When her taillights disappeared around the corner in the driveway, he shifted into gear.

His cell rang. "Dad, since you have a date tonight, I'd like to go to O'Reilly's for dinner with a group of kids from school."

"Sounds like fun. I'll be home shortly to shower and change. If you leave before I get home, don't be out past midnight."

"I won't. How late will you be?"

Michael scrubbed his face with his free hand and grimaced at the grit from the day. "Hard to tell. Liana got a call and has to show a house tonight. I might be home all evening, or out late. Be sure Lucky goes out and back in, before you go to bed. Oscar's in my room. Oh, and lock all the doors before you go to bed. I can use my key."

****

Liana nibbled on her bottom lip as she drove away from her soon-to-be beautiful house.

Michael tied her in knots. He implied he wanted her, and she wanted him too—desperately, but the moment she had to go back to work, he acted like he couldn't stand her. Probably just as well.

She'd acted on emotion with Jack and had ended up pregnant.

Emotion had driven her to marry Frank and look where it ended. As a college junior, all she'd thought of was the horrors of single motherhood. No husband, no help, no money and no degree.

Boy, had she made a mistake. The gratitude she'd felt for Frank's proposal had evaporated within the first year of marriage. She didn't love him, didn't want to make love with him, but was trapped in her impulsive decision.

For the past four years, she'd done well without a relationship. Why start now? There'd be plenty of time after Brittany went to college.

Liana puckered her lips and turned into the office parking lot. Yeah, but by that time, Michael Saxon would be long gone. If she thought she could protect herself from getting hurt, she was too late.

Snapping up her phone, she called Brittany to let her know they'd move to a condo first thing tomorrow morning.

****

Liana loved hotels.

Room service, maid service and oh yes, the honor bar. She inspected the booty of snacks and tiny bottles of liquor. She mixed a cocktail, excited to unwind and remember how it felt to be carefree.

She frowned and stirred her drink. Had she ever been carefree?

At least the new clients had been considerate and hurried through the two houses she'd chosen. One in Kalispell and Michael's remodeled house in Whitefish. They'd have an answer tomorrow.

She picked up her phone. Eight o'clock and no word from Michael. Well, if he couldn't understand she had to value every client, she didn't know what to say.

So what if he was the sexiest man she'd ever met? She'd be damned if she'd live with someone who didn't understand her needs. The gin and tonic tasted far too good and went down far too fast. She mixed another and settled into the club chair, her feet on the ottoman. She clicked through the cable channels, her mind only half on what she saw.

Cable was a luxury she'd denied Brittany. Homework took enough time without the temptation of one hundred and fifty stations.

She signed and glanced around the room. The past

few months had been crazy with business and the remodel. Here she could soak up some peacefulness. Liana leaned back and closed her eyes. Tonight she'd indulge in a couple cocktails; dinner downstairs.

Michael's face flashed through her mind. Dinner with him would have been marvelous. No kids, the anonymity of the hotel. Wow, what a fantasy. If only he understood her position, how she was a single mom with huge obligations.

She opened her eyes and gazed at the music video channel she'd selected. Damn, why had she lost it with him? Why so self-defensive? A nice explanation about the importance of each closing would have sufficed.

Oh well. Michael would finish her house, move onto the next project and her head would clear. She'd focus on Brittany and their new life in Montana. She'd focus on decorating her house for Thanksgiving so when her family arrived, they'd stop believing she lived in some cabin in the woods with no plumbing.

She giggled at the image of her mother's expression if Liana told her the bathroom was out back.

A firm rap on the door startled her.

The drink sloshed over the side of the glass and trickled down the back of her hand. She grabbed a napkin and dabbed at her hand and her sleeve. Great, she'd reek of alcohol. Pushing out of the chair, she wobbled on her feet.

"Whoa." Two cocktails on an empty stomach hit her with both barrels.

A louder, more insistent tap irritated her. "I'm coming!" She aimed for to the door, using the furniture and the wall for stability. A glance through the peephole ignited a familiar wave of heat. "Michael."

"Can I come in?"

She unlocked the door and inched it open. "Hi."

He blocked the opening with his foot. "Before you close the door in my face, I'm sorry I came down on you this afternoon. I don't have a right to dictate your time."

"No, you don't and I accept your apology." She smiled, floating on the gin. He'd showered and shaved and dressed in form fitting jeans and a crisp white cotton shirt.

She moved out of the way. "Come in."

He slipped between her and the closet door. His familiar musky-spicy cologne made her body tingle. He stopped at the foot of the king-sized bed before he turned to face her. "I wasn't sure you'd want to see me after the way we left things this evening."

"I wasn't sure either." Liana gripped the wall and wove her way toward him. "We have some differences we can't seem to get past."

"Can't isn't in my vocabulary. I'm not ready to give up."

He looked so damned good, so heartbreakingly handsome, Liana's resolve to keep things simple and uncomplicated, slipped. "Normally it's not in mine either, but there are issues we have to settle."

Snap up, Liana, she schooled herself. Don't go soft just because the man looks hotter than the pavement on the Forth of July.

The sight of him affected her more than the alcohol.

He shoved his fingers into the front pockets of his form fitting jeans. "So, are we still on for tonight?"

"Are you hungry?" She giggled and held her hand

over her mouth. Where had that come from?

One corner of Michael's mouth kicked up in the sexy grin she loved so much. "Looks like I missed happy hour, but to answer your question, yeah, I'm very hungry." He swept an intense gaze up and down her body.

Liana instantly went hot. What happened to her? A minute ago she'd made it clear they had problems they couldn't get past. Making love would complicate things to the max. She tamped down her libido and lifted her chin. "We could check out the hotel restaurant. I've heard it's good."

"Then let's do it—have dinner."

The room rippled before her eyes, Michael wavered with it.

"You haven't eaten today, have you?" He stepped toward her and gripped her shoulders. "Ms. Campbell, you're sloshed."

She dropped her chin to her chest. "I know. I'm embarrassed."

"Don't be. You work too hard and let down your defenses too seldom. When you're with me, you're safe."

A warmth that had nothing to do with alcohol or passionate thoughts, stole over her. He was so much more than a handsome man. Michael was a solid, dependable man who knew how to treat a lady.

"Thank you," she whispered. Moisture gathered in her eyes. "I do feel safe with you."

Dinner was magic. Michael lavished her with attention from seating her, to focusing on every word she said. Candles cast a golden glow over the table and deepened the bronze richness of Michael's skin.

He ordered a bottle of wine, but wouldn't pour her a glass until she'd eaten her salad and a piece of bread.

"Okay, I have to try that vintage. I'm better. I promise."

Michael smiled his special smile and poured her wine. "All right, but take it easy. I won't be accused of taking advantage of you."

Liana eyed him over the rim of her wine glass. Wow, what a lead in. With a simple response, she'd ensure a passion-filled night. "If something of that nature happens between us, Mr. Saxon, you might be the one who's taken advantage of."

Michael smirked. "You're a naughty woman, Ms. Campbell. Which reminds me—I'm curious—what made you keep your maiden name when you married?" He picked up another piece of bread and slathered it with whipped herb butter.

Liana took a sip of wine and set her glass on the white linen tablecloth. "I wasn't in love with Frank, so I didn't want to give him the wrong impression."

Michael's elbow connected with his bread plate and his knife skittered across the table. "You married a man you didn't love? Why?"

"Brittany doesn't know any of this, so if I tell you, you have to promise never to tell her or anyone."

Michael leaned his forearms on the table and squinted one eye at her. "Liana, you should know me better than that. I'd never tell Brittany anything of such a personal nature. Anything about your past life is your business."

Liana took a deep breath. If any hope of a relationship with him existed, she had to feed Michael the truth of her past. He deserved to know what he might be getting into. "Frank isn't Brittany's biological dad." She paused, and searched his amber eyes for disgust or disbelief. He didn't blink.

"Go on."

"I was in love with Frank's brother, Jack Nash."

Michael's dark brows shot up. "That explains it."

"What?"

"When I decided to take Oscar home, I looked for the cat carrier in Brittany's room. I accidentally bumped her photo album and knocked out some pictures. One of them was of a man I thought had to be Frank, until I turned it over and read, Uncle Jack."

"Brittany looks so much like Jack. It ate at Frank. He never mentioned it, but I'm sure he hoped the baby would look like me, so he wouldn't have to be constantly reminded she wasn't really his."

His mouth set in a firm line. Liana realized what he must think. "Oh, I wasn't married to Frank when I got pregnant. I was engaged to Jack."

"Go on."

She leaned toward him. "I found out I was pregnant not long before Jack shipped out to the Persian Gulf. I decided to wait to tell him about the baby and accept his proposal. I waited too long. His plane malfunctioned during a training mission and he was killed."

Michael reached across the table and grasped her forearm. "I'm so sorry."

The pesky tears she'd become an expert at shedding didn't appear. For the first time, discussing Jack's accident was more bittersweet than sad. Did Michael have something to do with the change?

"My father's a career Navy man. He's retired now,

but when my brothers and I were growing up, he was gone all the time. My parents divorced." She smiled at Michael. "Are you on overload yet?"

"Not at all." His voice was deep and soft. "I want to learn all the deep things about Liana Campbell."

"You're amazing." She grasped his hand. "Most men would have excused themselves by now, and I'd never see them again."

"Has that happened to you?"

"Truthfully, I haven't been this close to anyone." She cleared her throat. "Back to why I didn't tell Jack. I found out my father had an affair, and that's what ended my parent's marriage. I didn't want to marry a military man. I didn't want to stay home and raise my children alone, worry about him dying, or cheating on me. Both scenarios frightened me enough to refuse Jack every time he discussed marriage. Believe me, when I got the news, I regretted my hesitancy."

"So how did Frank come into this?"

Liana went on to tell him about Frank's crush on her and his jealousy toward Jack. How Frank comforted her at the funeral, and how she let down her guard and told him about the baby. His solution to marry seemed like the right thing. She wouldn't be a single mother, and Brittany would legally have Jack's name. Without Jack, she'd never love again anyway. She might as well be content.

"Were you content?" He fingered the inside of her hand, his gaze warm and intense in the candlelight.

"Rarely. I made a big mistake marrying someone I wasn't head over heels in love with. Marriage is too intimate of a relationship for lukewarm feelings."

Their dinner arrived. Michael thanked the server

and poured more wine.

"So, I get more?" Liana smiled, her heart lighter than it'd been for a long time. Telling Michael about her life with Frank had a cathartic effect.

"I think you can handle more." He winked at her. "Besides, I don't want you to get too serious. This is a date, after all."

"It is, isn't it?" She took a bite of sautéed scallops and moaned. "Oh, my gosh, this is so good." She lifted her wine glass and clinked it with his. "The wine is great and the company exceptional."

"To this evening." He took a sip, his eyes smoldering. After a long moment, he set his glass on the table and picked up his fork. "Do you plan to tell Brittany the truth?"

"I've wanted to so many times. For all his foibles, Brittany loves her dad. I'm petrified over how she might react. Will she side with Frank and want to live with him?"

"Why would she blame you for the divorce?"

Liana could swear the blood left her head. This was where she should tell him about Ryan, but how could she in public? She grappled to cover her panic. "Because I didn't love him, Frank blames me for the divorce."

"Sounds to me like you're transferring your parent's marital problems to your life and how it worked out. You blame your dad for their divorce. Have you seen much of him since?"

Pain pierced Liana's heart. "No. I haven't. Oh, my gosh, hearing it put like that does make the two situations seem closer."

"We're all shaped by the events in our lives, Liana.

It's how we learn." He patted his mouth with the linen napkin. "You can't help but judge one outcome by the other. Is your dad coming up for Thanksgiving?"

Liana sighed. "Brittany asked me the same thing. Come to think of it, so did Shari. I honestly don't know. I don't have his phone number, and Mom hasn't mentioned him."

"Making peace with your dad could help you and Brittany make peace with the decision you made sixteen years ago. Think about it."

Liana slowly ate the rest of her dinner. Michael was not only handsome and sexy, he was very intelligent. No one had ever "gotten" her like he did.

They opted to pass on dessert and took coffee to Liana's room.

The moment Michael closed the door, the intimacy of the bedroom wrapped around them. Without a word they set their coffee mugs on the small table in front of the window and faced each other. Liana pressed her lips to his. Her need bordered the edge of desperation.

She raked her fingers through his hair and down his neck to bracket his shoulders. It wouldn't hurt to enjoy some kisses and caresses.

Michael's testosterone went into over drive. He deepened the kiss and cupped her bottom, lifted her against him. Liana's legs came around his hips and set him on fire. He carried her to the bed, and gently lowered her to the comforter, following until her breasts pressed against his chest, her curves dipped and raised in just the right places.

Slow it down, Saxon. You didn't want to go too far, too fast.

Damn, he'd been on his own for three years and

was on the verge of combustion. They were both consenting adults. He didn't plan to walk away tomorrow. He cared far more than that.

So why did he start cooling down?

He tore his mouth from hers. "Liana."

"Hmm?" She rocked against him.

"I want you, baby, but I need to be sure you're ready for a deeper commitment. The sex will be damn good, but it won't resolve anything else."

Liana opened her eyes, her mossy green irises dreamy. "Why do you have to be so wise?"

She released a huge sigh, pulled away and lay on her back. She flopped her arm over her eyes. "Damn, damn, damn. Why do we have to think about tomorrow?"

"Because that's who we are." Michael took her arm off her face and gazed into her eyes. "We're not kids anymore and we're not irresponsible. Isn't that why we're no longer with our exes?"

Liana chuckled. "Good point." She sighed again. "So where do we go from here?"

Michael rolled to his back and laced his fingers over his chest. "Believe me, I have to use every bit of self control not to finish what we started. We've been through relationships that started for the wrong reasons. We need to be sure this is what we really want and not just good sex."

Liana rolled to her side and propped her head with one hand. "You're a strong man. Good sex sounds like just what I need right now." Tears spilled from her eyes and her shoulders shook with a sob.

"Whoa now, what brought this on? Come here." He gathered her into his arms and stroked her hair.

"Talk to me."

"I'm sorry, but it feels so good to lean on you, Michael. Frank doesn't let up. He's called either me or Brittany every day since I moved. He lays a guilt trip on Brittany and threatens me. On top of that, my house is torn apart, my entire family is coming for Thanksgiving, and I can't let down or I won't have the money to finish the repairs and remodel."

"Your house will be ready for Thanksgiving."

Liana buried her face in his crisp, white shirtfront. "I trust you, Michael." She gazed at him and fiddled with the buttons on his shirt. "You have such deep qualities. I see it in how you interact with the kids. Being with you would be far more than sex with a handsome hunk."

Michael pushed a lock of blonde hair off her forehead. "So, I'm a handsome hunk?" He couldn't stop a grin, or the warmth stealing into his heart.

"It can't be a revelation." Liana stared at him long and hard. "I'm sure you've heard it countless times, but you're more than handsome. You're solid and caring and good. That's why I'm so attracted to you."

"I'm very attracted to you. I want to spend time with you, and not just once every couple of weeks. I won't accept a casual relationship. Not for me and not for our children." He brushed a kiss across her brow. "Our work schedules have to mesh."

"Michael, I want to slow down. I want to pursue my design career. But I can't right now." She took a deep breath and slowly let it out. "Part of the reason I work so much—is because of the alimony I pay Frank."

"Alimony?" He jerked up on his elbow. "You've got to be kidding. I thought he had some big shot software career and paid a healthy child support for Brittany."

"He made good money until the dot com crash. After he lost his job, I supported us until he found another position. I stayed until we were financially back on our feet. I might have stayed longer, but...well, he's never paid child support."

"How did you end up paying alimony?"

She pursed her lips. "He claimed the divorce was my fault. He refused to give me a dime, even for Brittany's care. Instead he sends her money directly along with gift cards for department stores because he doesn't want me to benefit." She rolled on her back and waved her arms in the air. "I gave up a successful design career to move north with him. Ironic how I pay him support."

"I don't get it. How did the court rule you at fault? Wasn't the divorce on the grounds of incompatibility?"

She covered her face with both hands. "Can we not discuss this anymore tonight?"

He pulled one hand from her face and kissed the corner of her mouth. "If that's what you want." She held something back, he could sense it, but he didn't have a right to push—not yet. He rolled to the other edge of the bed and stood to tuck his shirttails back into his jeans. "Liana, I want to spend more time with you. I won't lie about where my head's been lately." He glanced at the rumpled bed and back. "I want our relationship to move to an intimate level. If there's something I should know before that happens...I hope you share it."

Liana scrambled off the bed, and stared at him over the expanse of the white comforter. "I want to spend more time with you too, but I'm not ready to open up completely. I hope you understand."

Michael smiled and backed to the door. "I'm not giving up. Sweet dreams."

Chapter Eight

Courtney Cummings called Liana shortly after seven the next morning and jarred her from a crazy jumble of dreams involving Jack, Frank and Michael. She and Courtney made plans to meet for breakfast to go over the offers the Cummings had been forced to increase. Their urgency coupled with a sleepless night, made Liana stress out.

Groggy, she stumbled to the shower and cranked on the water.

Michael's curiosity about the grounds for her divorce plagued her. Their relationship had moved past casual conversation. The subject would come up again and, gauging by his expression and tone when he talked about Meredith's affairs, she had two choices: confess or put him off again and risk losing him either way. Wow, not much of a choice.

She spent the morning with the Cummings's, giving her clients her full attention despite her tiredness and distress. Most likely Michael spent his Saturday's with Leif, doing whatever they did on the weekend. Strange how she'd almost slept with the man, but she didn't know more about his daily life than he built beautiful houses and had the respect of everyone he worked with.

Liana picked up Brittany right after lunch. They made a quick stop at the house to pack more essentials and empty the refrigerator into an ice chest for the condo Liana had rented for the next month.

They might not need it that long, but she didn't intend to uproot her daughter again if the house wasn't ready.

Settled into the condo, Liana popped a chicken in the oven and made a cup of tea. Somehow she had to stay awake and alert long enough to get through dinner.

"Hey, Mom?"

"Yes, sweetie?" Liana turned to Brittany, who had been in her temporary bedroom.

"Have you talked to Dad today?"

"No. Why?" Liana braced herself for what Frank might have said to her daughter.

"Molly has moved completely out. Dad's really down."

Liana took a deep breath and wrung the back of her neck with one hand. "Brit, I have a feeling where this conversation is going, and the answer is still no. You can't visit your dad before the Christmas holidays."

Brittany huffed. "That's kind of heartless. You have Michael. What if I can help Dad get back together with Molly? I won't know unless I'm there."

"First, I don't have Michael. We work together on the house and have had one date. Second, only your dad and Molly can work out their problems. Third, I resent being called heartless. I tried to work things out amicably with your father many times."

"I'm sorry, Mom. You're the nicest person I know. I just feel helpless since I'm too far away to really help him." Brittany turned back toward her bedroom.

"Hey, come give me a hug." Liana wrapped her daughter in her arms. "You have to stop feeling responsible for your dad's depression. Moving away wasn't an easy decision, but I decided and still maintain I made the best decision. Give him time to adjust."

Liana sank to the bar stool, her heart heavy. She wanted Brittany to be compassionate, but Frank played the victim well.

"All right, I'll assure him I'll be there for Christmas." Her shoulders slumped, Brittany returned to her bedroom.

Liana took a sip of tea and smacked her lips.

Frank Nash stepped over the line when he took advantage of Brittany's tender heart and she'd be damned if she let him get away with it.

****

Monday morning Liana drove Brittany to school on her way to the office. She tried to focus on her work, but ended up with her elbows on her desk and her head in her hands. She needed a plan.

For now she made enough money to work from home three days a week, but when this group of clients dried up, she'd still have alimony payments. She needed an approach to deal with Frank and eliminate the alimony.

Unable to accomplish a thing with so much uncertainty on her mind, she grabbed her jacket and left the office. She might as well wander the downtown streets where she could lose herself in the shops.

"Are you daydreaming about your tall, dark handsome contractor?"

Liana jumped. "Oh, my gosh, Shari, you startled me!"

"I know. You were in your own little world."

Liana hooked her arm through Shari's and steered

them into a coffee shop. "I need a latte."

"Hey, girl friend, I'm here for you. There's nothing a tall mocha latte can't solve. Oh, maybe some things, but then you call in straight chocolate."

Liana laughed. "Where's your mom?"

"A weekend of shopping wore her out, so she's home resting."

They paused their conversation to order coffees. Shari threw in a couple biscotti breads and pinned Liana with a probing stare. "So how'd the date go with Michael?"

Liana wove through the tables to a small bistro set in the corner. She settled in with her back to the wall. A stream of people came in and out of the shop for a midmorning caffeine fix. "We started to argue late in the afternoon when I had to show some properties and he didn't like the idea of a late dinner. I didn't think I'd see him later, but he showed up and saved me from a lonely night with the honor bar."

"Prince Charming has flaws?"

Liana took a deep breath. "The man is flawless."

"Honey, no man is flawless. Not even Richard. This means you're in really deep. What happened after that?"

"We had dinner in the hotel. I was so relaxed I told him about Jack."

Shari's auburn eyebrows shot up. "Wow."

"I know." Liana held up both hands, her fingers spread. "I want to be totally honest, but I couldn't tell him about Ryan. When I do, he'll be disgusted and call it quits."

"Yeah, for sure you have to wait until your house is finished."

Liana swatted at her friend. "Shari, I'm not that callous! Although realistically, I can't afford to make him want to leave. The house has to be done by Thanksgiving."

Shari leaned forward. "Honestly, Li, you've been extolling his virtues since you met him. Neither of us believes Michael will walk off the job just because you're not compatible."

"Of course he wouldn't."

"Now, tell me what else happened."

"We went back to my room with our coffee to talk, but—oh, my gosh—it was like something out of a romance novel. One of those hot, steamy ones I occasionally read. I wanted him to stay all night."

Shari rested her arms on the table. "And?"

"We kissed and held each other, but we both realized we need to move slow."

"Wow, you are working too much. Have you forgotten about the little joy called sex?"

"Hey, you've already lectured me about working too much. I get your point."

"Yes, and you know I'm right. You even changed your office schedule, but you still work long hours from home. How does Michael like your schedule?"

"My work schedule is the only issue he thinks we have. Wait until he learns I almost had an affair."

Shari grasped Liana's forearm. "You have to trust the man. He's a one of a kind, a real catch. Have faith in his feelings for you and in yourself. You slipped up with Ryan, but you stopped it from going too far."

Liana turned down her mouth. "Oh...if only I could believe Michael would see it that way."

Shari glanced around the shop. "I didn't hear them

call out our coffee order. I'll go check on it."

Liana leaned back in her chair and stared out the side window toward the city street. Friday night with Michael had been amazing. She loved the feel and strength of his arms, how his body molded to hers.

Shari returned with the lattes and biscotti. "So, what can we do to get your life on track?"

Liana clenched her fist and lightly tapped her knuckles on the table. "To start with, Frank needs to quit calling me or Brittany everyday. He threatens me and begs her to visit him over Thanksgiving. Can you believe that? He knows it's my favorite holiday."

Shari's mouth tightened. "I never liked the man."

"I've come to the conclusion that I need to hire a new lawyer. The one in San Francisco has to be in Frank's pocket. I'm going to quit paying alimony."

"Alimony!" Shari shouted. "You have got to be kidding me! You've been paying Frank alimony?"

Liana glanced around at the curious expressions on the other coffee house customer's faces. "That's exactly why I never told you. I knew you'd blow up."

"Well, it's the most archaic thing I've heard in a long time. How did it happen? Frank has a good job."

"When we went to court, he met me outside the courtroom and said he'd take Brittany from me if I didn't pay him. I refused at first, but he threatened to tell Brittany about Ryan if I didn't. It's another part of his blackmail scheme to keep me miserable."

Shari's mouth dropped open. She pushed her coffee cup to one side and reached across the table to clamp her hand over Liana's arm. "You have to stop this. All of it. You can't live the rest of your life, or even until Brittany grows up, under Frank's thumb."

Liana propped her elbows on the table and forked her fingers through her hair. "Oh, Shari, I'm in such a tangle, I don't know how I'll ever get out. I made way more money on my house in California than I spent on the house here. I have a healthy savings, but if I have to dip into it to pay Frank or my living expenses, I'll have no retirement."

"This is ridiculous! Richard will know a good lawyer. Why didn't you tell me before this? You never said a word."

"I couldn't. I promised Frank. He said if Brittany ever found out, he'd take me back to court for custody."

"Ha! Doesn't he realize he'd be hurting Brittany? Or does he care?"

"I don't know. I just don't want Brittany's life even more upset." She cupped her face with both hands. "She'll find out about everything and she'll hate me."

Shari picked up her coffee cup. "Piffle-paffle. Brit might surprise you and take it like the adult she's growing into. She isn't completely happy with Frank, Liana. She doesn't say anything to you, but she complains to me about his guilt trips and how he bad-mouths you."

Liana glanced up. "She does?"

"Yes, she does. She's unhappy he filed for divorce, and hooked up with Molly so soon after you moved out. It might be Michael's influence, but last week she confided in me. She thinks it's Frank's fault you left California."

"Wow, I wouldn't have dreamed she'd defend me after the conversation we had last night."

"I said she's unhappy with him, not ready to write him off. She's smart, but she's still young and in that high-charged state when everything is a drama. I think it's time you opened the can of worms and exposed Frank. You have nothing to be ashamed of. Don't play the bigger person and protect Frank at the cost of losing your daughter's respect and Michael's love."

Liana's chest tightened. "Love hasn't been mentioned."

"It won't be if you don't spend more time with him. Speaking of which," Shari forged on, "back to your sexless night with Michael. Frank's a moron. You have to stop the blame-game. Liana, you're human and you need to feel loved."

Liana blinked and hooted with laughter. Several people glanced their direction. She leaned closer to Shari. "Whoops. Didn't mean for that to slip out, but it hit my funny bone. Frank is a moron, but my night with Michael wasn't exactly sexless. The man is hot."

"I can see that." Shari's mouth turned up in a Cheshire cat smile. "Did you leave out something?"

"Not about our date. Thank you, Shari Collins, for being here for me, and making me feel more liberated. I'm ready to take Frank Nash down."

"Frank will lose it and attack through Brittany. You have to make a plan of what you're going to tell her when he does."

Liana drank the last of her latte, and set down the heavy ceramic cup. "When he does, I'll be honest and let the chips fall where they may."

The words were there, but the bravery was a little on the short side. Brittany loved her, but she was young and might be damaged by all the truth bound to come out of this battle.

She glanced at Shari and frowned. "Did my

marriage to Frank send me over the edge? Was he always irrational?"

"He was never like Jack. When you couldn't love him, no matter what he did, he lost it." Shari drank her latte, and patted her mouth with a paper napkin. "I always liked Jack. Brittany's a lot like him."

Liana gazed out the window. "She is, isn't she? I should have told him about her. I wish he'd known."

Shari laid her hand over Liana's. "Have you really dealt with Jack's loss? Liana, you've gone through more life-changing events than some people ever do.

"There are some things you never get over, Shari. Losing Jack might be one of them."

****

Michael spent the morning assessing the progress on Liana's house. Concrete was in the ground, and covered with blankets to speed up the cure. He might have been a fool to take on a project of this size alongside the other two houses he'd committed to, but he was determined to have it done for her holiday dinner.

At noon, he set his compact cooler on Liana's kitchen bar and took out the lunch he'd packed that morning. When he finished eating, he'd hurry across town to check on the new house. In the meantime he'd take time to think about Friday night and his date with Liana at the Outlaw Inn.

What in the hell had he done? He'd almost hopped into bed with a woman he'd only known for two weeks. Almost broke a cardinal rule he'd given his son about having sex before he was ready. He inflated his cheeks and blew out a frustrated breath. He was ready. At least his body was ready.

Until Liana dealt with her slime-wad ex and stopped the alimony, she couldn't afford to slow down and he had to quit hassling her about her hours. What bothered him was would she slow down when money was no longer tight? No way to know until it happened.

If he'd met her in Oklahoma City, they would have been on the same treadmill, racing out their days to make the almighty dollar, but not now. He loved to build houses and loved his home on the lake. He took joy in providing for Leif and helping Trinity through college, but there had to be a balance.

He opened a bag of chips and glanced around the room. He'd had some great times in this kitchen with Liana and the kids. He'd like to have more time with her, a whole lot more.

Friday night she'd shut down when he pressed her about the divorce. She'd shared so much; her parent's divorce, the choices she'd made with Jack and later, Frank. He wrung at the back of his neck with one hand and tilted his head from side to side. After he exposed Meredith's secrets, he'd vowed to never tolerate deception in any relationship. Throughout the messy divorce, he'd decided to stay single the rest of his life. That was before he met Liana.

Beautiful and intelligent didn't begin to describe Liana. She got under his skin and into his heart. Maybe if they'd made love Friday night, he'd have her out of his system and be back on his plan to stay unattached until Leif finished high school and went to college. Who was he kidding? Once wouldn't be enough and their lives weren't that simple.

"It just might be done in time."

Michael turned on the stool. "You snuck in."

The object of his tortured thoughts strolled into her kitchen.

"Not really." Her gaze moved from him to the tarps between the dining and living rooms. "You were deep in thought."

"I was." Michael turned back to his sandwich. "I called Sunday, but got your voice mail."

"I worked with the Cummings's all weekend. They had to leave Sunday afternoon, but we were able to finish a buy sell agreement on a house in Lakeside."

"Joy. I hope I'm not their neighbor."

"I wouldn't know. I've never seen your house." Liana moved to the refrigerator and took out a bottle of the flavored water she'd left behind.

"Hope you don't mind if I eat in your kitchen."

"You're always welcome in my home."

Liana opened the bottle and took a drink, screwed the lid back on and set it on the island next to him. Michael swiveled and brought his knees a hairs breath from her hip. Her fragrance wrapped around him and intensified his frustrations. Without thought, he pulled her toward him until she stood between his knees. "I can't get you out of my mind."

Liana placed a hand on each thigh. A bolt of lightning shot up his legs. "I'm sorry I wasn't available yesterday. I needed to spend time with Brittany. She's hounding me to let her go to Frank's before the holidays." She blinked against a sheen of tears. "I'm hiring a new lawyer to fight him, Michael. What comes out won't be pretty. You'll be glad you didn't stay over Friday night."

He wished she'd tell him everything. "Sure about that?"

"Yeah." She combed her fingers through his hair. "I ran into Shari this morning. I finally told her about the alimony. Richard will refer me to a local attorney."

"Is she as outraged as I am?"

"Absolutely, but she knows the rest of the story. She agrees it'll be ugly."

Michael ran his hands up and down her backside. "Shari's an old friend. You trust her. When will you trust me with the rest of the story?"

"It's complicated. I can't tell you right now."

A sharp pain of regret took his breath for a moment. "So, you don't trust me."

"I didn't mean that." Liana edged closer and slid her hands up the outside of his thighs until she framed his hips. "You're very trustworthy. I'm afraid when you know the whole story, you'll walk away. I'm not ready to see your taillights, Michael Saxon."

Michael barely controlled the urge to kiss her until her defenses crumbled. "If I didn't expect my crew back any moment, I'd make love to you right here. Right on that shiny granite countertop."

She buried her face in the side of his neck. "You tempt me, but it would be rather awkward if someone pulled back the tarp."

Michael gazed into her eyes. "Liana, nothing about us is coincidence. We've been divorced for about the same time. We both moved here to start over; we both have teenage children. Why can't you believe in us?"

"It does seem more than coincidence." Liana smoothed her palms over the front of his blue chamois work shirt. "I haven't wanted to be romantically involved until Brittany leaves for college. Maybe not even then. You're the first person who's tempted me to abandon my resolve to stay unattached."

Michael buried his face in her hair. "Since Jack, right?"

Liana sighed, her breath soft against his skin where the top buttons of his shirt gaped. "With Jack, I ran on teenage hormones. He was handsome, charming and adventurous. I thought I loved him more than I could possibly love anyone, yet even with him, I couldn't commit and risk my heart."

"Poor Jack. He missed out on a lot." He cupped her bottom and brought her against his hard need. "This isn't the time or the place, but it'll happen. Trust me."

"I do trust you." Her voice sounded deliciously breathless.

His ego expanded with the rest of him.

"Besides Shari, I've confided more in you than anyone."

"Glad to hear it." He ran his lips up and down her throat and traveled down to nuzzle her silk covered breasts. Her nipples hardened and perked through her lacy bra. Michael moaned. "After Thanksgiving, you and I need a date. A real one."

She tightened her legs and pulsated against him. "I'd like that."

Michael groaned. "Uh, we'd better get our act together or as sure as shootin', we'll get caught."

Liana released him and slid down his hips until her feet touched the floor.

Just what she needed to bring her senses back to earth. This man could make her forget her fears. She could almost spill her secrets, tell him about Ryan. Michael portrayed an exciting mix of trust and security. Not to mention wild passion and bone melting possibilities that scared her to death. She could lose focus and with it, her daughter and her independence, all for the dream of happily ever after.

Michael gathered the remains of his lunch and started for the door. Liana kept a tight grip on the edge of the countertop and willed her legs to stop trembling.

He turned, one hand on the doorknob. "Don't go past the tarp. The trusses are just tacked in place until the crew gets back. You okay at the condo? Can I have the address?"

"Oh, my gosh! Of course you can. I forgot to give it to you in all the hubbub. Here." She took a business card from her purse and scribbled the address on the back. "We're fine, but I miss my house and my cat."

"Oscar's okay with me, but if they allow pets at the complex I can bring him by tonight."

Liana closed the distance between them and pushed up on her tiptoes to press her lips to his. "Thank you. Oscar might cheer up Brittany. She's really attached to him."

"I'll drop him off at seven. Don't worry about dinner, Leif and I'll grab something on the way over."

"No. I insist you have dinner with us. Lasagna okay?"

He tilted his head and gazed into her eyes as if he couldn't believe she'd invited them. "Yeah, lasagna sounds great." Michael gave her a quick kiss and hurried out the back door.

Liana smiled at his hasty retreat. He really did want to make love to her. She straightened her clothes. Maybe things could work between them. Tears moistened her eyes, but this time, they were tears of hope and happiness, not despair.

****

The day before Thanksgiving, Liana picked her mom up at the Kalispell airport. "I can't wait for you to see my house. Of course, you won't appreciate the transformation as much as I do. The contractor did a beautiful job."

"How exciting! I hope you took some before pictures!" Cathy Campbell bubbled with enthusiasm and seemed younger since the last time Liana had seen her. She also acted evasive and avoided Liana's questions as to the cause of her effervescence.

"Why can't you just enjoy my good mood?" she answered. "I want to hear more about life in Northwestern Montana."

"Where's Gary?" Gary, her mom's long time boyfriend, usually participated in family events.

"He had business in North Carolina, so he decided to spend the weekend in Raleigh with his daughter."

Liana let the subject drop. Something didn't seem right, but she didn't want to ruin the camaraderie with her mom.

Later that evening, her brother Tim called to let them know he and her other brother, Mark had arrived with their families. They'd settled into a Kalispell hotel and would be over the next morning.

"Mom get in okay?" Tim asked.

"Yes, she had a good trip." Liana glanced around to make sure her mother wasn't within hearing distance, and lowered her voice. "I'm a little concerned with her new attitude. I mean, Mom's always been pleasant and positive, but she's a little over the top today. Do you think her hormones are off?" Concern flickered through her mind and set off a signal. Tim was the doctor of the family. He should have noticed if their mom wasn't normal.

Tim chuckled. "Calm down, sis. She's probably excited about all of us spending the holiday together."

Even with her brother's reassurance, Liana sensed something was going on. She worried more when, later in the evening, her mom avoided answering questions about her dad. Despite the circumstances surrounding their divorce, Cathy Campbell had always encouraged the kids to spend time with their dad. Liana usually declined and stayed home while her brothers went. She couldn't reconcile with her father when his thoughtless affair broke up their family.

Early Thanksgiving morning, she put the turkey in the oven and bustled around the kitchen, preparing the side dishes. Her mom and Brittany worked side by side, peeling potatoes while Liana chopped onions for the stuffing.

The doorbell rang at eleven.

Michael.

She almost said his name aloud. She hadn't seen him since Monday night and ached to wrap her arms around his big, strong body. Since Trinity planned to visit over the holiday and Liana's family were in town, they'd agreed it best to focus on their individual families until their relationship became clear.

The doorbell rang again. Liana hurried through her expansive new living room and pulled open the oversized, carved wooden front door Michael had personally installed.

Her stomach flip-flopped. "Daddy?"

"Hello, Pumpkin." Liana's dad stayed on the front step, his green eyes filled with uncertainty. "I hope you don't mind me showing up like this."

"Of course not." Liana's heart warred with her mind. He'd cheated on her mom; he'd left them alone too much; he'd split their family.

So did you, a little voice in the back of her head reminded her. Her chest contracted and her breath caught. Oh, my God. She'd been angry with her father for so long, she hadn't considered how similar her situation with Ryan might have been to her dad's affair. Michael had been so right about transference, and he didn't know the half of it.

"Daddy, please come in." Liana choked back tears.

Her dad walked into the foyer and blinked against the moisture in his eyes. She closed the door, and turned into his arms with a sob.

"I'm so sorry, baby girl. For everything." He smoothed her hair and kissed her forehead.

"I'm sorry I didn't call you. I've wanted to. I guess it gets more difficult if you let time build up."

Where had her mind been? She'd held against her dad the same thing she'd nearly done! Her mother and Brittany were halfway through the dining room when they saw her dad. Brittany whooped and hollered and catapulted herself into her grandfather's arms. Through the years Liana had never discouraged Brittany's visits with her grandfather. She'd just chosen not to accompany her.

Concerned over how Duncan Campbell's arrival would affect her mom, Liana glanced at her and gasped. Her mother absolutely glowed.

"Duncan."

"Cathy." Her father stepped forward and met her mother in front of the fireplace. "Glad to see you had a safe trip." He took her hands in his and kissed her cheek.

Liana had expected tension and awkwardness. She saw neither. Her heart filled to over flowing. She was afraid to ask questions and ruin the moment.

Her brothers and their families arrived shortly after noon, and the house turned into joyous chaos.

Brittany enjoyed the attention and interaction with her cousins, but Liana caught her glancing toward the door with a pensive look.

She started to take Brittany aside to ask if everything was okay, but her brothers drew her into their conversation about how much they already liked Montana, and wanted to consider buying a condo for vacations. She promised to look for one right after the holiday weekend.

When Brittany smiled and laughed again, Liana breathed a little easier and allowed herself to think about what else would happen next week. Michael would start on her bedroom remodel and be around every day. If she had her way, he and Leif would spend some evenings here too. She'd love to give him a quick call and tell him about her dad, and how much her family liked her house. She floated from hour to hour, wishing he'd knock on the door.

Trinity and Leif no doubt had him involved in dinner preparation and catching up on what had been going on in their lives. His former brother-in-law and new wife might have driven over from Libby.

The depth of her feelings for Michael alarmed her. She'd done fine on her own over the past four years. If she let her guard down and allowed her need for him to grow, could she rebound if it didn't work out?

She might have to.

Since she'd hired the new attorney two weeks ago, he'd put a settlement agreement together which ended the alimony payments to Frank and demanded he get counseling for the anger and bitterness. The packet should be with Frank's attorney by now.

At any moment, she expected a call from an irate Frank. She'd have to stay alert in case he reached Brittany first.

"You've been in your own little world for the past hour, Li." Her mother hugged her from behind. She propped her chin on Liana's shoulder and kissed her ear. "Are you all right? Um, you smell good."

"I'm fine. Just have a lot on my mind." Liana turned in her mom's arms. "Thank you for assuring me I don't smell like sweat and onions."

Cathy chuckled then turned serious. "Brit says you're working a lot. I'll tell you what I've told your brothers. Stop and smell the roses. Life goes by too fast."

Liana sighed. "I know, Mom. I'm working on those roses, but the market is still slow. If I don't grab every sale, someone else will. With the remodel and some other expenses, I'm close to dipping into my savings and I don't want to do that."

She gave her mom another hug and turned to check on the turkey. The house had been filled with the wonderful, mouthwatering scents of Thanksgiving dinner since about ten that morning.

"I understand how tight the market is right now, Li, but please don't burn yourself out."

"I won't. I have a plan." She shot her mother a reassuring smile and slipped two pans of dressing into the oven and took the lid off the roaster. She moaned as the full aroma of roasted bird hit her. Juice escaped from the skin, and sizzled on the side of the roasting pan. She filled the baster with juice, squeezed the rubber ball and doused the skin so it wouldn't dry out. Another few minutes and she'd keep the lid off to brown the skin.

If everything came together, this would be the Thanksgiving of her dreams. Only Michael and his kids could make it better.

Six pies lined the sideboard in the dining room. She'd baked four and her mom had insisted she buy two more at the bakery yesterday. Perfect. At this moment, her world was near perfect.

The doorbell rang. Liana's heart skipped a beat. Her breath accelerated. It might be Michael.

"Dad!" Brittany's voice echoed through the house.

"Dad?" Liana mimicked her daughter. "Frank?"

Stunned, she hurried to the living room and froze, her fears confirmed. Frank and his girlfriend, Molly, stood in the foyer. Obviously they'd reunited.

Brittany leaped into his arms like it was Christmas morning and she'd just opened the best present ever. "Dad you made it!"

Chapter Nine

"Made it?" Liana repeated like a parrot, while she stared at Frank through a tunnel of shock. "You planned this visit?"

Brittany stuck out her bottom lip and faced Liana, her back against her dad. "When you didn't want me to be gone on Thanksgiving, I asked Dad to come here so we could all be together."

Frank clamped his hands on Brittany shoulders, and looked over her head at Liana. "Don't be angry, Li. I wasn't sure I could get away from work. I didn't want to make a big deal out of it."

Liana's family gathered, her brothers flanked her like a military guard.

"Mark, Tim." Frank nodded at each of her brother's who had yet to say a word.

"Frank." Mark finally held out his hand.

Frank accepted the gesture. "Good to see you." He moved into the living room and held his hand out to Tim, who had never been a Frank fan, but a glance from his wife made him accept the gesture.

Liana motioned toward the living room. "Come in. Molly, I'm glad you came." She really was glad. Molly could act as a buffer when Frank dropped his congenial bull shit and went off the deep end.

Because he would go off the deep end. He'd received her settlement papers, of that she was sure.

Something wasn't right. He didn't seem angry. His casual air worried her more than if he'd burst in swearing and yelling.

"Thank you, Liana. I'm sorry we showed up without warning." Molly smiled apologetically, and shook hands with the family.

Liana wanted to run and hide. "Can I offer you something to drink?" She forced a smile and listed the beverages she'd stocked up on for the weekend.

In auto-motion, she handed Molly a glass of wine, and Frank a scotch and water.

"Please make yourselves comfortable. I have to check on dinner." She couldn't escape the living room fast enough. In the kitchen, she leaned against the granite counter top and took a deep breath.

"Can I help with dinner?" Molly had followed her.

"Dinner's under control. Would you like to set the table?"

"I'd love to. Did Brittany tell you I'm taking interior decorating courses?"

Liana froze. "No, she didn't. What does Frank think of your choice of careers?"

"Oh, he's very supportive. He said you tried it a long time ago, but it didn't work out."

Liana silently fumed with volcanic rage.

"I've started redecorating our condo." Molly looked oblivious to Liana's anger. "Frank's happy for me to do anything as long as I stay. It sounds pitiful, but he's really a great guy. I hope we can work out our differences."

She suddenly covered her mouth with her fingertips. "I'm sorry to go on and on. That wasn't an appropriate comment, considering you and Frank didn't make it."

Liana poured a glass of wine and took a gulp, and lifted it toward Molly. "Don't apologize. It's awkward for you too. Being here, I mean. Here's to you decorating Frank's world."

Molly smiled and clinked her glass against Liana's. Amazing; Molly didn't have a clue that interior design had been Liana's dream, and she was very good at it. The fault lay with Frank. The rat!

Liana pointed to the dining room. "The tablecloth, napkins and candles are in the buffet. Please arrange them to your liking while I pull out the turkey and make the gravy."

Molly clapped her hands in delight and hurried into the dining room to begin the transformation.

Her perfect day tarnished, Liana took another drink of wine and turned to the oven willing herself to calm down. It would all work out.

Laugher and teasing drifted from the living room. What in the hell was Frank doing? A comedy act? The nerve of him to show up on her favorite holiday. He'd known her family would be here. She blinked back tears of anger and frustration. How dare he!

Her mom could be heard, occasionally adding to the conversation, and her dad's chuckle wove through the melee like a satin ribbon on a gift. No matter what Frank ended up doing to her holiday, having her entire family together was amazing.

"Everything coming along?" Her mother, accustomed to having the holiday dinners at her house, couldn't stay out of the kitchen for more than a few minutes. Liana understood. An active woman, Cathy Campbell loved to be in the middle of whatever was going on.

Liana swiped away the tears and lifted her chin toward the stove. "Molly's busy with the table, but if you whip the potatoes, I'll work on the gravy. The food will be served in thirty minutes."

"I'm impressed. Even Frank's untimely arrival hasn't thrown you off schedule." Cathy touched Liana's shoulder. "Honey, I hope he hasn't ruined your day."

Liana turned to her mom. "I refuse to give him the power. I've lived in fear of so many things for too long."

"Fear?" Her mother stepped closer to Liana. "Was Frank violent with you?"

"No, not physically. Oh hell." Liana threw her hands in the air. "Not mentally violent either, just controlling and manipulative. Can we talk about this later?" Maybe the time had come for her to fill in her parents. They'd always believed Frank fathered Brittany and had never commented on Brittany's "early" birth. They were intelligent people. They had to suspect all was not what it seemed.

"Of course. We have so much to catch up on." Cathy whipped the potatoes until they formed fluffy peaks. She covered them with a sheet of foil and helped Molly find the serving utensils.

Liana appreciated her mother's help and concern. With the ugly facts of her marriage and divorce about to come out through the courts, she owed her parents the truth.

"Sis, if you don't have some food on the table soon, I'll start to nibble." Her oldest brother wrapped an arm around her and snagged a piece of turkey from the platter.

"Ah-ah." She slapped the back of his hand and laughed. "It's almost ready."

He enveloped her in a quick squeeze and kissed the top of her head. "Brittany said you're working long hours. Everything okay?"

Liana's stomach dropped. Her brothers had always been good at reading her expressions. "You know how it is with a new business. It takes time and hard work to build a clientele."

Awkward didn't begin to describe the atmosphere; discussing finances with Tim while Frank's woman rushed in and out of the kitchen.

"Let me know if you need anything. We're doing well and can afford to help my baby sister."

"You're a dear." Liana wrapped her arms around his lean middle. "You've always been there to save the day."

"I've never gotten over losing Jack either, sis." His voice dropped so only they shared the words. "Don't forget he was my best friend."

"I know." Liana couldn't stop the crack in her voice.

"Now isn't the time or place, but I understand why you married Frank and it wasn't because he reminded you of Jack."

Liana froze. "No, now isn't the time, but this weekend is. Do you think we could have a heart to heart family meeting tomorrow?"

"You bet." He kissed her forehead.

"Looks like something serious." Cathy sailed into the kitchen. "Sharing family secrets?"

Liana frowned at her mom. "Not yet, but I have a feeling there are things I don't know about."

"Not at all, dear. What else is ready to go to the table? I think food will calm the tension out there."

Liana helped her mom set the holiday meal on Molly's beautifully arranged table. She took a minute to drink it in, her first family dinner in Kalispell. Once seated, everyone joined hands while her dad asked for a blessing on the meal. At the last amen, Liana looked around the table and lifted her wine glass.

"Here's to sharing my new home with my much loved family. I'm so happy you could make the trip."

"Here's to your new life, sweetie." Her father lifted his glass. "No offense Frank, but I hope it's a happy one."

"None taken, sir." Frank joined in the toast with a sip of wine.

"Thank you, Daddy. I'm thrilled you're staying for the weekend." Liana forced her smile to stay in place for her dad's sake. Even with Frank darkening her door, she didn't intend to let the opportunity to rebuild her relationship with her dad pass them by.

How long did Frank plan to stay and why didn't he mention the court papers? Was he stalling before he tortured her about the new financial arrangement? The one where she paid him zippo each month?

Despite Frank and Molly's presence, the dinner went well. For Brittany's sake her family included them in the conversation, careful not to go too far down memory lane.

Liana forced herself to eat the delicious food she'd looked so forward to. Her stomach roiled and tied in knots. How could Frank act like they were on amiable terms? Was he a sociopath? She set her fork down, patted her mouth and pushed back her chair. "Dessert and coffee now or wait awhile?"

Mark froze with his hand halfway to the turkey platter. "Does this mean I have to stop eating?"

Liana laughed. "No, you can eat until you can't stand. We can wait on dessert. It'll give me time to cleanup and let my food settle."

She wandered into the kitchen, and started to organize the leftovers and pots and pans.

Her mother followed. "Dear, allow me to help. I can't kick back when there's work to be done."

"Thank you, Mom." Liana opened the storage container cupboard next to the refrigerator. "Use whatever you need."

Her mind went a thousand miles a minute while her mother hummed and moved food from their dishes to the containers. "Mom, I'm curious."

"About what, dear?" Her mother stopped transferring the dressing to a bowl and turned with a raised brow.

"What's changed with you and Daddy? I haven't seen you together for years and when I did, you could barely stand to be in the same room. Today, I swear you're flirting with each other."

Cathy shrugged. "We're adults and it's time to act civil." Her mother caught her upper lip between her teeth, but didn't stop scrapping the gravy into a container. "A lot has happened since you left California."

"Do you plan to tell me about it?" Liana folded her arms and leaned against the bar, carefully watching her mom.

"I didn't plan to talk about it today, dear. I wanted to wait until things quieted down. Maybe tomorrow."

"I've already asked Tim if we can have a family meeting tomorrow. I have some announcements as well. Can you and I talk now?"

Cathy washed her hands and glanced over her shoulder at Liana. "You have some announcements? Hmm, now I'm curious."

"One thing at a time. We're talking about you and Dad."

Cathy dried her hands and propped them on her hips. "How about tea in the den?"

"I think I'll stick to wine." Liana put a tea bag in a tall mug, held it under the hotshot spigot at the sink, and handed it to her mom. "It keeps me from wrapping my hands around Frank's neck."

Her sisters-in-law came into the kitchen, loaded down with dirty plates.

"The cook should not cleanup," Laurie, Tim's wife announced. She set the plates on the counter next to the sink and shoed them out of the kitchen. "You two go visit while Dottie and I take over."

Liana hugged both her sisters-in-law and led the way to the den, her mother on her heels. Once her mother entered the room, Liana closed the pocket door. "Okay. What's happening?"

Cathy blew on her tea before she took a sip. "I've broken it off with Gary. We're no longer dating."

Liana sank to the over stuffed leather chair. "You're what? What happened, Mom? You and Gary were so happy."

"I think you'd better drink more wine before I continue." Cathy rolled Liana's office chair around the desk. She sat down and scooted forward until their knees touched. "I'm having an affair."

Liana swore the air got sucked from the room. She drew in two quick breaths and forged on. "How could you do that to Gary? After you left Dad because of his affair?"

Cathy leaned back and folded her hands. "Liana, you're thirty-five years old, it's time you heard the truth. Your father wouldn't allow me to talk about it at the time. Later I found it easier not to bring it up. He wanted to protect me. The truth is I didn't leave your father because he had an affair. I filed for a divorce from your father because I had an affair."

Liana gasped. "What?"

"He was gone so much. I got lonely and lost focus of what I really wanted in life. I met Gary and well the rest, as they say, is history."

Astonished, Liana set her glass on her desk. "Daddy didn't have an affair?"

"No." Cathy slowly shook her head. "I was the one who cheated. Your father was and still is the model of honor."

The years she'd missed with her father, harboring resentment and anger toward him, tumbled though her mind. Liana forked her fingers through her hair. "I can't believe this. What else don't I know?"

"Well..." Cathy dragged out the word. "The person I'm having an affair with is your father."

The room spun. Liana didn't know whether to be appalled or elated. "You and Daddy are back together?"

Cathy slid to her knees in front of Liana and held her hands. "Yes, dear. Your father and I are back together. I'm so sorry for the pain you suffered all those years. The divorce was all my fault. I knew when I married your father he'd make the Navy a career. I had no right to resent his absences. Things can get crazy. You kids were growing up and life seemed to be slipping by. Call it a mid-life crisis—I don't know. My behavior can be blamed on numerous things, but it boils down to the facts. I was wrong. I should have talked to your dad and worked it out with him. Instead, I used divorce as the answer."

Liana's chest ached from emotion and holding her breath. "I need to process this, Mom. You and Dad back together is a dream come true, but I need time to reconcile with the pain from early adolescence. I believed Dad abandoned his family for another woman. You should have told us the truth."

"Yes, you're absolutely right. I should have overridden Duncan's plan to shoulder the blame. I hope you can forgive both of us."

Liana blinked against a rush of tears. "Poor Dad. I missed so many years with him." She gazed at her mother. "That's what hurts the most. When he arrived today, I realized I couldn't hold the affair against him anymore, because I've done things I shouldn't have too."

Cathy framed Liana's shoulders with her delicate hands. "I've always known the truth, Liana. Brittany is Jack's child, isn't she?"

Liana opened her mouth, but for a moment, couldn't form the words. "She's Jack's daughter. I'm sorry I didn't tell you but—"

"I was in a constant state of crisis and you didn't want to burden me."

Liana rested her head on her mom's shoulder. "I wanted to share it with you. I was so embarrassed about being pregnant and not married. When Jack died, I told

Frank. He urged me to marry him so Brittany wouldn't be illegitimate. For all his faults, Frank really did want to do a good thing, but living with a man you don't love—have no passion for—the good will evaporates."

"He may have seemed admirable, but you know as well as I do, Frank's motive was his jealousy of Jack." Cathy smoothed Liana's hair like she had when she was little and hurt.

"It didn't take long for me to realize his motives, and his jealousy." Liana sighed. "I suppose we should join the others before Brittany sends out a search party. Mind if I slip into my bathroom and freshen up first?" She kissed her mother's cheek.

"I'll cover for you. Are you all right with your dad and I?"

"Are you kidding? Once I get over the shock, I'll be elated. Poor Gary." Liana hesitated. "But, I feel worse for Daddy. I treated him terribly. It'll take a while to make up for a fraction of the hurt I caused him."

"It'll take me even longer. To Duncan, and my children. Too bad it took me twenty-three years to get my act together." Cathy gripped the doorknob. "Ready?"

Liana dashed through the corner of the living room, relieved her guests seemed happy to linger in the dining room. She closed the bedroom door and locked it.

Wow, she needed more than a few minutes to recover from her mother's revelation, but right now, she had a houseful of family and her conniving ex to deal with.

Her mother and father were having an affair? She plopped on the bed and laid back, spreading her arms on either side. She itched to share the news with someone. But who? Shari? Her best friend was busy with her family today. She wouldn't mind Liana's call. They'd always been there for each other, but Liana wouldn't bother her.

Michael?

His name popped into her mind for the umpteenth time and filled her with warmth. She grabbed her pillow and hugged it. She was in a house of happy couples. Even Frank and Molly seemed happy. She ached to have such a strong connection with Michael. He'd become a steadying force in her sometimes crazy world. His caring and strength were impressive and she wanted him in her life every day. She wanted to lay her head on his broad shoulder, breath in his spicy scent and press her body to his.

Reaching for the nightstand, she snapped up her cell phone and punched out his number before she lost her nerve.

It rang three times.

"Well, hello there. What makes you call me when you have a houseful of family?" His voice spread over her like warm honey.

"I have a houseful of family."

He laughed. "I've had an interesting day too. Meredith showed up three sheets to the wind complaining about the hotel she checked into."

Liana covered her mouth and laughed. "Sorry, but I'm so rummy from family dynamics, I'm losing it."

"Uh-oh. Wish I could be there to hold you, sweetheart. It's been too long."

She sighed. "Oh, Michael, Frank and his girlfriend showed up right before dinner. Can you believe it?"

"You're kidding. Did he get the papers?"

"I don't know. He acts like nothing's wrong and it's ordinary for him to drop in to spend the day with his daughter."

"Strange. Did Brittany invite him?"

"Oh yeah. I'm sure his guilt trip persuaded her. She's been upset about his depression and the supposed breakup with Molly."

"How are things with your mom?"

"Oh, my gosh! Would you believe my parents are here together and I do mean, together? They're having an affair—with each other! I just found out and I'm still stunned."

"Sounds like you need a shoulder." His voice lowered and went gravely, sending goosebumps over her entire body. "How about we meet and find out if we're sexually compatible?"

Liana's groan of frustration turned into a giggle. "You're outrageous! Do you have doubts about our compatibility?"

"Not at all. I'm concerned about Frank's presence."

"Never fear, my brothers and dad have my back."

"They sound like good men."

Damn, she loved the sound of his voice. She longed to be in his arms and erase the guilt haunting her because of her final meeting with Ryan. The past couldn't be undone, but treated as a lesson learned.

"Maybe if we rendezvous, we'll discover the magic was exaggerated."

"Think so?"

"You don't?"

"Campbell, making love to you once won't get you out of my system." He groaned. "Why did we have to start this conversation when we both have obligations tonight?"

"Can you trust Meredith with the kids?" She didn't have any business leaving her family or asking him to. Especially with Frank on the scene, but seeing Michael would give her the strength to get through whatever evil Frank planned and the family meeting tomorrow.

"Trinity can handle her mother. Meredith will be passed out before the pies are cut."

"If you're sure, I'll see if I can go out for a while. Where should we meet?" She'd love to meet Michael's daughter, but not with Meredith around. Their relationship hadn't progressed far enough to suggest it.

"How about The Lakeside Inn? It's right off the highway."

"Sounds good and not too far away. I'll freshen up and make my excuses." She looked at her bedside clock. "Meet you in an hour?"

"I'll be there with bells on."

His voice stirred her senses into a frenzy of excitement. She was crazy to meet him at all, and at an inn to boot.

****

Liana climbed into her SUV and guided it around the cars parked in her yard. When she'd emerged from her room to announce a friend had called and needed help, her mother raised a brow; Frank narrowed his eyes, and her Dad nodded and laid back in the club chair to snooze off his dinner.

Brittany volunteered to set up board games for her cousins, and her brothers and sisters-in-law helped themselves to the brandy. They seemed fine with her story about a friend in need who had holiday depression. They assured her they could serve dessert when everyone was ready.

Her nerves twanged like an old guitar and her heart fluttered with anticipation. For now she felt young again and the heavy responsibilities of life melted away with every mile she drew closer to Michael. The logical, grown up part of her wondered what in the hell was she doing, meeting Michael in board daylight on Thanksgiving when Frank was in town.

Three vehicles sat in the inn parking lot. A red pickup, a blue sedan and a vintage red Corvette. She shifted in her seat and decided to stay put until Michael arrived. She stared at the sports car and imagined herself gliding down the highway, the top down, the wind in her hair.

Of course, Michael would be in the car too, driving or riding, it made no difference to her.

Knuckles wrapped against the window next to her head. Liana jumped and twisted in the seat. Michael stood outside, a grin on his handsome face.

"Are you coming in?"

Liana slipped her keys from the ignition and opened the door. "I didn't see your truck so I decided to wait out here."

His grin widened. "You didn't see my truck because I drove my toy." He lifted his chin toward the corvette.

"You're kidding? It's yours?" She hurried to the classic car and peeked in the driver's window. Black leather interior with burl wood trim, took her breath away. "This is awesome."

"Well, well." Michael slid his hand up her back and under her hair. "If I'd known my car would turn you on so much I would've played this card earlier."

Liana giggled. "Is that what it is? A chick magnet?"

"It's working, isn't it?" He pulled her against his side. "The only chick I'm interested in is you. Want to take a spin before we go inside?"

Liana tried to act cool, but she didn't do a very good job. Her face must have reflected her excitement. "I'd love to. Do you mind?"

He shook his head. "Nothing like a beautiful woman in a fast car to make my day." He pulled keys from his jeans pocket and unlocked the door, his gaze on her, one dark brow raised. "You driving, or riding?"

Liana couldn't believe it. "You'd let me drive your baby?"

"If it makes you smile like that, I'd let you do anything within my power. Here." He handed her the keys. "Reach across and unlock my door, would you?"

Liana slid into the interior and sighed when her bottom sank into the soft leather. She'd only dreamed of sitting in a car like this, let alone driving one.

"Hey, can I come too?" Michael tapped on the passenger window.

"Oh!" She leaned across the seat and unlocked the door. Michael's potent presence filled the space beside her.

He pulled a lever and pushed the seat back. "Whew, whoever sat here last must have been short."

"Another star struck woman?" She couldn't stop the twinge of jealously at the thought of another woman riding with Michael. Don't be ridiculous. Of course he'd dated other women. He'd hinted he hadn't been intimate with anyone for a long time. Had that been a line to get her in the sack?

"Probably one of the kids. I don't bring the old girl out much. Not like I'd like to. Have you ever used a stick shift?"

Liana adjusted her seat forward to reach the pedals. "Of course. As a teenager, my brother, Tim, had a '69 Mustang. He let me drive it a few times."

Michael explained the gear-shift pattern and the idiosyncrasies of the car. "Just take it easy and you'll be okay."

Liana took a deep breath to calm her nerves and her excitement. She pushed in the clutch and turned the key. The engine roared to life and then settled into a purr. So did she. "Wow." She glanced around before she shifted into reverse and backed out of the parking spot. She crept toward the highway and stopped. "Okay, which way?"

"How about the open highway?"

"Sounds good." Waiting for a car to pass, she turned onto the highway and accelerated, listening for the engine to signal when to shift gears just as her brother taught her.

"Very good," Michael said when she reached forth gear. "I'm impressed." He settled back in the seat, looking every bit like a man who didn't have a care in the world.

"Did you doubt me?" Liana couldn't help but tease. She spared him a quick glance. What a rush. A hot man in a hot car.

"Not at all. I figured you could manage, but you exceed my expectations—as usual."

"Hmm." Liana's body went into a slow burn. Driving his car was like foreplay. Michael's cologne and magnetic male energy wrapped around her. Her sensitive fingers luxuriated over the burl wood steering wheel, every nerve in her body aware of the power of the car and the man.

"You're full of surprises too, Michael."

"What do you mean? I'm an open book."

"Ha! You've more than exceeded my first impression of you as just another handsome face." She giggled at her own wit, the exhilaration of driving the open road pushed away every bit of tension. "You turned out to be a man's man, driving a truck, building houses. Kind of a, shucks ma'am, kind of guy."

Michael hooted with laughter. "Oh really? That's how you see me?"

Liana shrugged. "Kind of. Don't get me wrong, I'm madly attracted to you. Learning you have a wild side makes me crazy."

He shook with laughter. "You think I'm wild, huh? Turn at the next road. Yeah, that one to your left. It'll take us to the lakeshore."

Liana reluctantly geared down and hit the blinker. Confirming the car behind her slowed, she turned off the highway and crept down the gravel road to park where several trucks with empty boat trailers rimmed the lakeshore.

She cut the engine and glanced around to see what made Michael want to come here. "It's beautiful, b—"

Her seat belt released. He lifted her over the console and planted her in his lap before she could object. His lips claimed hers, turning her body into a million sensitized nerve endings. She wrapped her arms around his neck, wiggling to get even closer. Michael slid his hands under her sweater and cupped her breasts.

"I don't know how I walked out of your hotel room that night, Liana, but I'm ready to make love right now."

"Here?" She wanted him to quit talking and keep kissing.

He chuckled. "I don't think it's possible right here. I reserved a room at the inn. Let's go back and check in."

"Michael, I have a houseful of company and so do you. I didn't intend to be gone that long."

His cupped his hand over her aching female core. She moaned and rubbed against his amazing fingers.

"Baby, I've backed off to give us room to think—to do the right thing. I've gone crazy without you this past week." He plied his agile fingers to the best advantage. She moaned louder.

"I've ached for you too, but remember, we haven't made love because of our differences."

"I've thought about our differences. We have more going for us than most couples, and we're just getting started. Come with me."

The play on words sent her over the edge and into a sparkling world she hadn't visited in so long. "Oh, my, my." She covered his face and neck with kisses.

Michael's chuckle rumbled through his chest. "Like that?"

"Like it? If we go to the inn, can we make ourselves leave in an hour? I can't be gone too long. Who knows what Frank will pull."

Michael pulled back and looked at her with narrowed eyes. "He's not staying at your house, is he? You did say his girlfriend came with him, didn't you?"

Liana sighed and snuggled against his lap, a little

guilty over her release when he was still rock hard and wound up. "Yes, Molly's there, thank goodness. Can we talk about them later?"

She kissed his full firm lips one more time and shuffled across the console into the driver's seat. Her body and mind glowed with satisfaction and the anticipation of being alone with him in the privacy of a room. Something about the time crunch heightened the excitement of their rendezvous.

Michael settled back into the seat, maneuvering until he was halfway comfortable. Being with Liana would fulfill his every fantasy, but he wished she'd open up completely about her past with Frank. What finally ended the marriage. He wanted more than a physical relationship, as mind blowing as that would be.

Despite her recent bout of inattentive driving, she was a good driver. The corvette purred at her every command, just like the car's owner. "I hope Meredith isn't giving the kids too bad of a time." Maybe if he talked about his ex, she would reciprocate.

Liana glanced at him, taking her eyes off the road for a split second. "Should we postpone this until our families are back to normal?"

Michael hooted with laughter. "There is no normal when it comes to Meredith." He sighed and reached across the seat to play with her hair. "Damn, why did my mind have to go there? I guess you have a point. We should be happy with the time we had today and rescue our children."

Liana nodded and flipped on the blinker to turn onto the gravel parking lot in front of the inn. "Can you get your money back?"

"Maybe not, but that's okay." He wanted to toss

responsibility to the wind for once and act on his emotions, but when he made love to Liana, he wanted to take his time and do it right. He wanted her to open up and tell him what bothered her. He was prepared to answer any question she had for him.

Liana slid out of the car and shut the door. With reluctance, she handed Michael the keys. "Thank you for an unbelievable ride."

Michael's impulses took over for a moment. "Not the ride I had in mind, but I enjoyed it too."

Liana's delicious mouth tilted in a private smile and a thrill shot through him. "We have something to look forward to. That is if you still want to go out with me."

"If I still want to?" Michael pointed at his chest. "Uh, yeah, slightly."

"Okay, so when?"

"Okay, let's set a date."

"What works for you?"

"I'm not the one with the tight schedule."

"Don't go there. I can't work less until this alimony thing is revoked."

Michael rubbed his bristly face with one hand and pursed his lips. Shoot, he'd been so excited about meeting Liana he'd forgotten to shave. "How about next Friday night?"

Liana pulled her smart phone from her purse. She looked at the screen and frowned. "Brittany called me and I didn't hear the beep. Excuse me a moment." She punched a key, and turned away.

Michael waited for her to listen to the message. He pulled his cell phone out of the holder on his belt and flipped open the cover. Damn, he'd had a call too. The call log showed his house number, but no voice mail. Hmm, not good.

Liana turned toward him. "I have to get back. Brittany called. Her father won't leave until I return. Why, I have no idea when my parents and brothers are there." She shrugged and shook her head. "I'm sure Frank has figured out my friend in crisis might be a man."

Michael chuckled. "You told them you had a friend in crisis?" He stepped closer and pulled her against him. Her eyes widened. He smiled. "You weren't far off the mark. The way I see it, I'm still in a crisis. Maybe more than before you got here."

Liana chuckled. "I would have to agree." She puckered and batted her lashes at him. "I wish I could stay. Call me tomorrow?"

"You can bet on it." Michael escorted her to the SUV and helped her behind the wheel before pressing a kiss to the side of her neck. "Um, you smell so good. I'm going to have one hell of a night."

"You're not alone." She turned her head and pressed her lips to his, giving him a kiss to ensure a restless night. "Think about that, Cowboy."

Michael groaned under his breath and stepped away to close the door. He waited until her vehicle disappeared around the corner before he went inside to cancel his room. Maybe they'd give him a gift certificate to use next time.

Because there would be a next time.

Chapter Ten

Liana moved through the rest of Thanksgiving Day like a robot, her senses on overload. Over the past twelve hours, she'd learned the truth about her parent's divorce, unwillingly shared dinner with her ex and his girlfriend, and steamed up Michael's corvette windows in the hottest intimate moment she'd experienced to date.

Back at her house, she was dismayed to discover Frank waiting at the door. He questioned her about her "friend in need" until an embarrassed Molly insisted they check into the hotel room they'd reserved. They'd get some rest and be fresh for spending time with Brittany the next day.

Liana's stomach twisted into a knot. She should pull him aside and ask him about the settlement papers. They'd been delivered over two weeks ago, so why hadn't he brought them up? Fear flashed through her. Maybe he came to kidnap Brittany?

In a daze, she shut the door and turned to her family. Oh. my God, how could she handle one more thing? She'd already set up a family meeting for tomorrow morning. Her brothers would never let her cancel, or pass it off as just a time to spend core family time together. Tim was too sharp and in tune with her distress.

She had to continue with her decision to tell them

everything; things no one wanted to confess to their parents and siblings. But this wasn't about just her. If Frank fed an exaggerated version of Liana's indiscretion to Brittany, her future with her daughter could be in jeopardy. Brittany might choose to live with Frank and he wasn't mentally stable enough to be the kind of father Brittany needed.

By the time everyone started to yawn and her brothers and their families left for the hotel, Liana teetered on the edge of hysteria. To top it off, her father followed her mother into her bedroom, his bags in tow.

Brittany glanced at her with raised brows.

"I'll explain later." Liana kissed her daughter and wished her a goodnight before escaping to her room. She went through her nighttime routine; washing her face, brushing her teeth, taking her vitamins. Out of things to do, she sat on the bed, rocked back and forth and rehearsed what she'd say to her family at the meeting.

At two o'clock in the morning, she crawled under the covers and fell into an exhausted sleep.

****

Liana glanced at her brothers and parents. "I can't express how much it means to have you here." Her throat tightened and her eyes burned with tears she couldn't stem. "You didn't come to Kalispell to listen to me wade through my past, but because of some current events, it's time I brought you up to date. I so appreciate Dottie and Laurie for taking the kids to the skating rink so we won't be interrupted."

"All right, sis. This looks serious, what's happened?" Tim shifted in the burgundy leather chair.

She twisted her hands together. "Um...I don't know

where to begin."

"How about admit Brittany is Jack's daughter." Tim drilled her with the older brother stare she'd grown up dreading.

"Okay, let's start there. For those of you who haven't known or suspected, I was pregnant with Brittany when Jack's plane crashed. I could have been his wife, but I was scared. Too scared to marry a man who planned to fly all over the world for the next twenty years."

Her father looked away and rolled his lips, his jaw set against the emotions she'd dredged up.

"Daddy, I don't mean to hurt you." She sighed. "I've hurt you enough over the past twenty plus years. I think it was because I-I loved you so much." Her voice choked on cleansing tears.

Duncan came out of his chair and closed the distance between them. He folded his daughter in his arms. "Don't cry, darling girl. You're right. I wasn't home like I should have been. I chose your mom and a family, but I gave more precedence to my Naval career."

Liana buried her face against her father's still firm shoulder. "You were gone a lot, Daddy, but I blamed you for things you were never guilty of. Can you forgive me?"

"Of course." Duncan bracketed her face in his large hands, his green eyes, so like her own, soft with love for his only daughter. "I never blamed you for turning away from me. I made the decision to be the bad guy." He glanced over his shoulder toward her mother.

Liana wished she could see his full expression, but she saw her mom's. Cathy's was a classic reflection of regret, pain and deep love for the man she'd been unfaithful to.

"I should never have agreed to your plan, Duncan." Cathy stood and moved to wrap her arms around her ex-husband and Liana. "You've always been the stronger one."

"Uh, what's happening here?" Mark shot out of his chair and began to pace. "I have a feeling I've been left out of some vital pieces of information."

Duncan and Cathy stepped back to face their sons. Liana pressed her hands against her chest. "I thought I was the only one who didn't know. You did, didn't you, Tim?"

Tim nodded. "Sit down Mark. I only knew what happened because I'm the oldest and probably paid more attention to adult things. Mom had the affair, not Dad."

Mark sank into his chair. His mouth open, he darted a puzzled look between his mom and dad. "What? Why did we understand Dad ended your marriage?"

Tim leaned forward and rested his elbows on his thighs. "If we'd tuned in instead of acting like self-absorbed teenagers, we would have noticed Mom started dating Gary right away. Mom didn't tell me— we didn't have this conversation—I just had the feeling."

Liana shook her head. "I'm sorry, Mom and Dad. I didn't call this meeting to air your business."

"It's okay, honey." Cathy squeezed Liana's hand. "It's time we all start fresh. You know from our conversation yesterday, but your brothers don't. Your father and I are dating, and plan to remarry."

"Woo-hoo!" Tim sprang from his chair and gave his dad a bear hug before he scooped his mom into his arms and kissed both her cheeks. "I'm so glad." He turned to Mark. "Come on, bro. This is great news, you can feel slighted later."

Mark inflated his cheeks and let the air slowly escape before he joined his family in front of the wall of bookcases. "All right, I am happy about this reunion, but it'll take me awhile to reconcile with what happened."

"As it should." Duncan hugged his younger son. "But think about this, do your children know everything that happens between you and Dottie?"

"Of course not." Mark had the grace to look sheepish at his father's point. "Okay, I hate to admit it, but Tim's right. I'll comb through all of this later. Right now, Liana has something to tell us so we should move on."

"I do have something to tell you, and it's not pretty." Liana waited until her family settled back in their chairs. "I have to just say it and get it over with. I never loved Frank."

"That's not news to any of us. We all wondered when you'd get enough courage and leave him." Tim crossed one leg over the other and leaned back.

"I wanted to end the marriage countless times. There were days, weeks, years when things weren't that bad between us. Times when I thought if we built a friendship, we could stay together for Brittany, but a friendship would never happen. Frank wouldn't let it. He wanted me to love him like I'd loved Jack. When I didn't reciprocate his passion, he became very bitter and belittled me. He hurt my feelings to make me feel worse about not loving him. After nearly ten years of marriage, I went off the deep end and almost had an affair with a client."

Silence.

"Wow." Mark stood and began to pace again. "What do you mean, almost? What happened?"

"Mark, sit down." Tim played the older brother. "Liana, go on."

She fought against extreme embarrassment and wished she didn't have to air this particular piece of history. "I'm not proud of how I handled myself. I met Ryan through a client. At first, we met for drinks and dinner to discuss the sale of a downtown office building. By our third meeting, I became swept up in the attentions of a handsome, charming man who seemed to want me. All I could think of was my self-esteem—more exact, my ego. After dinner, I went to his room. The moment I stepped into his room, reality hit and sanity returned. I could never have forgiven myself if I'd gone all the way. I apologized and left."

Silence pervaded the room. Liana wanted to crawl away and hide, but she had to finish what she'd begun. "Frank played so many games to make me stay with him, the worst of which, threats to take Brittany away if I left him. So what did I do? I handed him the perfect trump card. He saw me leave the hotel. Brittany was with him, but she was so excited about the ballet they'd just attended, she didn't see me. If Frank has his way, he'll tell Brittany I had an affair—I was at fault for the divorce and ruined his life. She'll hate me."

Tim folded his arms over his chest. "It won't happen, sis. Brittany will not hate you. She's nearly sixteen years old, old enough to know a little about the world. Kids these days are far more sophisticated than we were."

"True." Liana fiddled with the drawstring on the workout pants she'd slipped into that morning. "Brittany is my life, and I can't risk losing her."

The tears started again. Liana accepted a tissue from her dad and wiped her eyes. "So, are you all totally disgusted with me?"

"Only because you should have left Frank way before you did and confide in us. We would have helped." Mark wrapped his arms around her. "Somehow you have an erroneous vision of Tim and I. We respect and love you, Li. We both loved Jack and wished to hell he hadn't died. When you married Frank right away, we knew something wasn't right. You could have come to us, sis." He pushed back and looked into her face. "So where does this put you now? What in the hell is Frank doing in Kalispell?"

Liana chuckled. "Good question. My attorney served him with new settlement papers over two weeks ago." She sniffed and dabbed at her eyes. The love and understanding from her family had her on overload. All the years she stood strong and independent and denied herself their support, made her shake her head. "Over the past four years, each month like clockwork, I've paid Frank what amounts to blackmail money. The judge didn't know about his demands, and I was in too much of a fog to report it."

"That piece of scum." Tim abandoned his chair and began to take Mark's path across the hardwood floor and back. "Frank Nash needs some fear put in him."

"Now, Tim, we won't resort to violence even though I'd like to do some myself." Duncan took

Liana's hand. "Go ahead, sweetheart."

"I can't believe Frank's here. He acts like nothing's happened. Something isn't right. Last night when they left, a fear of him kidnapping Brittany almost made my knees buckle. Would he try to kidnap her?"

Tim stopped mid step. "All right, don't get ahead of yourself. How much do you pay him?"

Liana named the figure.

"Holy—"

"Mark, watch your language." Cathy spoke for the first time since Liana disclosed her near affair. "Li, what can we do to help?"

Overwhelmed with emotion, Liana sat down before her legs collapsed. "I'm not sure what you can do. I just couldn't let Frank tell you his version first." She stared at the area rug. The swirls of dark brown and beige began to hypnotize her.

"Let us know if you have to go to court, we'll be there." Duncan scooted to the edge of the leather wing-back chair.

"Thank you, Daddy."

"What about when Brittany finds out about her paternity?" Tim threw his hands in the air. "Poor kid, she has some hard facts coming down the pike."

Cathy rose to put her arms around her daughter. "Liana, we are all committed to support you through this. Don't forget, we're just a phone call, or plane ride away, aren't we?" She turned to the men in her family.

"Of course we are." Her dad and her brothers agreed in unison.

They all gathered around and hugged Liana. She might feel exposed, but she also experienced a huge sense of relief. She prayed they'd still back her after they had time to digest everything she'd told them.

****

Liana glanced at the clock and groaned. Monday morning and she'd forgotten to set the alarm. Rolling out of bed, she hurried to Brittany's room.

"Brittany, are you awake?"

"No, I'm not. What time is it?"

Liana couldn't blame her for being tired. Thanksgiving weekend had been wonderful, terrible, restful and exhausting. She'd experienced a bevy of emotions she wouldn't have thought possible in one segment of time.

"It's seven-thirty. Come on, you have to get up."

"Please don't shout." Brittany rolled toward the wall and shielded her eyes from the bright overhead light. "Do you have to shout?"

"I'm sorry, Pumpkin. I blew it and forgot to set the alarm."

Brittany's eyes flashed wide open. She threw back the covers and sat up in one movement. "I can't be late. I have an English test this morning!" She raced to her closet, stripping out of her pajamas as she went. "Oh, no. I don't have time for a shower."

"Wear your hair up. What time's your English class?" Liana hurried back to her room to get dressed. Luckily she didn't have any morning appointments so she'd drive Brittany to school before she got ready for work.

"My class starts at eight-thirty."

"We'll make it." Liana hopped around on one foot, pulling on a pair of black velveteen sweat pants. She pulled on the matching zip up jacket and fluffed her hair. She brushed her teeth and slipped on a pair of clogs. Good enough until later.

Back in Brittany's room, her daughter was dressed and peered into her vanity mirror while she brushed on mascara. "I'm so sorry, Brit. I didn't mean for your week to start out on the wrong foot. Can I do anything to help?"

"Could you make me a smoothie?" She didn't turn toward Liana, but her tone had mellowed.

Had Frank's visit been a good thing, or a bad thing? Had he fulfilled Brittany's need to spend time with him, or had he promised her something he shouldn't have? Liana bit back a moan as she hurried to the kitchen to make the smoothie and pack a lunch for her daughter.

She'd walk on eggshells until Frank reacted to the settlement papers.

"I'll have your breakfast and lunch ready in about ten minutes. I'll run out and start the car so it can warm up."

"Thank you, Mom!"

Tossing blueberries, flax and whey powder into the blender, she pushed the button and started to make a turkey cranberry sandwich.

The smoothie in a portable cup and the lunch in a bag, Liana ran outside to start the SUV. The cold morning air sent a shiver through her. Not for the first time, she wondered if she'd been crazy to move to Montana. Soon there'd be snow on the roads. At least her house was winterized, right down to insulation in the new rafters of her studio. The next phase of remodel would be chaotic, but warm.

"Mom, are you ready?" Brittany's voice snapped her out of her thoughts.

"I'm ready! The car should be warm. Let's go."

She normally dropped Brittany in front of the school and left, confident her daughter was safe. Today she waited until Brittany disappeared into the building. Frank and Molly hadn't communicated before they returned to San Francisco yesterday. Had they really gone? Shaking off her paranoia, she made a quick phone call to her broker.

"I have a referral for you. The prospects are interested in the Saxon Construction house in Whitefish." Stan gave her the phone number.

Liana's breathing accelerated. "Saxon Construction? Wow, I had a couple interested in it last week."

"Competition is good. Did you show it?"

"Yes, I love the house. I used several of the features for my remodel. Could you text me their number? I just dropped Brittany off at school. Do you have office coverage today, Stan? I'd like to focus on this client."

He assured her the office was well covered and wished her a profitable day. Liana hurried into the house to get ready for a day of business. She hesitated in the center of her living room and soaked up the transformation. Her family had been impressed with the workmanship in the remodel and were excited about the studio. Her financial struggle had been worth every tear and dollar. If the stream of clients kept up, she could enjoy working out of her home. Brittany would come home to warmth and light and a home cooked meal.

Liana took a quick shower before she poured a fresh cup of coffee and fired up her computer before she called the Martins. She learned they'd been referred by the Cummings. Wow, all the running around, late nights and early mornings had paid off. Courtney Cummings had given them a glowing report on her expertise and high level of service.

The Martins wanted a walk-through today. She connected with the listing agent and arranged to meet the Martins in an hour at the mall off the main highway to Whitefish. She imagined Michael's pleasure if she managed to sell the house. Her diligence to help him might soften the blow when she confided in him about Ryan.

Not sure how long she'd be in Whitefish, Liana jotted a note for Brittany to bake a frozen pizza if Liana wasn't home by five.

The Martins were from Calgary and on their way to a software company in Seattle to negotiate some business. They didn't have time to shop around and wanted to make a quick decision. Luckily, Liana was accustomed to high-energy business people, or they would have drained her with all their brain storming on the drive to Whitefish. They loved the area and planned to rearrange their obligations to spend more time there.

When she pulled in front of the Artisan style house, the sight of the Saxon Construction sign in the yard made her heart flutter. Okay, she had it bad for Michael Saxon.

The Martins loved the house.

"Can you recommend a home inspector?" Mac Martin's voice was muffled as he shot questions over his shoulder from under the kitchen sink.

"Rick with Northwest Inspections is very good." She frowned. "Is something wrong?"

"I'm not happy with the drain pipe connection. I'd

like the builder to do a walk through with the inspector."

Liana took a deep breath. Working in tandem with Michael had seemed like a cool idea, but to pick apart his ability as a general contractor might be lethal to their relationship. She'd been in business long enough to know some people were impossible to please.

She nodded. "I'll check with him. Coincidentally, Saxon Construction is remodeling my house. He does a beautiful job." She hoped Michael wouldn't be offended by her request.

****

Michael glanced at his watch. Two o'clock. He'd planned to finish this job in time to get started on Liana's bedroom today, but the electrician was behind schedule and wanted to go over the plans with Michael.

They no sooner had the wiring schedule stretched out on the bar in the kitchen when his phone vibrated. "Saxon Construction."

"Michael."

His body went hot at the sound of his name in her breathy, feminine voice. "Liana, what's up?"

"I have a huge favor to ask."

"Sure, what is it?"

"It's work related."

"Okay..." As promised, he'd called her on Friday. She'd sounded so emotional he'd been worried about her ever since. If she hadn't been so busy with her family, he would have stopped by to make sure she was all right.

"I'm at your house in Whitefish. My clients from Canada are very interested in making an offer, but they'd like to set up an inspection and include you in the walk through. They have to leave early in the morning so Rick from Northwest Inspections will be here at five."

Torn between the urgency to sell the house and not being home to coach Leif with his math, Michael grimaced. "Rick normally gives me a list of his findings." He forked his fingers through his hair and clamped his teeth in frustration. Damn, he didn't want to get caught up in petty discussions over personal preference on a speculation house.

"I'm sure he will." The tension in her voice carried through the connection. He could picture her beautiful mouth tightening and the little crease between her brows. "The Martins have requested you walk through with them and Rick. Can you make it?"

"Just a second." Michael pressed the phone against his thigh. "Jake, how much longer will we be?"

The electrician glanced over the schedule and shook his head. "Can you stay another fifteen minutes? Sorry I'm late with this, Mick. There were issues at my other job."

"No problem. When can I get the sheet-rockers in here?"

"Wednesday, the minute I finish the rough-in."

Michael held up his index finger. "Great. Be right back." He walked out the front door before he put the phone to his ear. "Okay, Liana. Only because I need to sell the house, I'll make an exception and work late. In the future, I'm not a realtor. I don't work all hours of the day."

"Yes, sir." Liana's voice went from soft and breathy, to succinct and clipped. "Will five work?"

"Five it is."

No sense in starting anything at Liana's house today. He'd work here until time to head for Whitefish.

Dammit, he hadn't meant to be short with her, but he had no desire to work crazy hours just because she did. He liked his life in Montana and never planned to go back to the rat race. When the Whitefish Lake house sold, he'd be on track financially with one house at a time.

At four, he flipped open his phone and called Leif. "Hi son. I'm almost finished for the day, but I agreed to do a walk through on the Whitefish house with an inspector. I'll pick up dinner. In the meantime, there's some left over turkey in the refrigerator for a sandwich."

"Not a problem, Dad, and don't pick up dinner. I can make a sandwich. I'll slap some cream cheese and cranberries on it and call it good."

Michael pushed back his cowboy hat and rubbed his forehead. "How'd you get so responsible?"

"Uh, well, I think we both know I didn't get it from Mom."

"Now, now. For all her faults, she has her moments of dependability." Michael tired to keep his disappointment in Meredith to himself. "I'll be home before seven." Michael closed his phone, and stuck it back in the holster on his belt.

The change in his schedule allowed time to help the electrician so the sheet-rockers could get on the job tomorrow instead of Wednesday. The change wasn't all bad.

When he'd told Liana he'd learned to slow down, he'd meant it, but he'd over obligated himself with the speculation house in Kalispell. He had no business starting a new project before the Whitefish house sold. Downsizing his business had meant downsizing his business line of credit, so he'd had to dip into his savings. With the crunch in commercial lending, he was a little tight on money. The house in Whitefish needed to sell, and soon.

He jumped into his truck and cranked up his stereo in hopes George Strait would put him in a mellow mood. By the time Michael pulled into the driveway of the Whitefish house, his anxiety level had dropped a notch. Now, if Liana's clients didn't jack him around, he should be home by six-thirty.

Liana met him at the door. "Michael, thank you for coming. Rick's running late, but should arrive in about fifteen minutes."

Michael raised a brow and stepped past her into the tiled foyer. "I hope so. I have a son at home who needs a prod with his homework."

"I know, and I'm sorry." She lowered her voice and nodded toward the kitchen.

Michael got it. Her clients were in the kitchen and she didn't want him to undo all of her schmoozing. "Let's get started."

"Why don't I introduce you to the Martins?" She gestured toward the kitchen.

"Sure." Michael tried not to sound short. The drive from Kalispell had mellowed him out, until he saw her in the doorway. He wasn't angry with her, just tied up in knots from wanting her. If they didn't have some intimate time soon, he'd go crazy.

The Martin's were a techie looking couple from a large software company in Calgary. People from a completely different world. He shook Mac Martin's hand.

"Good to meet you. Do you mind if we get started? Rick can look at everything when he gets here."

Mac Martin glanced at Liana, his brows meeting below his artfully arranged bangs. "Shouldn't we wait for the inspector?"

Michael pulled his shoulders back and took a deep breath. "I left a job early to walk through the house with you."

Liana stepped closer and laid her hand on Michael's arm. "Mac saw something he didn't like under the kitchen sink. Uh, here's the list we've made."

Michael's patience teetered. He took the list and stared at Liana for a moment before he looked at the paper. She'd raved over the job he'd done with her remodel, but when it came to her clients, he wasn't good enough.

"This house was built to code and inspected by the appropriate agencies before a certificate of occupancy was issued." He sounded like an ass, but dammit, he didn't appreciate some desk jockey questioning his work.

Mac Martin broadened his shoulders and clasped his hands behind his back. "Mr. Saxon, if you aren't willing to address our concerns, I'm not interested in buying your house. I have no desire to pay someone to redo these items later."

Through a haze of irritation, he walked through the issues with the Martins and Liana. Each time Mac Martin noted an item he'd personally like changed, Michael bit his tongue until he was surprised he had one left. After the tenth complaint, he couldn't keep quiet. "Mr. Martin, even though this was a remodel, it's still a spec house, not a custom build. My designer chooses the finishes and colors to fit a range of homeowners." The house was damned fine in Michael's book.

While the Martin's pondered changing out the windows in the breakfast nook, Michael grabbed Liana's hand and headed to the powder room to take a look at the pocket door.

"He's right on this one. Something's out of plumb, so I'll fix it tomorrow. The rest I'll go over with Rick." He turned to Liana, his hands planted on his hips. "What in the hell is this all about?"

"Welcome to my world." Liana stood on her tiptoes and peered into his face. "I deal with demands on a daily basis. It's one of the reasons I work so many hours."

"The other reason?" His breath brushed her forehead making her bangs flutter.

A thrill shot deep in Liana's body. She wanted to be closer to him. Every day, always. She stepped back. "Can you stay and talk with the inspector?"

Michael glanced at his watch. "Liana, it's almost six o'clock. My son's home scrounging for dinner. I don't work these hours anymore, remember?"

Liana tilted her head to one side. "Yes, you've made that point. Okay. I'll assure the Martins you'll connect with Rick tomorrow and make any needed repairs. Rick will email the report to both of us. I really do appreciate your willingness to come so late in the day."

Michael moved toward her, eating up the space she'd put between them. "I don't want to wait until Friday night to see you."

Liana smiled. "You still want to go out with me after I disrupted your evening?"

"Of course. Hey, every couple has rifts. I'm irritated over the situation, not you."

Her heart warmed. "I'm glad. How about Wednesday night?"

"Wednesday? It's a work night, remember?"

"Throw my words back at me, will you?" She glanced toward the kitchen. The Martins were still wrapped up in the changes they'd make to the otherwise satisfactory house. She turned back to Michael. "Even I break the rules sometimes. I get tired of toughing it out, don't you?"

"Sure do. Wednesday is as long as I want to wait. How about dinner at Ciao Mambo? I'll pick you up at six?"

"Sounds good." Liana pecked a kiss on his cheek and backed away. "Better run before Rick shows up."

Michael nodded and slipped out the front door.

Liana waited until he'd closed the door before she practically skipped to the kitchen where her clients were going over the tile work with a magnifying glass. Well, they weren't really, but it seemed like it. Sometimes her clients went over the top, but the really cool and patient people made up for the cranky, picky ones.

Rick arrived fifteen minutes after Michael left. Mac Martin followed Rick through the house to point out the items he'd covered with Michael. Darkness had fallen, but Rick produced a flashlight and humored Mac with a look at the foundation, while Liana discussed possible decorating ideas with Mrs. Martin. The men returned within a few minutes.

"I can't see under the house tonight so I'll swing by tomorrow to check it out."

"That's reasonable," Liana said before either of the Martins could respond. "We really appreciate your time, and at such short notice." Liana walked with him toward the door.

"Thank you, Liana." Rick lowered his voice when the Martins followed them to the door. "I should have the report emailed out tomorrow. I can tell you one thing,"—he raised his voice—"I've worked with Michael Saxon on several houses and the inspectors love his work. The man is a perfectionist."

"Perfection would mean copper pipes," Mac Martin said, his mouth turned down.

Liana glanced at Rick with a raised brow. "See you later."

****

"They expect me to do what?"

Liana glanced around the office to see if anyone had heard Michael bellow through the phone.

"Rick convinced them you were absolutely right about the drain pipes being PEX, but they want the intake water pipes changed to copper. Just under the sinks."

Michael paused long enough that Liana expected another explosion. "This is ridiculous. The rest of the house is plumped with PEX. But if it means selling the house right away, I'll humor them and call the plumber for a bid. I won't reduce the price another dollar, or pay for the change out. I price my houses right where they need to be with some wiggle room for bargainers."

"I understand, Michael. The request is crazy, but the Martins are my clients and they're willing to pay just under full price for your house."

Michael sighed. "This is one of the reasons I left my big business in Oklahoma City."

"Just one of the reasons? What's the other one?" He'd asked her the same question last night.

"I hope to have the opportunity to tell you all about it."

She lowered her voice and sighed into the phone. "Thank you, Michael. I'm fortunate to work with such a competent, reasonable and, may I add, handsome contractor."

"Hmm," Michael moaned. "Get personal with me, lady, and we won't wait until Wednesday."

Liana's awareness spiked. "Speaking of tomorrow night, Brittany asked permission to stay with Meagan after ballet practice so they can study together. I wonder what brought that on?"

"I told Leif about our date. I have a feeling they compare notes at school." Michael chuckled.

"Really? It's rather disconcerting when kids start to arrange private time for their parents."

"Whatever it takes. I can't wait to be alone with you."

Liana shifted in her chair, and glanced around the office. She hoped no one heard her conversation. It seemed a little like phone sex. "Back to business. Rick emailed the inspection report this afternoon. Did you receive one?"

"Yeah, I got it."

"Could you let me know how soon the changes can be made?"

"Does my agent have the offer?"

"Yes, I sent it over with the repairs as contingency

to close the sale. She should call you soon to sign. The Martins like the house or they wouldn't pay for the inspection and changes."

"You're good, Liana. No wonder you have so many referrals. See you soon." Michael hung onto the connection a few seconds after she said goodbye.

He slid out of his truck and unlocked the front door of the house. He'd fix the silly pocket door and meet the plumber in about thirty minutes. Lucky for all concerned, the subcontractors were happy for any little job that came along.

No matter how much he tried not to, his mind flashed back to Thanksgiving night in the corvette with Liana. Even the thought of her in his arms, moaning and coming apart ignited a wildfire in him.

He cleared his throat and his mind. The Martin's list of repairs wouldn't get done with him daydreaming. He still had work to do at the spec house in Kalispell and be home early enough to shower and change for Leif's basketball game.

Damn, his date with Liana couldn't come soon enough.

****

Brittany wandered into the kitchen and leaned against the island. "I'm happy you're seeing Michael."

Brittany's statement almost made Liana cut herself with the freshly sharpened filet knife. "Where did that remark come from?"

"Well, ever since you met him after dinner on Thanksgiving you've acted younger. Less stressed out."

How did Brittany know she'd met Michael last Thursday?

"I'm glad you approve."

"Leif and I agree you and Michael are good for each other. My friends think it's weird you don't date. Most of their parents are already remarried."

Liana cringed. "Sounds like you and your friends have some personal conversations. I'd rather keep my life private."

"Oh I wouldn't tell them anything really personal. Just regular stuff. It's part of making new friends, Mom."

Liana washed and dried her hands. "I know the divorce and the move to Montana have been hard on you. I didn't date because I wanted to focus on you and make a stable home."

"You don't have to wrap me in cotton. I'm almost sixteen. Besides, Leif told me his dad hasn't really dated since his divorce either."

"I can't help being protective. I want you to be happy."

"I want you to be happy too, so enjoy yourself with Michael. He's a great guy." Brittany turned toward the den. "I'm going to check my Facebook account!"

"All right, honey. Dinner will be ready in about thirty minutes."

Liana sautéed the cubed chicken breast and tossed it with Caesar salad.

Since cutting back her work hours, she and Brittany had started eating dinner in the dining room every night. Breakfast was usually a hurried affair at the island, but Liana tried to make dinner an extra special time to eat good food and catch up on their day.

What would it have been like if Jack had survived his military stint? Would their marriage have lasted? Would he have been the good father Liana had always pictured? Questions streamed through her head, but couldn't be answered.

Wednesday morning, Liana wrote up the offer for the Whitefish house, and Michael's agent accepted it. The Martins were happy with the house and the price.

When they asked Liana to recommend a decorator, her heart fluttered. She'd love to start her design business alongside the Realtor business. The Martins were amazed and delighted when she showed them her portfolio from San Diego and offered them a bid. Life was looking up.

She couldn't wait to tell Michael. Maybe kicking off her business was a sign of more good things to come.

****

Liana rushed into the house shortly before six. Damn, she'd lost track of time and wouldn't have the leisurely bath she'd planned. She laid her purse on the island and a note from Brittany caught her eye.

Shari had picked Brittany up after ballet and brought her home to pack an overnight bag and feed Oscar.

What would she do without her dear friend? She'd always been able to count on Shari through the ups and downs in life. When Brittany and Meagan were born, they'd become like sisters. Thank goodness they also became best friends.

There were so many good things in Liana's life she couldn't allow herself to get bogged down with the negative influences. Like Frank for instance, and the games he continued to play, like not calling her about the new settlement agreement.

Determined to push Frank out of her mind for the

night, she took a shower and sorted through her closet. She wanted to wow Michael with her ability to adjust to the cold Montana weather and still look sexy.

She pulled on a pair of formfitting stretchy jeans and a thigh length, fuzzy sweater with a scooped neckline. She didn't have western boots so the tall Italian leather pair would have to do. Turquoise earrings, bracelets and a long strand of turquoise and silver beads looked good against the black cashmere. She blow-dried and ruffled her hair in the messy style Michael liked.

"I'm ready." She added color to her lips. "I think."

Liana hadn't been on a formal date since right after Brittany was born. Well, except for the night Michael came to the Outlaw Inn.

The previous date had been when Frank insisted they go out to celebrate the birth of their daughter. She'd tried to act like a happily married woman, but the chemistry just wasn't there and ten years of marriage didn't change her feelings. She never loved Frank.

Glancing at the bedside clock, Liana's stomach fluttered. He'd be here in ten minutes. Ten minutes until her first real date with Michael. The memory of what happened in the corvette set off intense ribbons of heat. She hurried to the kitchen and poured a glass of wine. She'd forgotten to eat lunch so the wine immediately mellowed her. She wrapped her fingers around the stemware and slid it back and forth on the granite counter top.

Were things going her way at last? Her family knew about her past and still loved and supported her; she had a design contract with the Martins and she was about to spend an intimate evening with Michael.

Liana ate a couple of crackers with brie and drained the glass of wine. Anticipation curled through her and heightened her taste buds and the awareness of everything around her. Michael made her feel things she'd thought impossible to experience. Along with the thrill, came the fear it wouldn't last after she told him about Ryan, but he deserved to know that side of her. Tonight, she needed to tell him.

Chapter Eleven

He'd driven the corvette.

Michael helped her into the passenger seat. He leaned across her and buckled her in before he slid behind the wheel. Tonight, he didn't offer for her to drive. He was in command. After years of fighting for independence, the sensuality of being pampered fueled her libido.

Jack had owned a sports car and liked to show her and the car off. He had made the moon rise and the world turn. He'd been handsome and charming, but immature and more of a thrill seeker than a family man. Michael was everything she'd ever dreamed of in a man and completely focused on her. "I thought you'd like another ride in the 'Vette." Michael gave her thigh a light squeeze.

"You thought right." She missed his touch when he pulled into the traffic and shifted gears. The combination of man and car was downright sexy.

"What's Leif doing tonight?"

"He's home doing schoolwork." Michael shrugged one shoulder. "I picked up his favorite pizza. To tell you the truth, I ended up working late today too."

Liana held up her index finger. "At least it wasn't my fault this time."

Michael chuckled. "No, it's my own fault. I overextended my time and money when I agreed to build a spec house for my buddy." He accelerated until they left Kalispell behind. "I really appreciate how you made the sale happen."

"After what you've done for us it's the least I could do. Really, timing is the key. I can't take all the credit."

He slid his hand to her knee, hesitating before he moved it halfway up her thigh, his gaze on the road. "You're good, Liana. I completely understand why you're so busy. I had no right to ever criticize you. I hope you believe everything I said was out of concern."

Liana touched his cheek and traced her fingertip down his handsome face. "Thank you for the compliment and the apology. Your opinion matters to me."

He grabbed her hand and pressed a tender kiss on the back of her fingers. "I'm glad."

She sighed at the old fashioned gesture.

They entered the outskirts of Whitefish. Michael slowed the car and turned left to park in front of the restaurant they both loved even before they'd met there on Liana's birthday. Liana reached for the door handle. Realizing Michael hadn't moved, she turned toward him. Her breath caught at the slow heat radiating from his amber eyes.

They stared at each other for a long moment before he slipped his arm around her and pulled her close for a kiss.

Liana moaned and floated in a world of sensation filled with Michael's heat, scent and touch. He drew back and studied her expression. Her body heated to a low simmer and her skin felt every yarn in her cashmere sweater.

"What is it about this car?"

Michael chuckled. "I think we'll enjoy kissing wherever we are. Hungry?" He raised one dark brow.

Liana cleared her throat with drama. "Extremely."

He gave her another quick kiss, unfolded his tall frame from the car and rounded the hood.

Liana stretched and wiggled. She was so much more connected to Michael than she ever had with Jack. Poor Jack. She didn't want to discount her love for him. He'd been her first, the father of her child, but the intensity with Michael surpassed any emotion she'd ever dreamed of.

Michael opened her door. "I think I'll drive the old girl more often. You didn't react like this to my truck."

"Do you only bring her out when you have a hot prospect?"

He laughed again. "If you knew how seldom I go out, you'd realize what an off base question that is. I meant it when I said I hadn't dated in over a year. Longer than that since I tried to impress someone." He took her arm and escorted her into the Italian restaurant. "Leif is elated we're dating, but when I mentioned I might be very late, he looked at me like he was the father."

Liana laughed. "Brittany gave us her approval last night. It scares me how much the kids know these days."

"Me too." Michael stopped at the empty host station, looped his arm around her waist and kissed her forehead. "By the way, you look incredibly hot tonight."

"Thank you. So do you."

The host returned and led them toward a corner table. She loved the way Michael pressed his hand against the small of her back and guided her through the busy dining room. She didn't even mind the possessiveness radiating from him when a good-looking man smiled at her as they passed his table.

Michael's attentiveness was completely different from Frank's, who had bordered on obsessiveness. Even before Ryan came to town.

"I'm glad we moved up our date night." Liana touched his hand as he scooted her chair into the table.

He kissed her earlobe. "Me too."

Crazy sensations shimmered down her neck. Liana smiled. "It's difficult to act polished and professional when you kiss me like that."

"Wait until later." He wiggled his brows and made her laugh.

The host hovered with a smile. She handed them menus, announced Sarah would be their server for the evening, and left.

"I have some exciting news." Liana leaned forward, her forearms on the menu. "The Martins have hired me to personalize the house for them."

Michael's eyes widened. "That is great news. Are you sure you can handle working for Mac Martin?"

Liana tilted her head. "Oh, he'll no doubt be a pain, but if they like my work, I'm sure they'll refer me to their friends and business associates."

Michael cased her hands with his. "If it makes you sparkle like you are tonight, I'll back you all the way."

"The job isn't the only thing making me sparkle tonight." Liana turned her hands and grasped his fingers.

They ordered dinner and relaxed over a glass of wine from the bottle Sarah presented and served. At least Liana tried to relax. The anticipation over what might happen later made her giddy and on edge. If only she could just tell Michael about Ryan and be done with it. She owed him the truth before their relationship progressed. She'd had enough secrets in her life. She needed to wipe the slate clean and start over.

However, life didn't work that way. Life was composed of mistakes and poor judgments, and she'd had her share. The immediate question blared through her mind and dimmed the excitement of the evening. How would Michael react to the revelation that she'd been the Meredith in Frank's life? Well, kind of...she didn't drink excessively, or take prescription drugs and freak out, but she'd almost followed through with a one-night stand with a man she barely knew.

"Hey, have I lost you?" Michael clinked his glass against hers.

She wanted to cry. Across the table sat the most handsome, sexy, considerate, intelligent—well, the list went on—man she'd ever met and he wanted to be with her. Why couldn't she open up and tell him about Ryan?

"To our first date." He completed the toast, took a drink and rolled his lips together.

Liana ached to kiss those lips, kiss his bare skin, lay with him through the dark night. *After you tell him you almost cheated on Frank.* She blinked and forced a smile.

"To our first date."

"Liana, do you have second thoughts about us?" Michael's smooth voice intensified her inner conflict.

"Absolutely not." She sipped her wine.

"Are you okay?" He dipped his head and gazed at

her. The candlelight shot gold through his amber eyes.

Liana gulped. "I sometimes slip into a depressing thought pattern, but I'm through going there tonight."

Completely through.

Everyone had secrets in their past, didn't they? Her family certainly did. If she never told Michael about Ryan, would it be unethical? She'd kissed Ryan and he'd unzipped her dress, but she'd stopped him and herself from doing something unredeemable. It had nothing to do with Michael.

"Glad to hear that." He squeezed her hands and leaned back. "I meant it when I said I'm not interested in a casual relationship. When things get tough, I'm here for you."

Tears pricked her eyes. Liana smiled. "You are amazing. I need to buy Lucky some special treat for running in front of your truck."

He chuckled. "Believe me, sweetheart, Lucky's getting very special treatment." Michael had called about three weeks ago to announce the birth of five puppies.

"Brittany's upset with me for not inviting ourselves over to see the puppies. Is Lucky ready for visitors?"

"Sure, why don't you and Brittany come over tomorrow night? I'll make dinner and we can have puppy time."

Liana floated on a cloud of bliss. The man melted her into a puddle every time she turned around. How had she been so—she'd almost thought—lucky? Liana Campbell, you don't believe in luck, remember? "We'd love to come over. Brittany's hinted about getting a puppy when they're old enough. She's been through so much, maybe a pup will give her something to center on when Frank hits the ceiling."

"Hey, listen to me. You're an excellent mother. Everything you've done has been in her best interest. Don't forget that when things get ugly."

Sarah arrived with their dinner. The food looked and smelled heavenly. Michael ate his meal with relish, but saw to her every need. He poured more wine, asked about her food, touched her arm several times. Liana almost melted down when he slid his cowboy boot between her designer Italian boots.

His amazing eyes heated to a rich topaz. Her body tightened and her lungs refused to work right. Too many sensations, thoughts and pesky regrets whirled through her mind for her to relax.

"Wait until you try their desserts."

"I can't possibly eat dessert." Liana glanced at the plateful of food in front of her.

Michael stared at her across the stoneware, crystal glassware and flickering candles. He rested his fork on his empty plate and clasped her hand in his. "We can take it to go and have it later...much later."

Liana literally felt her breasts firm and her nipples peak. How did he do that? "Sounds good." Everything he said sounded good.

When Sarah returned for their plates, she requested a carton for her leftovers and finished her glass of wine.

Michael smiled at Sarah and winked at Liana. "How about some decadent chocolate dessert for later on."

"Certainly, Mr. Saxon. I'll just add it to your check and be right back." Sarah deftly gathered up the plates and flatware.

He pulled out his debit card and laid it on the table.

"Go ahead and take care of the check. I don't need to see it."

"Uh, wait a minute." Liana held up a finger and reached for her purse. "I'll pay for my dinner."

Michael slipped his card into Sarah's apron pocket and nodded at her. Sarah left the table. "In my day when a man asked a woman out, he paid the bill. I'm old fashioned enough to believe it still should be that way."

He pulled Liana's chair out before she could gather an objection, and laid her jacket over her shoulders. Sarah returned with their cartons and Michael's card and receipt.

Liana noted the large tip he added to the bill, and warmed as his work-roughened hand signed with a flourish. The man was an artist with everything he touched.

The thought coursed through her as he took her arm and escorted her to the corvette. Before she could slip onto the passenger seat, he pulled her close and pressed his lips against her temple. "Ready for the rest of the night?"

Liana's brain froze for a moment before going into a spin. "Of course."

He slid his hand up her back and under her hair. He cupped her scalp. "You hesitated. Liana. When I make love with you, I want you to be completely sure it's what you want."

When he held her like this, her mind went to mush. "Honestly? There's nothing I want more."

"I still sense a 'but' in your response. We're heading to your house before it turns into a no." He helped her with her seat belt and closed her door.

Torn between her damnable need to be completely open and honest and the intense sexual awareness only Michael could arouse, Liana struggled with a way to tell him about Ryan. The ride back to her house was laced with anticipation. Between shifting gears and commanding the powerful car, Michael touched her leg several times.

He drove to the end of her street where her lot sat on the outskirts of town. Parking behind her SUV, he switched off the heater, lights and engine. "Am I coming inside?"

Liana's stomach flip-flopped. She'd much rather fall into each other's arms in a fit of passion. The more intentional method made her think twice. Yeah, she was on fire for him, liked and respected him, but if she acted on the response he evoked in her lonely body, their relationship would never be the same.

She took a deep breath and turned toward him on the supple leather seat. "Michael, I've thought about this moment since we met. Making love with you will leave an unforgettable impression on my mind and body. I just don't want you to ever regret it."

Michael tucked a stray piece of hair behind her ear. "Life's too full of regrets. You'll never be one of mine."

Liana's past relationships shattered around her like ice crystals. She'd loved Jack and mourned his loss; she'd tried to love Frank and couldn't. Out of desperation for love, she'd almost cheapened herself with an affair. What she already had with Michael made every relationship pale in comparison. "I can't imagine ever regretting one moment with you either."

Not waiting for a reply, she fished her house keys

out of her purse and headed for the front door. Her hands trembled as she tried to fit the key to the lock. Her heart raced. Was she doing the right thing? She'd only known Michael a short time. What had happened to her vow to wait until Brittany grew up and left for college?

Michael gently took control of the key and unlocked the door. Liana visibly trembled from head to foot. Was she excited or afraid?

Working on her house—getting to know her—his attraction to her had grown into more than a casual emotion. She affected him like no other woman.

"How about I pour some wine?" Michael set the chocolate dessert on the bar.

"I thought we were having coffee." She moved into the kitchen and started to make a pot.

"I'm not in the mood for coffee." He poured wine into the glasses they'd used before dinner and handed her one. Lifting his glass, he clinked against it hers. The ring of crystal seemed to signal the change in their relationship.

"To the rest of our first real date."

She trembled, but placed the rim of the glass to her lips and took a sip.

Michael took a drink, set the glass on the bar and moved toward her. "I've tried to be a gentleman, but I'm on fire for you." He took her glass and set it next to his.

Liana's gaze turned hazy as she wound her arms around his neck and buried her face in the side of his throat.

"Hey, are you okay? We don't have to make love tonight. I want it to be right for you." He meant every word. In his mind, he'd already taken their relationship to the next level. He cared too much about Liana and her daughter to walk away.

"You're so good to me." Her voice vibrated against his neck.

He pulled back and feathered his lips over hers. Moaning against her mouth, he scooped her up and carried her to the couch where he held her in his lap while he explored the soft texture of her black sweater.

"This outfit drove me crazy all night."

"That's why I wore it."

Michael treaded his fingers through her hair and traced his thumb over her lips. "It doesn't matter what you wear, you turn me on."

Liana's mossy gaze entranced him and touched his soul. "Even in a chenille robe with no makeup?"

"I wanted to strip that robe and teddy off and kiss you from head to toe. You can't turn me off, sweetheart." Three years of celibacy broke like a dam. Michael framed her face with his hands and claimed her mouth. He slid his palms over her shoulders and down her back, tugging at the long sweater to gain access to her soft, creamy skin. He worked at her bra clasp, freeing it before he eased her back, sliding his hands over her stomach and up to cup her firm, full breasts. "Damn, we have on too many clothes."

"Let's go to my room." Liana gripped his shoulders and arched against his throbbing body.

"Good plan." Living the next part of his fantasy, he carried her into the bedroom and released her legs until she stood by her bed. She ran her lips over his throat and down his chest, freeing shirt buttons as she went.

He moaned, his head in a fog of need. Suddenly he

realized more than her kisses dampened his skin. He tilted his head. She was crying. "Sweetheart, if you're not ready, it's okay. I'm a patient man."

She blinked against the tears balanced on her bottom lids. "I'm overcome with emotion, Michael. I've never felt such overwhelming need."

He pulled her against him and cradled her face against his shoulder. "I want to be the one who really understands you, inside and out."

Liana wrapped her arms around his middle and nuzzled his bare chest. Michael choked back tears. She touched his carefully guarded heart. She was confident and professional, yet had a vulnerability few people saw. He was privileged to be the one who got beyond the capable, independent businesswoman.

He gently lowered her to the bed and caught the hem of her sweater to pull it over her head. Tossing it to one side, he finished removing her bra and took a moment to stare at the beauty of the woman before him. Her skin glowed a soft peach in the filtered light from the hall.

Liana rose up on her elbows and sizzled him with green eyes no longer mossy and soft, but dark and hot with passion.

He kicked off his boots and quickly shed his jeans and underwear. With care, he draped his shirt over the back of the chair in the corner of the room. Leif might be up when he got home. The last thing he needed to do was excite his son's imagination. He turned toward Liana and relished the exquisite torture of watching her undress.

Naked, she moved to the bureau next to the bed and fumbled with something before a match flared. She touched the flame to the wick of a large gold candle.

Michael shut the bedroom door. Liana sashayed toward him on a wave of sandalwood, her every step driving him over the edge. He stayed put—just to torture himself—drawing out the moments before his life changed forever. Because he knew in his heart, after he made love to Liana, he'd never be the same.

Liana drank in his grace and strength. She should tell him about Ryan, but the words wouldn't come.

"You are a work of art, Liana Campbell."

His words flared through her like a raging fire and pushed her concerns away to a dark corner she'd deal with later. Later when he walked out of her life. Tonight was special and unique.

Liana stopped in front of him, a breath away from the bronzed man who was every woman's fantasy. For tonight—for this moment—he watched her like she was his every fantasy.

She slid her hands over his broad shoulders, and gently pushed until his legs pressed against the mattress. Michael sat on the edge of the bed and glided his large, calloused hands over her thighs and hips and settled at her waist. She took control and moved between his knees, brushing her breasts against his lips until he groaned and paid homage to her hardened nipples.

Emboldened, she planted one knee on the mattress next to his hip, then the other and rubbed her aching body against his naked skin, sinking into his lap until they melded into one. Mindless, seconds later she soared through the stars, but Michael didn't stop.

She held his head, loving the feel of his dark, silky hair, loving the intimacy of sharing her body with him.

She mumbled words she'd never say in daylight. Michael moaned and growled in response. He swung them fully on the queen-size bed without breaking their connection and braced his hands on either side of her, slowing his pace to pull her into an amazing world she'd never imagined entering.

His movements, his hot, sweat slick skin, and masculine scent overwhelmed her senses. How could he keep going?

Liana ran her hands down his muscled chest and flat stomach, fascinated with his strength and control. He'd been right. Once would never be enough.

Reaching his peak, he buried his face in the side of her neck and shuddered and groaned. Liana soared into a wonderful universe of exploding stars and quivering, tingling flesh.

"Liana, Liana," Michael mumbled. "You're so perfect." He pushed up on his elbows, holding his full weight off her.

She brushed his hair from his forehead and smiled. "What we did was perfect."

She should have told him.

They'd made love. Their relationship had changed and he'd gone into it without the truth he deserved.

She fell to the earth, the pall of yet another deception hanging over her.

"Dammit, sweetheart, I'm sorry." He rolled to his side, taking her with him.

Liana pushed up on her elbow and looked down into his handsome face. She cherished this moment of being skin against skin, wrapped in his strong arms. "What are you apologizing for?"

"I went crazy and forgot about the condom in my

jeans pocket. We just had unprotected sex." He scrubbed his face with both hands. "The good news is, I'm clean. Boy, am I clean." He laughed without humor. "I haven't been with anyone since my divorce. After Meredith confessed her affair, I had some tests done to make sure she didn't bring more home than heartbreak."

Liana was stunned. It hadn't entered her mind. Not birth control or diseases. She'd been so wrapped up in her need for Michael, versus confessing her near indiscretion with Ryan, she hadn't thought of all the responsible reasons why she shouldn't make love with him.

"You're on birth control, right?" The soft glow of the candlelight illuminated his amber eyes.

"No." The word echoed through the room like the gong in a Tibetan temple.

Michael pushed up on his elbow, bringing his face a breath from hers. "Baby, talk to me."

Liana let out a gush of air and sank into the pillows, covering her face with both hands. "No, to everything. I'm not on birth control. I haven't been tested for diseases. I'm unfit to be a lover, or a mother or anything else that resembles responsibility."

Michael moved her hand from her face. "What are you really talking about?"

Liana slid to the other side of the bed and sat up, her back to him. She wrapped her arms around her bare middle and stared out the window toward the side yard. "When Frank wouldn't give me a divorce, I despaired ever feeling like you just made me feel. I had a big deal going with a firm from Chicago. Ryan was their real estate procurement officer. We met for dinner and drinks. He was charming, attentive and made no bones about wanting more than a business deal. The meeting moved to his room."

Silence.

"You had an affair?"

"I almost had an affair. Whatever you want to call it, I kissed Ryan. When he unzipped my dress, sanity returned. I told him I couldn't go through with it. I might not have loved Frank, but I couldn't compromise my own ideals." Tears welled and tracked down her cheeks. Liana swiped at them. "When I left the hotel, Frank and Brittany were walking toward me. They'd gone to the Nutcracker. Thank God Brittany didn't see me. Frank instantly turned her toward the crosswalk and they went into the parking garage."

She pulled her feet onto the edge of the bed and wrapped her arms around her legs. "Wow." Michael finally spoke. "You've harbored this guilt for a long time, haven't you?"

"He wouldn't believe I didn't have sex. He used it as a bargaining chip in the divorce and every day since."

The bedding rustled and the mattress shifted. Liana waited to say more, listening to him dress. He was leaving.

"I should have told you."

"Yeah, well we've both made some assumptions we shouldn't have." He walked around the bed and pulled the sheet around her shoulders. "I need to go. Leif's home alone."

She couldn't stop the flow of tears or the ache in her heart. Liana nodded, but her voice wouldn't work.

Michael knelt in front of her and wiped her tears

with his thumbs. "Honey, a lot happened tonight. I wanted this as much or more than you did, but I didn't mean to expose you to a pregnancy you might not want. As for what happened with that guy...if you think it compares to Meredith and the end of my marriage, it doesn't. I won't lie. Trust is crucial to me, but you didn't break my trust, honey. Frank was a fool to treat you like he did."

Liana shook her head. "I'd never hold you responsible for something I let happen."

"Well, you should. It's time you stopped wearing the weight of the world on your shoulders." He kissed her cheeks and moved his mouth over hers. "I'll call you tomorrow. Will you be all right?"

She nodded and sniffed. Michael handed her a tissue from the box on her nightstand. "Baby, if I didn't have an impressionable son at home, I'd stay and hold you all night." He kissed her forehead, turned and left the room.

Liana sat on the edge of the bed until the roar of his truck echoed into the distance, and the night chill crept through the sheet. He'd said he didn't see the resemblance between his marriage and hers, yet he'd been shocked; his silence spoke volumes. He'd said he'd call her, but he wouldn't. She'd lost the only man she could ever love.

Stiff and cold, Liana snuggled under the down comforter, and cried herself to sleep.

Chapter Twelve

Thursday morning moved like an eternity. Liana stayed in bed until ten, exhausted and broken. Michael didn't call about last night, and Frank didn't call to blame her for every wrong in his life. She stumbled into the kitchen to fix a pot of coffee, and a popped a piece of bread in the toaster. Since she planned to work from home today, she stayed in her loungewear and checked emails.

At noon, Brittany called for permission to go shopping with Meagan after school. She'd leave for her dad's on the first day of her holiday break, so she wanted to start her Christmas shopping. Liana agreed, partly to make Brittany happy and partly to give herself more time to pull herself together before her daughter found her red-eyed and miserable. Restless, she started a load of laundry and took meat from the freezer for dinner. In robotic motion, she made a sandwich and took a couple of bites.

Michael had promised to call. He probably woke this morning and thanked his lucky stars he'd gone home last night. Did he regret his involvement with her?

At two-thirty, Stan called to relay a message from a new client. She forced a cheerful tone she didn't feel and jotted down their email address and cell numbers.

"Are you all right, Liana? You don't sound like

yourself."

So much for her act.

"I'm fine, Stan. I'm having pre-holiday depression since Brittany's going to her dad's for vacation."

"Hang in there, kid. It'll all work out. Say, aren't you going to San Diego to visit your family for some of the time Brittany's with her dad?"

"Yes. I'll fly back on the twenty-seventh." She assured her broker she'd be fine and ended the call so she could email the prospective clients.

Good lord, what was she doing? She looked down at her attire and shook her head. She might own attractive loungewear, but she didn't intend to become a recluse who never got dressed.

One thing at a time.

Frank wouldn't remain silent for long. He'd plan a new strategy to spring on her. She had to toughen up and be ready. Her heart ached over losing Michael, but Brittany had to be her first concern.

She slipped into sports socks and running shoes and braved the cold air for a run. Physical exertion opened the valve on her stress and drained the tension from her neck and shoulders. She ran for twenty minutes before she circled and returned home to shower and dress in a pair of comfortable jeans and a long sleeved T-shirt.

Regardless of what happened with Michael, it was time to start over, begin a new life—this time for real. Geography hadn't accomplished the deep down changes she needed.

She'd clean out her closet—sort through the boxes she hadn't unpacked from her move—get rid of stuff she should have tossed when she packed up the house in San Francisco.

If Michael continued with the remodel, her bedroom would be the next project and he needed space to work. Brittany's bedroom would be like new when she returned from Frank's. If Michael wanted to work in her house; if Brittany returned from Frank's.

"Stop it! Just stop it!" She stepped in front of her bedroom mirror and braced her hands on the dresser. Staring at her reflection, she narrowed her eyes. "Snap out of it! You made one mistake, but you didn't go as far as you could have. You stopped and did the right thing, so why do you still punish yourself!"

Steely determination looked back at her. Her determination. The backbone that had given her the strength to stay married to Frank for ten years. The strength she'd pulled on to get through the divorce and the bevy of emotion that followed.

She loved Michael, but if he couldn't handle her near affair over four years ago, while she was married to someone else, she'd survive and move on. Liana pushed away from the dresser and brushed her hands against her denim covered thighs. Like her literal baggage, she'd start weeding out her personal baggage. No more guilt trips over her dinners and drinks with Ryan, or the night she so easily could have lost herself in his arms. No more guilt for not telling Jack about her pregnancy before it was too late.

Enough.

Life was a jumble of choices, good and bad, and she'd learned from every one of them. They all shaped the successful—yes dammit—successful woman she'd become.

Tearing into her closet, she made piles in

categories, stringing two of them into the living room. One to box up and take to the thrift store, one to go through at a more leisurely pace. Liana wasn't in the mood to go through the sentimental items. Today, she had to be tough.

Halfway to the bedroom for another armload of stuff, a thought flashed through her mind. "Frank could be harassing Mom." She grabbed the landline and punched out her mom's number. Cathy answered on the second ring.

"Liana, it's so good to hear from you. How are you and Brittany?"

"Has Frank called you?"

"No, I haven't talked to Frank since Thanksgiving. Why?"

"I was afraid he might harass you and Daddy." Liana sighed and sank to the couch.

"I pity the fool if he tries to turn us against you. You know how your father and I feel about Frank and what he's done to you."

"I know. I'm just on overload today."

"From the big weekend? We all covered a lot of personal history, but it was healthy."

"The meeting isn't what distresses me, Mom. I went out with Michael last night."

"Ah, the famous Michael Brittany keeps talking about."

Liana smiled for the first time all day. "Brittany talks about Michael?"

"Oh yes, it's clear she likes him. She's called me twice since we left on Saturday to tell me about her life in Montana and how much she likes it there. The conversations always include Michael and his son,

Leif."

Liana sighed. "I finally told Michael about almost having an affair. I should have told him before we ever went to dinner."

"I have a suspicion dinner wasn't the crucial part of the evening." Cathy drew out her words to make her point clear.

"You're right." Liana punched her favorite red pillow and fluffed it. "For the first time since my divorce, I allowed myself to be intimate with a man. Not just any man. Oh, Mom if you could meet Michael, you'd know how safe I am with him."

"Judging by Brittany's enthusiasm and the way your voice sparkles when you mention him, I doubt he's having second thoughts. He's probably at work and possibly processing how quickly your relationship has moved."

"Really? I mean, he's attracted to me and he's stuck it out through some challenges."

"Honey, Frank did such a number on you. You're a successful businesswoman, but you have no confidence in yourself as a person. Don't chase Michael off with self-recriminations."

"I'm trying, Mom. I had a face to face with myself a few minutes ago and realized I'd fallen into the same trap I've criticized in other people. The victim. A victim mentality that I'm guilty for all the misery in Frank's life, and I owed Jack the truth, and I should have told Michael more, and on and on and on."

"I'm glad to hear you talk like this, Li. I've been worried about you for a long time. You deserve to be happy, honey."

"Thanks, Mom. Right now, what matters is

Brittany and supporting her in her dreams and hopes. I need to be an example of stability for her to learn from."

"Wow. I'm impressed. No matter what happens with Frank or Michael, Li, keep that goal and your spirit. If you need, Dad and I will fly up and spend time with you and Brittany."

Liana pushed out a rush of breath. "I appreciate your offer, but I'll be fine. I know that now." She said goodbye and wandered into the den to set the cordless receiver back on the cradle.

New strength and well being started in her heart, and spread through her entire body. Her family understood and backed her. She'd taken control of her life.

She returned to the living room and looked at the piles of clothes and memorabilia. She pressed her palm to her belly. She'd had unprotected sex last night. Michael's baby could be growing inside her at this very moment.

"Wow. I could have another child." Another child to raise on her own? No. She wouldn't be alone regardless of how her relationship with Michael turned out. He'd never abandon his child. She'd never get so involved with a man incapable of taking care of his child. If she was pregnant, they'd always be connected, even if not in the way she longed to be connected with him.

She loved him.

She'd fallen head over heels for Michael Saxon and what he thought had the power to hurt her far more than anything Frank could say or do.

She'd go insane if he didn't call soon!

Needing to keep busy, Liana dug into her cleaning project with a vengeance. She retrieved empty totes from the shed behind the house and designated one for keeping and two for going.

The phone rang.

Her heart fluttered.

Michael or Frank?

"Just answer the damn phone." She glanced at the caller ID and hit the green button.

"Hello, Frank."

"What in the hell are you doing?" His voice blasted through the connection.

Liana blinked and tightened her lips. "I'm cleaning house, Frank. Getting rid of things I should have tossed a long time ago."

"Is your daughter one of the things you're tossing?"

Liana resisted the urge to throw the phone across the room. The bastard! "No, Frank. I don't toss people away like you do. I don't hold things over people and manipulate them. Brittany is the most important person in my life. She doesn't deserve to be lied to for another day."

"You're right. That's exactly why I'm calling to tell her everything unless you call off your hot shot attorney and cancel this court date."

"Why didn't we have this discussion when you blessed us with your presence last weekend? Why call me now like you just saw the paperwork?"

"I wanted to check out your life in Montana. It's clear you plan to wipe me out of my daughter's life. No doubt with the help of your boyfriend."

"What are you talking about? I've never wanted to

take Brittany out of your life. When you started to act so unstable, distance seemed to be the answer. We're happy here, Frank, and Brittany has made new friends."

"Cancel the court date or I'll tell her about the affair."

"I'll only cancel the court date if you agree to drop the alimony. You forget you have more at stake than I do. Tell Brittany about Ryan, and I'll tell her about Jack. Actually, you know what? I'm going to tell her anyway. She deserves to learn about her real father."

"Real father! I'm the one who raised her. I was there from her birth until the day you took her away from me."

The doorbell rang. Liana glanced out the window. Michael's big black truck sat in her drive way. She hurried to the door, swung it open, and drank in the sight of him.

Michael raised a brow. His gaze darted from her to the phone and back. She nodded and gestured for him to enter.

"Liana, are you there? Did I hear the doorbell?" Frank shouted so loud, Liana held the phone away from her ear.

Her gaze hungrily followed Michael as he walked into the kitchen and helped himself to a cup of coffee. Worn blue jeans and a chambray shirt covered the body she'd learned so well the night before. He leaned against the counter, his demeanor casual, but his shoulders tense and his amber eyes alert.

"Yes, Frank. A very good friend of mine came over to help. So, what's it going to be? Will you honor my request about the alimony, or risk losing Brittany completely?"

"Brittany won't turn against me."

"Don't overestimate yourself, Frank. If you handle this like an adult, you can stay in her life."

"Adult as in, adultery?"

"Can you honestly say you didn't have affairs during our marriage?"

"Always making me the bad guy, aren't you?"

"Frank, we had a dysfunctional marriage from day one. You never listened to me, or concerned yourself with my needs. Even after ten years of life with a man I couldn't love, I didn't cheat on you, but you didn't believe me. I'm sick and tired of the blackmail and what you've done to my life and self-esteem."

"I'm tired of being blamed for a loveless marriage. You were like sleeping with a corpse. Can you blame me for looking for some passion? You were an unfit wife, and you're an unfit mother. I'm filing for full custody. When I'm finished, you can add child support to your alimony check."

Liana gasped. "Are you delusional? No judge will give you full custody. You've gone over the edge, Frank. I don't think you're safe to be around. Where is Molly in all of this?"

Click.

Liana stared at the phone. "I don't believe it! The SOB just hung up on me! He's going for full custody and plans to force me into paying child support!"

Michael pushed away from the counter and walked toward her. "Does Brittany have her phone?"

"Of course." Liana shook her head. "Would he call her now, before he calls his lawyer?"

"The man's not rational. He's going to do as much damage as he can." He glanced at his watch. "Brittany's out of school. Is she coming right home?"

"No." Liana shook her head, her mind reeling. "She's Christmas shopping with Shari and Meagan."

"Call her and get them over here."

Liana glanced around the room at the piles of mementos and old clothes; her resolve to reclaim her life and be strong. Now she trembled with anger and fear.

"What if he tells her everything? Who will she turn to?"

"You'll fight him. Better the truth comes out now, Liana. You can't protect Brittany anymore." Michael flipped open her phone, searched the contacts and selected one before pressing the phone to his ear. He asked Brittany to come home immediately and not to answer any other calls. Not even from her dad.

Michael set Liana's phone on the bar and pulled her against him, breathing in the floral scent of her hair. He'd hardly slept last night. He'd tossed and turned, reliving their lovemaking until he almost crawled out of bed and returned to her house.

The rest of the time, he agonized over joining his life with a woman who could turn to another man when her needs weren't met. He'd lived through that situation one too many times. He didn't plan to repeat history. Over the morning, he'd started to call her several times, but realized what he had to say needed to be said in person.

His arrival had been timely. Hearing Frank scream at Liana through a phone connection from clear across the room, showed what her life must have been like. Michael never treated Meredith like that, he'd never shout at her or guilt her into making love with him.

Frank had driven her into the other guy's arms and Michael was thankful she'd ended the relationship with Ryan before it began. She might have mistakenly thought Ryan was the man of her dreams and Michael would never have met her.

He'd never justify infidelity, but circumstances were as individual as the people who created them.

"I'm sorry I couldn't stay last night."

"I didn't think you'd be back."

"Your confession blew me away."

Liana wrapped her arms around his waist and kissed the tanned skin between the top two buttons of his chambray work shirt. She rested her head against his chest. "Infidelity ended your marriage. I understand how my indiscretion would cause doubts. Unhappy marriage or not, an affair is never the answer. Fortunately, I learned my lesson before it went too far. I wanted to tell you—give you the option of trusting me or not—but every time I started, I froze. Our relationship moved on and I found myself wanting one night to hold onto for the rest of my life."

Michael pulled her closer. "Baby, Frank should have let you go years ago. You were never in love with him. A man knows when he's the only person holding a relationship together."

Liana's phone rang. Michael reluctantly let her leave his arms to answer it. She bumped a stack of old greeting cards and sent them off the edge of the table to the floor.

He braced himself for another rude call from Frank.

"Hi, Mom."

Liana's greeting to her mom gave him a measure of

relief. Brittany was on her way home and Frank could be up to more no good.

"Oh, great. Mom. I'll keep you posted. Sorry you had to get dragged into this." She ended the call and set her phone on the coffee table.

Michael glanced at her from his crouched position while he gathered up the mementoes. "He called your mom."

"It's all happening just as I feared." Liana covered her mouth with one hand and clutched her head with the other, her mossy eyes filled with tears.

Michael set the stack of cards on the coffee table and pulled her into his arms. Damn Frank Nash for hurting her.

The front door swung open. Brittany ran into the living room with Meagan and Shari right behind her. Michael stepped away from Liana. Brittany enveloped her mom in a big hug and a lump lodged in his throat. "Mom, are you all right?"

"I'm fine, honey." Liana gazed into her daughter's face. Brittany's height and larger frame made her mother look small and delicate. Michael pressed his hands against their backs and completed the family connection he longed to expand.

"Oh, my God. Do you have cancer?" Tears welled in Brittany's mahogany brown eyes.

"Heavens no, it's nothing like that." Liana's breasts lifted on a huge breath. "Brittany, I need to tell you something very important. Do you want to talk out here, or in your room?"

Brittany glanced from Michael to Shari and Meagan. "We're all family. We can talk here."

Michael kissed Brittany's forehead. "Why don't we

sit down?"

Liana laughed, her voice breaking. "I chose today to clean out my closets. Now look." She gestured to the piles of stuff on every available surface.

"We can sit in the dining room." Shari took charge and led the way.

Brittany's eyes grew wider as they sat around the table. Michael's bravado wavered. He feared for Brittany and Liana's relationship. Being a teenager was difficult enough without having the parental rug jerked out from under her.

"Brittany, we're in the midst of a crisis with your dad—with Frank." Liana glanced at Shari and took a deep breath.

"So much happens over the years of our lives, Brittany. Some good, some not so good. Sometimes we make unwise decisions, even if at the time we think it's the best thing to do."

"Mom, will you just tell me? You're really scaring me. Has something happened to Dad?"

"Only anger and bitterness, Brittany."

Brittany's phone rang. She started to reach for it. Michael took her hand and shook his head. "This is important and not easy for your mom to say. You can get that later."

A chirp signaled a message had been left.

Liana rubbed her collarbone and met Brittany's fear-filled eyes. "There's no easy way to say this." Her eyes teared. She shook her head. "No gentle way, so I have to come out with it." She grasped her daughter's hand.

Michael ached to wrap them both in his arms, but what he wanted would have to wait. Their history was about to unfold and he had no part in it, but dammit he wanted a big part in their future.

Liana stood and walked around the table. At Brittany's side, she sank to one knee and took hold of her hand. Shari stood at her other side.

"Frank isn't really your dad." Liana's words shot through the room like a cannon.

Brittany's eyes widened and her creamy complexion turned pale. "What do you mean, he's not my dad? What do you mean?" Her voice raised several octaves. She tried to stand, but Shari bracketed her shoulders with her arm.

"Listen to your mom, Brit. She'd never lie to you."

"Someone lied to me," Brittany shrieked. "Since I was born, they lied to me! If Dad—if Frank—isn't my dad, who is?"

"Jack Nash." Liana choked out the name.

"Uncle Jack?"

"Oh, Brittany, I've wanted to tell you so many times, but I made a pact with Frank. He would give you the Nash name and be a father to you, if I never told you about Jack."

"Did you have an affair with Uncle Jack? I don't understand how this happened." Tears streaked down Brittany's pale cheeks, her full lips puckered.

Liana ran her gaze over Michael and turned back to Brittany. "Not an affair. I fell in love with Jack the moment your Uncle Tim brought him home from college. They were buddies. I was seventeen at the time. Jack and I dated. When he finished college, Jack went into the Navy. He became a pilot. He was a thrill-seeker and wanted to fly F-17 fighter jets."

Liana brushed Brittany's dark auburn hair back

from her damp face. "He proposed to me, but I said no. I'd always blamed my parent's divorce on the Navy. I didn't want to live that life, so I told him I'd have to think about it. When he shipped out to the Middle East, I found out I was pregnant, but I decided to tell him after he settled in at his new base. I was too late. He was killed in a training exercise."

"Uncle Jack is my dad?" Brittany's eyes brightened like she'd crawled out of a hole and saw daylight for the first time. "Is that why Da—Frank never wanted to talk about Jack? I have his photo, I could see how much I looked like him, but Dad wouldn't discuss it."

Liana trembled and her heart raced. "You should never forget Frank was a good father to you for many years, Brittany. He's very irrational right now. Things will be ugly until we sort out a new legal arrangement." She let a pent-up breath rush through her lips.

"It's sad, Britt, but I never loved Frank. I wanted a divorce years ago, but he'd never agree. I always loved Jack and it ate at Frank."

"Jack was killed in the plane crash." Brittany sniffed and swiped at her tears. Meagan ran and got her a tissue.

"Yes, Jack was killed. There's so much to my story, Brittany, and someday you'll have all the pieces. For now, Frank wants to take you away from me."

Liana glanced at Michael before she continued. He sent her as much encouragement as he could with just a look.

"Brittany, there's something else he'll use against me. Something I wish I could change, but I can't."

"What? What is it?" Brittany dried her tears with the tissues Meagan handed her and drilled her mother with a look so like Jack's, goosebumps scattered over Liana's body. She could swear she faced Jack with the truth too.

"Frank finally agreed to the divorce." She didn't want to tell her daughter about her weak moment, but if she didn't, Frank would. "Because he saw me leave a downtown hotel and thought I had an affair."

Brittany and Meagan gasped. Liana's heart sank, but she had to go on and set the record straight. "I wasn't. Not really, but my relationship with Ryan had turned from all business to more personal interaction and I couldn't let that happen, so I left the hotel. No one would have known about it, but you and your dad—Frank—had attended the ballet and were walking up the street. Frank saw me leave the hotel. Later, he wouldn't believe me when I told him the truth."

She looked at her fingers. "Frank filed for the divorce before I could—on the grounds of adultery. I was in a fog and couldn't think. I just wanted out of the marriage so I didn't contest the grounds. He's going to tell you I cheated on him. I'm sure the call you just got was Frank leaving a message. He wants to turn you against me. Every month since the divorce I've paid him what amounts to blackmail money.

"The judge didn't order it, Frank did for his silence. I'm tired of all the hours away from you, and I'm tired of being the bad guy. Frank has a good job. He doesn't need, or deserve my money. Other than the six months I took off to have you, I've worked. I've paid him back many times over for the minuscule amount of support he ever gave me."

Out of breath and strength, Liana stopped.

Michael got up and flipped on the hot water kettle

and made a fresh pot of coffee. Having him move around her kitchen helped to ease Liana's brittle nerves. She turned back to Brittany. Her heart ached over the shock in her daughter's expression. "I'm sorry you had hear this and to find out about Jack so abruptly. Do you have any questions, sweetheart?"

Brittany slowly shook her head. "I've always been interested in Uncle Jack. I look a lot like him, don't I?"

"Boy, do you." Shari gave Brittany a hug. "You're a lot like him all the way around. Jack was a good man, and intelligent to boot. Did you know he was an officer in the Navy?"

Liana's recent jealousy over Shari's close role in Brittany's life turned into gratitude. Shari gave validity to everything Liana told Brittany, and gave Liana a chance to gather her emotions.

Michael set cups of coffee and cocoa on the table and sat back down. The atmosphere reminded Liana of the gathering after a funeral. In a way it fit. She'd just laid to rest the lies of the past. They were dead and held less power.

"Mom, what should I do about Dad? I mean, Frank?"

Liana hugged her daughter much like Shari had a few moments before. "Honey, Frank has acted as your dad your entire life. Don't worry about what you'll call him. Give yourself some time to decide." She ran her hands down the front of her jeans.

"I'm sorry, but I don't think it's a good idea for you to visit him over the holidays. Maybe after we settle in court. How about you change your plans and visit Grandma and Grandpa's instead? You can spend time with your uncles and their families. Doesn't that sound fun?"

Brittany slowly nodded. "I can't help but feel bad for him. Frank, I mean." She looked down at her cocoa. "He has to be sad over all of this. If I desert him, what'll happen?"

"I know I'm not really part of this family." Michael glanced at Liana. "So tell me to butt out if you want. Brittany, I was here when Frank called your mom. I heard his angry voice from across the room. He needs time to cool down and get a grip on his emotions. Let him have that time. Later, if he's receptive, you can go visit him." He held up both hands. "That comes from a guy who's been through an ugly divorce and custody battle."

"Were you angry, Michael?" Brittany leaned her elbows on the table, her auburn eyebrows angled in question and sympathy.

"I was very angry. I was also concerned about my kids because their mom had some serious issues. She was and still is, an alcoholic and had branched out into prescription drugs. I couldn't live with the craziness another day. I didn't want my kids to either."

"Is that why Leif lives with you?"

"Yep, and Trinity did for a short time before she went off to college."

Liana rotated her head and messaged the back of her neck to relieve the stress. She glanced at Shari and realized she'd done the same thing. They chuckled in comic relief.

Shari stood. "If you're all right, Meagan and I need to get home. Richard's probably wondering how this is all unfolded."

"He knows? Daddy knows?" Meagan asked. "Does

225

Cash?"

"Of course your father knows. We've been close friends of Liana's for many years. Your dad and Jack were good buddies through high school. However, your brother does not know about Frank and Jack. We'll have a family meeting later today when Cash is through with basketball practice. You, young lady, need to keep all of this to yourself."

"Of course I will." Meagan shot her mom an indignant glance. "I'd never say something to hurt Brittany."

"Of course you wouldn't." Shari patted her daughter's hand. "Let's give these guys some time to themselves." She picked up their cups and carried them to the sink.

Liana hugged Shari and Meagan and thanked them for their support and friendship. When they left, she turned to Michael and Brittany. Brittany might be mature and sophisticated for a nearly sixteen year old, but she'd been handed a heavy set of facts. Some adults wouldn't handle it nearly as well as she seemed to be.

Frank Nash for one. Frank hadn't handled it well at all.

Michael stood by while Brittany listened to her voice mail. Her face crumpled. Michael held her while Liana listened to Frank's spiteful message.

Liana deleted the message and handed the phone back to her daughter. "Michael's right. Frank needs time to deal with his anger. He refuses to take any responsibility for what's happened. A marriage and a divorce takes two people, sweetheart."

Brittany nodded and hurried to her room. Liana started to follow, but Michael stopped her. "Let her cry and have some time alone. Heck, she might even call Meagan and rehash everything."

"What a day!" Liana wandered into the kitchen and pulled out the bottle of wine they'd opened the night before. She poured two glasses and handed one to Michael. She sipped her wine and soaked up the image of him in her house for however long it lasted. "I'm sorry you got caught up in my drama."

"Hey." Michael let his hand fall from his hip as he walked toward her. "Relationships have tough times as well as good." He stopped when they were toe to toe and cupped her chin. "What happens in your life matters to me."

Liana grasped his hand and gently squeezed it, her heart full of emotion.

His eyes were warm and his full bottom lip curved in a sexy smile she'd like to taste.

"I'll throw some dinner together. Would you and Leif join us?" Her voice caught and her eyes watered. She'd never had a man like Michael in her life. Only her family had so obviously cared this much for her.

"You should have some private time with Brittany." He set his wineglass on the counter and pulled her into his arms for a kiss reminiscent of last night. "When you're ready to talk, call me."

"I will." She stroked his jaw. "You didn't shave this morning. I like it."

"Oh yeah? Remember that when you have a whisker burn."

He lingered and kissed her again. His eyes eating her up, he backed away. On his way to the front door, he detoured into Brittany's room.

Liana listened to the hum of their voices, savoring

his caring presence in their lives.

He came through the living room, raised his hand in a wave before he disappeared behind the fireplace. The front door opened and closed.

Chapter Thirteen

"Hey, Dad, what happened?" Leif took a gigantic bite of the overstuffed roast beef sandwich he'd made.

"It's a cinch your appetite's good." Michael pointed to the half empty plate in the center of the table. "Is that your second or third sandwich?"

"I don't know. I'm just hungry. Basketball tryouts were brutal today. I think I made the team."

"That's great, son. Just don't let your grades slip."

Michael slowly ate his sandwich, his appetite dimmed by what Liana and Brittany must be going through.

"So, did things fall apart with Liana? You weren't out as late last night as I thought you'd be."

Michael quit pretending to eat his lunch and set the sandwich on the saucer. "Aren't you the Einstein of the social scene? Since when do I need to tell you about my dates?"

Leif held up both hands. "Hey, I'm just sayin'. Something's off."

"You're right." Michael puffed his cheeks and released the air in a long slow breath. "It does have to do with Liana, but probably not what you think. Liana's ex shook things up today. Brittany had to hear about some stuff from the past; events she didn't know about. It upset both of them."

"That's too bad. I like Brittany. Well, I like Liana

too. She's really a cool lady, and attractive for her age."

Michael hooted with laughter. "Her age! She's five years younger than I am. Does that make me a dinosaur?"

"No, you're still active and everything. So, how'd it turn out?" Leif's amber eyes reflected his concern.

Michael only disclosed how Brittany learned Jack, Frank's brother, was her biological father. Leif should know about Frank's crazy behavior in case Frank showed up, or Brittany needed someone to talk to.

"Wow." Leif pushed his plate away and crossed his arms. "Poor Brittany. Her dad—well the guy she thought was her dad—sounds whacked. Do you think he'll come here? I mean, if he's as freaked out as he sounds, he could try to kidnap her."

A chill spread up the back of Michael's neck. "Good God, I hope not." He pushed his chair back and stood so fast the chair rocked on its legs. "I should call Liana." He scrambled to his landline and punched out her number. She answered on the third ring. "Liana, have you heard from Frank since I left?"

"No, I haven't heard from him since the voice mail on Brittany's phone. I'm sure he's in touch with his attorney."

"I don't want to scare you, but there's a possibility Frank could show up in Kalispell and either guilt Brittany into going with him, or take her anyway. He was here for Thanksgiving. He knows the lay of the land."

"The thought crossed my mind when he and Molly took Brittany out last Saturday. But now? Would he make another trip here to take her away?"

"Calm down, sweetheart. You need to be aware it

could happen. Is it okay if we come over?"

"I don't want to monopolize more of your time. You have a son to take care of and houses to build."

"Right now, I need to know you and Brittany are okay. I'll bring steaks and make dinner."

Silence.

Could a two-month relationship survive so many life-changing events?

"Are you sure it's not an imposition?"

He released a breath he didn't realize he'd been holding. "We'll be right over." Michael glanced at his son who made a face, but shrugged and nodded.

Michael almost skipped down the stairs to the basement where he filled the firebox of his wood-fired boiler heating system. When he reentered the kitchen, Leif had Lucky outside for a walk. He stood at the window and enjoyed the sight of his son playing with the dog.

Life could be so odd and unpredictable. He vowed to appreciate every moment he spent with his children, and with Liana and Brittany.

****

"That didn't take long," Liana said when she opened the door to let Michael and Leif inside.

"I couldn't wait." Michael claimed her mouth in a wet possessive kiss.

Liana didn't want to stop, but with Leif in the entry behind Michael, and Brittany behind her, now wasn't the time. She pulled away and smiled at Michael's grinning teen.

"Hello, Leif."

"Hi, Liana. Sorry you're having such a bad time."

Liana hugged him before she looped her arm

through his and turned to Brittany. "How about you two duke it out on a computer game while Michael and I make dinner?"

Brittany lifted her chin toward the den. "Okay, Saxon, let's see if you can win this time."

Liana sighed as they disappeared into the den. "Kids are so resilient. Brittany and I had a great talk. She's upset, but she's trying to adjust. She's much more sophisticated about my other revelation than I was at her age."

"Have you heard from your lawyer?"

Liana put the steaks on a plate. "Did you and Leif eat lunch, or should we start the steaks now?"

"When we're ready to eat, I'll cook dinner. You didn't answer me. Have you heard from your lawyer?" He rounded the bar and wrapped his arms around her. He pulled her back against his front and buried his face in the side of her neck.

Liana wiggled against him and moaned. "Just what I needed. Yes, I called my lawyer. He doesn't think Frank has a chance in court since the alimony was never court ordered."

Michael pressed his lips to her ear, sending goosebumps over her entire body, and whispered, "Good point."

Liana lifted her chin to give him better access to her sensitive skin. "I could charge him with harassment take him to court for child support, but I don't want to. I just want this to be over."

She turned and looped her arms around his neck. "Even if Frank decided to resurrect the grounds for divorce, California is a no-fault state. The law doesn't care about the supposed affair."

"Sounds like you've had a busy afternoon."

He claimed her mouth and his probing tongue sent her senses reeling. Liana wiggled closer and discovered the hard evidence. He wanted her as much as she wanted him. She moaned against his mouth. "I guess that answers my question."

"What question?"

"Was one night enough?"

"Forever won't be enough." Michael kissed her again. "If I don't stop, we'll have some explaining to do to the kids."

Liana's heart lifted from the deep hole she'd been in all day. "I'm so glad you came over."

The phone rang. Michael raised a dark brow. Reluctant to allow anyone into their evening, she glanced at the caller ID. "I have no idea who's calling. Guess I'd better answer." She hit the green button and put the phone to her ear.

"Liana? It's Molly Matthews."

"Molly." Liana turned toward Michael and pointed to the phone with a frown. "What's happening?"

"I'm worried about Frank. He told me the shocking news about Brittany's paternity. I can't believe he didn't tell me the truth long ago. He loves her so much, Liana. Why does their relationship have to change?"

"It didn't have to, Molly. Frank's the one who drove a wedge between them. Brittany loves him."

"He said you're dragging him to court to get full custody of Brittany."

"That's not true. I finally stood up for myself and served him with settlement papers to end the alimony I've paid him every month for the past four years."

"Alimony? Are you kidding me?"

"It's a long story, but I never intended for Brittany to stay away from Frank. Frank wouldn't let me stop making the payments without the penalty of him disclosing certain things to Brittany. Lies, basically. Frank's ruining his relationship with everyone."

"I'm sorry for you and Brittany, but I'm really worried about Frank. When he called this morning, he sounded a little unhinged and said he'd see me later, but he hasn't shown up or called."

Uneasiness curled in Liana's stomach. "Please call me if you hear from him, and I'll do the same. Should I call you at this number?" Liana verified the number with Molly before she disconnected the call. "That was Frank's fiancée."

"So I gathered."

"Molly hasn't heard from him since early this morning. I'm really worried, Michael. She said when he told her about Brittany's paternity, he sounded unhinged. He told her I'm trying to take Brittany from him."

"He's probably been unstable for a while, Liana, you just didn't see it. It's easy to adjust to certain behaviors in people. Believe me, I know."

Michael put his arms around her. "I'll stay as long as you want me to." He tilted his head and gazed into her eyes. "I think we should call Richard and get some law enforcement advice."

"Now, I really feel creeped-out." Liana rested her head on Michael's chest. "Frank could be on his way to snatch Brittany."

"Forewarned is forearmed."

"Brittany's ballet recital is tomorrow night. I don't want her life disrupted."

"We'll do what we can. Whoever Richard recommends can keep an eye on her when she's out of the house. You'll take over when she's at home. I plan to work on your bedroom tomorrow, so if you have an outside appointment, I'll watch for anything suspicious. If you have a photo of Frank, I'll show it to my crew."

Liana rubbed her upper arms to dispel the chills. "I hate this! It didn't need to happen. He was always so possessive, but I attributed it to his jealousy over Jack. Now, I see it as mental illness. I should have done something about it a long time ago."

"Stop it." Michael bracketed her arms, and gave her a gentle shake. "Quit heaping the blame on yourself. Frank's an adult, not a child. Doesn't he have a family?"

Liana nodded. "His parents live in San Francisco and used to visit often." She grabbed her head with both hands and closed her eyes. "Oh, I don't know. One day you think you have so many problems, so much stress. Out of the blue something happens and it all boils down to elemental survival and protecting your loved ones."

"Realty can be a harsh thing, but not always a bad thing. It's a check to get us back to what's important."

"I just don't want Brittany hurt. Physically or emotionally."

Michael handed her the cell phone. "Call Richard, or I will. You should dig out a photo of Frank so I know who to look for."

****

Every creak in the house, every breath of wind through the trees startled Liana. An evening with the Saxon men should have been fun. She and Michael had weathered her confession and Frank's unstable

235

behavior. Instead, each time the phone rang or a branch scraped the window, she jumped.

Liana told Brittany about Molly's call. The best defense against Frank's craziness was for Brittany to know everything.

Michael and Leif were a godsend. They made her feel safe and kept Brittany's mind at least partially off her father. Leif suggested they play a board game, so Brittany pulled out her old version of Monopoly.

Liana's usual enthusiasm for buying and selling properties was dulled by her fear of Frank prowling around her house. She had just paid Brittany the rent for Park Place when something occurred to her. Frank spent Thanksgiving Day in her house. He'd stayed when she left to meet Michael. He could have checked out the house, learned all the entrances, what windows belonged to which rooms.

She shivered.

"Need a sweater?" Michael's question startled her out of her paranoia.

Liana glanced down. She'd been rubbing her arms and probably looked like a maniac.

"Yes. I'll be right back." She slipped from the living room and closed her bedroom door. Oh, my gosh. Would she make it through the night without falling apart?

She took the phone into the bathroom and called Shari.

"Liana, is everything all right?"

"I'm hiding out in my own house. The upside is, Michael and Leif came over for dinner and we're playing Monopoly. Shari, what if Frank takes Brittany? I'll lose my mind if anything happens to her."

"Do you really think Frank would harm Brittany?"

"I don't know what to expect from him anymore."

"For heaven's sake, don't shake up Brittany. She has to be completely off-kilter already."

"You're right." She sighed and lowered the toilet seat and sat down.

"Hmm, I think I'll call Richard just to make sure we're not overlooking something. He's at an Elk Foundation meeting. Have you met the guy he sent to watch the house tonight?"

"We did. He's seems very compassionate and sharp. I can't thank you and Richard enough. You've done so much for us." Liana straightened the roll of toilet paper. "I must confess, I was jealous of your relationship with Brittany. I think I had a slipped cog."

"Jealous?" Shari sounded genuinely amazed. "Liana, Brittany loves and respects you. You're her mom. She'd never want to replace you. I just wanted to help, to take some of the pressure off until you were settled into your job and new home."

"I realize that now." She leaned back and jumped when her back hit the cold tank. She giggled and stood up to peer at her reflection in the mirror. "I'm a ninny!"

"What happened? What did you do?"

"I'm in my bathroom so the others wouldn't hear me call you. I'm supposed to be getting a sweater. I'd better get back to the game before they send out a posse."

"Yeah, if the posse is Michael, you might be detained even longer." Shari giggled.

"You're naughty, my friend, but accurate!" Laughter lifted some of the heaviness from her chest. "I'll see you at the recital tomorrow night."

She left the bathroom and grabbed a long cashmere cardigan before she hurried into the living room. Michael glanced at her and an image of them locked in the bathroom flashed through her mind.

"I almost went after you." His eyes warmed to a slow burn.

Liana tingled from head to foot. Her awareness of Michael helped dull her fear of what Frank might do. She smiled at Leif and Brittany. "Whose turn is it?"

Michael struggled to tamp down his fantasies. He ached to hold her and kiss the worry from her brow. With the kids around, he'd have to wait to show her how much he wanted her.

Brittany playfully punched his arm. "It's your turn, Michael. Are you too tired to play?"

Michael chuckled and rolled the dice. "Kensington Palace. I'll buy it."

"Dad,"—Leif peered at the board with tired eyes— "it's Boardwalk."

"Wouldn't you rather own Kensington Palace?" Michael winked at Brittany.

"No, I'm happy in Lakeside." Leif yawned with all the abandon of a growing teenage boy.

Liana laughed at their antics, folded her arms on the edge of the table and glanced between the kids. "Maybe we should call it a night. I'm so grateful for your company, but we're all exhausted."

Michael reached across the board-game and clasped her hand. "Are you sure you'll be all right?"

"The detective is parked outside. I'll lock all the windows and doors the moment you leave."

"No, we'll check the windows and doors before I leave. Remember, I'm only a quick call away." Michael cringed at Brittany's worried expression. "I'll bet Lucky wonders where we are."

Brittany brightened. "I want to see Lucky. It seems like something always happens and we don't go to your house. How are the puppies?"

"Squealing, eating and growing like weeds. Your recital's tomorrow night. How about dinner at our house next week sometime?" He raised a brow at Liana.

Brittany wiggled in her chair and smiled. "I can't wait to see the puppies. Can we go over Monday night, Mom?"

"Do you have ballet Monday night?"

"Nope. The Nutcracker performance tomorrow night is our last recital until after the first of the year."

Michael gathered up the game pieces and money. "It's settled. Dinner on Monday night with puppy time." He smiled at Brittany. She'd accepted his presence from the start and seemed happy about him dating her mom.

Brittany hugged him goodnight. "Would you and Leif come to my recital?"

Michael's throat tightened. He glanced over her head and met Liana's approving smile. "We'd love to, wouldn't we, Leif?"

"Sure." Leif shrugged and stuffed his hands in his jeans pockets.

"Let's check those windows and let you ladies get some sleep." Once Michael confirmed the windows were all firmly shut and locked, he and Leif said goodnight and headed for the truck. Clamping his hand on his son's shoulder, he grinned. "You okay about watching a group of girls dance around in tutus?"

Leif grinned. "I'll suffer through it."

Michael waved at the private eye, relieved the guy looked alert. He'd rather spend the night on Liana's couch, but it wouldn't be fair to Leif or the dogs. They needed to go home.

He had a feeling Frank was more hot air than physical danger. At least he hoped so. Nevertheless, he'd learned a long time ago to never underestimate an enemy.

****

The night dragged by.

Michael dozed off and on, his mind on Liana. Each time he roused, he reached for the phone, but pulled back before he dialed. She should be asleep and he didn't want to disturb her. At three in the morning he gave up and stumbled to the kitchen to make coffee.

Before he'd met Liana, he'd believed his life was complete and satisfying. He built quality houses, spent time on the lake, and both his kids were doing great. Meredith, well, she was only a mild pain in the ass.

He'd been content and only occasionally missed female companionship. By some quirk of fate, he met Liana. She created something so big, so mind blowing, he didn't think he'd ever be satisfied with the way things were before Lucky brought them together. He hadn't known what he missed until that gutsy little blonde with the big green eyes shook up his quiet, low-key world.

The coffeemaker gurgled and sputtered before it expelled the last ounce of dark, rich coffee. Michael filled a mug, wandered into the dark living room and gazed through the floor to ceiling windows. The clouds had moved out during the evening, and the moon cast a bright silver glow over the backyard and across the lake in a column of iridescence. He glanced at the dark outline of his boat and froze.

Something on the dock moved.

Michael blinked a couple of times to lubricate his tired eyes and stared hard at the area around the boat.

A shadowy figure emerged. He stepped away from the windows, glad he hadn't turned on a light, other than the one over the sink in the kitchen. It faced the side yard, so wasn't visible from the boat dock.

Lucky ambled out of Leif's room. Her tail swished from side to side. Michael crouched and patted her head. "It's okay, girl, I see him. You go protect our kids." He herded Lucky into Leif's room where they kept the puppy box at night.

For a few seconds, he watched his son sleep. If something went bad, Leif needed to be aware and alert. "Son, wake up."

Leif moaned and rubbed his eyes and peered through the darkness at his dad. "What? What time is it?"

"Three-thirty. Someone's at the boat. I want you awake in case we need to call the sheriff's office."

Leif sat up, his eyes wide. "Why don't we call the sheriff right now? That's what they get paid for."

Michael ruffled his son's wild hair. "Don't let them hear you say that. Maybe you're right. Stay in your room and keep Lucky calm. I don't want her to bark and scare the guy away."

Michael's boat wasn't a small fishing craft, but a cabin cruiser with a full galley and bunks. An RV on the lake. It'd cost a chunk of his retirement money, and he didn't intend to let some bum live in, or vandalize it. He dialed 911 and reported the prowler. Dispatch assured him they'd have a couple of patrol cars headed his way in about two minutes.

Michael moved toward the windows and buttoned his Levis as he scanned the moonlit backyard and dock. Nothing. He barely breathed, waiting for something to move.

A light flared. The prowler leaned over the edge of the boat. The idiot had set off a flare!

"Leif! The boat's on fire—call the fire department!"

"Dad! Don't go out there!" Leif hollered from his bedroom, but Michael kept going. His bare feet crunched against the frosty grass, his shirttails billowed. Someone threatened his home, and he wasn't going to get away with it.

He pounded onto the dock and blinked. The bastard was gone. He glanced around the deck before he leaped into the boat to use one corner of his shirt to grab the flare.

"Ouch! Dammit!" He stumbled over some ropes on the deck and barely reached the side of the boat before his shirt ignited. His heart hammering, he pitched the flare into the lake and smothered the flames on his shirt.

From the house, Lucky barked and snarled. A chill of premonition spread up his neck and scalp and adrenaline coursed through him.

"Leif."

Michael raced to the house and slammed through the door into the pitch black living room. In the glow from the kitchen light, a large man dragged something toward the front door. Lucky's barks were earsplitting as she danced around the intruder. The man didn't seem to realize Michael had entered the house and continued his slow movement toward the foyer.

Michael wished his hunting rifle was handy, but he'd locked it up in his bedroom. He stayed close to the wall and edged around the living room. Where was Leif?

Lucky snarled and grabbed at the man's leg.

"Damn dog, let go of me!"

Michael took advantage of the distraction and leaped on the man's back. They both went down. Michael's elbow connected with the slate floor. In the jumble, he realized Leif was the thing the man had dragged to the foyer.

Sharp fear sliced through him. "Leif? Son? Are you okay?" His eyes on the shadowy figure, he hoped his voice would rouse his son.

Leif groaned and tried to roll away from the scuffle.

With a shriek that would make his Cherokee ancestors proud, Michael pinned the intruder to the floor and pummeled him until he harmlessly lay groaning.

Breathing hard, Michael pushed off the floor and hit the switch and flooded the entry with light. His mind rapidly registered two things: Leif was pale and unconscious on the floor and the intruder was Frank Nash.

Frank struggled to his feet.

Michael's blood ran cold. "What the hell are you trying to prove, Nash?"

Filled with rage, Michael knocked Frank against the wall. Frank surged toward him and pulled off a punch. Bells rang through Michael's head.

"You're took my daughter from me. I want you to

know what it's like."

"You crazy son-of-a-bitch." Michael slammed into him, knocking him to the floor. "I'm not taking Brittany from you."

Frank yelled, and with insane strength, threw Michael against the entry wall. Before Michael could react, Frank grabbed Leif's arm and pulled him toward the living room. Michael rebounded, snarled and raced through the house. He slammed Frank into the French doors. The glass shattered and showered the carpet and Leif with sparkling shards.

Michael waded through the glass and cold-cocked Frank. The bastard crumpled.

Lucky's frenzied barking and the wail of sirens penetrated Michael's rage. He dropped to Leif's side. "Son." His voice broke and his eyes watered. "Leif, wake up."

"Mr. Saxon?"

Michael glanced over his shoulder. Two officers and a paramedic had entered the house. "Please, help my son."

The paramedic hurried to Leif's side, a medical bag in his hand. He lifted an eyelid and flashed Leif's eye with a penlight and took his pulse. "He's coming to."

Michael rocked on his heels and flinched.

"Mr. Saxon, your son got quite a knock to the head, but he's young and strong. I've seen him at basketball practice. He's a tough kid."

"Mr. Saxon,"—another officer touched Michael's shoulder—"I know you're worried about your son, but I have a couple questions."

"Yeah, sure. Whatever it takes to get that scum behind bars."

"He's cuffed and in the patrol car. Do you know the identity of the man?"

Michael scrubbed at his face with both hands. "His name is, Frank Nash. His ex-wife, Liana Campbell moved to Kalispell with her daughter about six months ago. She and I are seeing each other." He paused and rubbed his forehead. He wished they'd drill him later so he could focus on Leif. "Liana lives on Evergreen Road. We figured Nash might show up, so we hired a PI to watch over her. Here is his number." Michael fumbled for his wallet before he remembered he'd left it on the dresser.

Everything moved in a slow motion haze even though he hurried into his bedroom for his wallet and truck keys. He handed the private investigator's card to the officer.

"Thanks." The officer read the card and scribbled on a pad. "Go to your son. We'll take Nash in and notify the private eye. An officer will inform Ms. Campbell in person. We'll have more questions for you later. In the meantime, you'd better get your feet looked at. You have some nasty cuts."

His feet could wait. Michael rushed to the living room where the paramedics were lifting Leif to a gurney. "We're taking your son to the hospital for observation. He's been awake, but drifted off. His vitals are good. His pulse is a bit high, but that's to be expected. He likely has a concussion."

Michael took Leif's hand and walked along the gurney. "Son, wake up. It's Dad. You need to wake up."

Leif groaned and opened his eyes a crack. "Dad? What happened?"

"You were knocked out. We're taking you to the hospital to make sure you're all right."

"I came out of my bedroom to call the fire department and my head exploded." Leif grimaced and tried to touch the back of his head, but the paramedic caught his hand.

"Take it easy, champ. We've stopped the bleeding, but you need to leave it alone." The paramedic placed Leif's hand on his chest. "It's gonna hurt for a bit. They'll give you something for the pain once we get to the hospital."

Michael checked on Lucky, who had calmed down and rejoined her pups in their box. "You were a good girl, Lucky. You probably saved Leif's life." He choked back tears. "Rest with your pups now. I'll see you later."

He started for the door and realized he was still barefoot. His feet hurt like hell. No way could he wear his boots. He slipped on a pair of flips-flops and left the house.

****

"Dad?" Leif lifted his arm and patted the air.

"I'm here, son." Michael caught up with the nurses rolling Leif's gurney from the ER to his room, and grasped his hand. Leif had been examined by two doctors. The test results showed no permanent damage. The doctor's advised Leif stay overnight to be monitored.

"Who was it, Dad? Who set fire to the boat and hit me?"

"Frank Nash, Liana's ex."

"So he did show up. Is the boat okay?"

"You're all I care about, son." He grimaced when

every step ground the tiny shards of glass into his feet, but he didn't want Leif to worry about him. His son needed to heal and he needed the security of his dad being in charge and okay.

When they stopped at the elevator, Michael brushed his son's shiny black hair away from his forehead and kissed his brow. "We'll see to the boat later when you feel better."

"What about Liana and Brittany? You should go tell them, Dad. Liana shouldn't hear about this without you."

"Liana is a strong woman. She's also a mother and she'd want me to stay with you. I'll see her later."

"Man, he came out of nowhere. Lucky went crazy."

"Lucky is why I ran back to the house. She tried to protect you." Michael's voice caught. He dragged his shirtsleeve across his eyes and sniffed.

The nurses wheeled the gurney into the elevator. Michael squeezed in beside them, keeping hold of his son's hand.

Leif looked at his dad and tightened the grip. "I'm okay, Dad. It's going to be okay."

For the second time that night Michael did something he hadn't done in a very long time. He kissed his son's brow and cried with relief.

****

The doorbell peeled through the silent, dark house and jerked Liana out of what had already been a very restless night. Her heart hammering, she threw on her robe and hurried to the foyer. A glance out the side light showed the private investigator and two officers on the porch.

"It's okay to open the door, Ms. Campbell." The PI stepped forward and raised his hand in greeting.

Liana unlocked the dead bolt and opened the door a crack.

"Can we come in? We have some news."

Liana stepped back and motioned for them to continue into the living room.

Brittany stumbled from the hall, her eyes squinted, her hair a mass of auburn lights.

"What is it, Mom? What happened?"

Liana hurried to her daughter and looped her arm around Brittany's waist. Her daughter might be tall and turning into a woman, but she was still young enough to need Liana's strength from time to time.

"I'm not sure, honey. Officers, wh-what's happened?"

"Ms. Campbell, there's no easy way to put this. Your ex-husband was involved in an incident at the home of Michael Saxon. Mr. Nash is under arrest and in the Flathead County jail."

Liana wobbled and sank to the couch. The officers related how Frank had broken into Michael's house. The fire on the boat. Frank knocked Leif unconscious. Her stomach roiled.

One of the officers kneeled in front of the couch. "Can I get you some water, Ms. Campbell?"

"No, I'll be fine. I need to call Michael and check on Leif."

"He's at the hospital. Would you like for one of us to drive you there?"

"I'll be fine. Thank you so much for telling me in person."

"Ms. Campbell, do you want me to stay until

daylight?" The PI hesitated at the front door.

Liana searched her mind. Frank had been the threat and he was locked up. "No. I think we're fine now. Thank you for being here."

"Of course. I'll check in with Richard in the morning."

The officers and PI left.

"Oh, my gosh! I can't believe he did this!" Brittany sobbed. She wrapped her arms around herself and rocked on the edge of the couch. "Dad hurt Leif?"

"I'll call Michael." Her brain in a fog, she dialed Michael's number twice before her fingers worked. It went directly to his voice mail. "Oh, Michael, I'm so sorry you got tangled up in this mess. What can we do to help? We're so worried about Leif. Please call us."

"I can't believe he did this!" Brittany repeated, and sprang from the couch to pace the length of the room. "What's wrong with him?"

Liana wanted to race to the hospital this instant, but she had to assure Brittany first. She caught her in her arms and stroked her hair. "I don't know, honey. I guess he had problems we weren't aware of. A person can't change this quickly and do something so terrible out of the blue."

"I should have gone to see him. Maybe if I'd been there, he wouldn't have done this."

"Don't blame yourself. You can't feel responsible for the actions of others. It's taken me years to learn that lesson. I bogged myself down with guilt over things I couldn't change or control. I don't want you to do the same thing."

"You did?" Brittany sniffed and hiccupped.

"Yep. I wasted so much time and emotion. I

blamed myself instead of finding a solution."

Brittany wrapped her arms around her mom and hugged her tight. "You deserve to be happy, Mom. I think you should marry Michael."

A pang shot through Liana's heart. "Right now, Leif is all that matters." After what happened tonight, Michael might never want to see her again.

"Of course, but I know Michael loves you, Mom." Brittany's mahogany eyes took on the wisdom of a much older woman. "I see how he watches you. I like Leif too. He'd make a cool stepbrother."

"Are you up to a trip to the hospital?"

"Yes. I'll throw on some clothes and be right out."

Liana watched her daughter disappear into her room, before she returned to her bedroom to dress. Michael had to be going through hell. Even if Leif's prognosis was good, Michael's son had been injured, his life threatened. No parent should have to go through such trauma.

Her mind raced as they locked the house and hurried to the frost-covered car.

The trip to the hospital was a nerve-wracking blur. Leif's recovery was the most important thing, but she couldn't stop believing Frank had ruined any chance of her and Michael being together.

Parking outside the ER, Liana and Brittany entered the hospital. Their wet boots squeaked against the polished tile as they hurried to the reception desk.

"May I help you with something?" The tired eyed receptionist pursed her lips.

"We're here to check on Leif Saxon. He was just admitted through the ER." Liana clasped her shaking hands. The impact of Frank's actions swept through her. Her knees shook. She gripped the countertop.

The receptionist tapped something into her computer and read the screen. The sterile silence of the lobby, the tick of the minute hand on the wall clock and the muffled voices from somewhere beyond the secure door, made Liana want to scream with frustration.

"Yes, he was admitted, and he's on his way to a room for the night. He can only be seen by close family." She peered over the black rim of her glasses. "Are you close family?"

"No. He and his father are close friends of ours." She gestured toward Brittany and back to herself.

"In that case I'm sorry, but you can't see him tonight. You'll have to check with Mr. Saxon tomorrow."

Liana glanced at Brittany, who nibbled on her bottom lip and sniffed. Tears balanced on her lower lids. Her daughter had been through so much in a very short time. Neither of them could rest or think of anything else until they confirmed Leif's condition. "Can you call the room and let Mr. Saxon know we're here?"

"No, I can't disturb them while the nurses are hooking up the monitors. You'll have to connect with them later."

Liana turned to her daughter. "All we can do is go back to the car and wait for Michael to call."

The electric doors swished open and the winter chill hit them. Liana shivered and picked up her pace. In the car, she started the engine and flipped the heat on high.

"What should we do?" Brittany turned in the seat and pulled her jacket closer.

"Wait." Liana sighed. "Now I know exactly how other people feel when there's a crisis and they can't access the people they care about. We have to wait. Maybe Michael will check his messages."

Her cell phone rang. Her stomach churned. She hit the connect button. "Michael. How's Leif?"

"Physically, the doctors say he'll be fine in a few days. His concussion is mild, and there's no internal bleeding."

Physically. The word echoed through her head.

Liana pressed her hand to her forehead. "What do you mean, physically? My god, they don't believe there's brain damage do they?"

"No, but he's been through a trauma, Liana."

"I'm so sorry. Brittany and I are in the parking lot. They won't let us come up." She caught a sigh through the phone connection.

"He's drowsy from the pain medication. Take Brittany home and get some rest. I can't think past getting Leif back on his feet."

Liana's chest tightened and her heart ached. To contemplate losing Michael was too unbearable. She'd never expected to fall so completely in love. Thanks to Frank's retaliation and her secrets, her chance to spend her life with Michael might have ended before it began.

She fiddled with her key chain and tried not to cry. "Go back to Leif and please give him our love. If you have a chance later, we'd like an update. Day or night." She slumped against the seat. *Please, please forgive me for everything that's happened.*

"I should know something later this morning. Bye." Click.

Liana bit her bottom lip. She'd been through

heartache before, but this was different. She'd never loved a man like she loved Michael. Somehow, she'd have to survive. She had to for Brittany's sake.

She struggled to compose herself. Damn Frank Nash for the damage he'd done, and the hurt he'd caused. She turned toward Brittany. "Michael has enough on his hands without worrying about us. We'll go home and wait."

"Did he say Leif is all right?"

She repeated Michael's update. "Michael is rightfully upset."

"I hope he doesn't blame us for what Frank did." Brittany swiped at her own tears and sniffed.

Liana shifted the SUV into gear and her fragile emotions into parent mode. "Leif and Michael won't really blame us. Sometimes when a tragedy happens there's too much pain to go back to the way things were before."

"I hope you're wrong!" Brittany flounced in her seat. "I'm sure Michael's in love with you! How could he hold what Frank did against you?"

"Please, Brittany, don't worry about it. Right now, we need to go home and try to sleep. Your recital's this afternoon."

Brittany sighed and leaned her head against the door.

Liana needed to reach the solitude of her bedroom before she fell apart and cried her heart out.

Chapter Fourteen

He'd been too abrupt.

He couldn't help it. The fear, the angst of Leif's injury, the threat to their home and security, roiled inside him until he wanted to go to the jail and beat up Frank Nash. Again. Luckily, logic overrode his innate need for physical retribution.

He wasn't a Neanderthal. He was a hard-working businessman. A father. Right now his son needed him to stay sane and strong, not get carried away with his tangled emotions. He also had to make things right with Liana. He'd taken his frustrations out on her and she didn't deserve it. She must hate him.

Michael braced his elbows on his thighs and leaned forward to cup his face with his hands. He couldn't think about Liana right now. God, he could have lost his son forever. Leif deserved his full attention.

Over the next few hours, he dozed and woke intermittently to make sure Leif slept. He'd watch his son's chest rise and fall until his eyelids went heavy and he dozed off again.

The nurses were great. They quietly entered the room and moved around to check on Leif's vitals and make him comfortable.

Through the haze of the night Liana's hurt tone played through the back of his mind. She'd been hurt enough and he'd added to it as if she could control

Frank. He'd probably ruined any chances of weathering this storm.

Daylight peeked through the window blinds of Leif's hospital room. His son slept like a log, the beauty of youth allowed him to turn off his fears and relax. Oh, to be young again and have such resilience. He straightened his stiff back and stifled a moan as he pushed out of the orange vinyl chair. The moment his inflamed feet pressed into the rubber soles of his flip-flogs, he flinched. Before he'd drifted off to sleep, he'd picked out the larger shards of glass, but didn't want to make a big deal about his injuries. Now, he'd pay the piper. An old song about likening a relationship to walking on broken glass flashed through his mind.

He hobbled to the window and turned the wand to open the blinds a touch. Purple and gold hues shadowed the Flathead Valley, gently waking the inhabitants before the sun shot its rays over the cold, winter day. Michael released a breath and inflated his cheeks. He hoped if he pushed out all the old air and sucked in the new, his angst would loosen and flee.

Dammit, he couldn't ignore it. He had to do damage control with Liana. She wasn't part of some mid-life crisis. He wouldn't have made love with her if he didn't care for her. A lot.

Did he have what it took to maintain a lasting relationship? Maybe being single for three years with the freedom and flexibility to call his own shots would prevent him from wanting to compromise when he needed to. Marriage was a partnership.

Marriage? Where in the hell had that thought come from?

Wow.

He stared at his sleeping son for another moment before he left the room.

To combine his family with Liana's would mean tons of compromises. Was he ready for the commitment? He checked with the on-duty nurse and asked her to tell Leif he'd gone home to take care of the dogs. He left the hospital and climbed into his frost-covered truck. The drive home was surreal. Life had suddenly taken a sharp left hand turn.

He pulled into the driveway and parked. Even his house seemed different. He fumbled with his keys, his hands shaking. Finally he fit the key to the lock and turned the bolt. He stepped into the foyer and into a wall of frigid air.

In a daze, he moved into the living room and stared at the shattered French door. His stomach clenched. Shards of glass on the carpet; the coffee table overturned, all evidence that last night hadn't been a nightmare, but real. A lunatic broke into his house and tried to kidnap his son.

Lucky shot out of Leif's room, her tail wagging like a windshield wiper, but her expression worried. "I'm so sorry, girl. I should've come home sooner." He squatted and ruffled her fur. "Leif will be fine. You're worried about him, aren't you?" he crooned to the dog, blinking back tears he'd managed to stem once the machines were attached to Leif and his vitals were normal. "When Leif gets home, we'll celebrate. You're a hero, Lucky. You probably saved Leif's life. You were there for him, girl."

Michael forked his fingers through his hair and braced against the pain stabbing his heart. If he had stayed in the house instead of racing out to protect the boat, Frank would have attacked him, not Leif. Urging Lucky to the front door so she wouldn't cut her paws on the glass, he let her outside and watched as she rounded the house and sniffed the trail to the boat dock like a detective on the job. Michael used the broom and dust pan to gather up the large shards of glass. The shop vacuum brought up the small pieces. By the time he turned off the vacuum, Lucky was ready to come in. She darted to Leif's room to check on her pups.

Michael stared at his son's door. He'd putt off entering the room where things could have turned out so different. Frank could have hit Leif harder and Michael would be facing indescribable grief.

"For God's sake, quit making things worse than they are," Michael chastised himself and strode to the bedroom door. Everything was just as Leif left it the night before, including the signs of a struggle. The overturned lamp and nightstand chilled him to the bone.

Leif would recover and, according to all the early test results, wouldn't have physical repercussions from the attack. No physical issues, but he'd never be the same again. A well balanced kid, he'd still be well balanced, but life wouldn't look the same. He'd view the world differently.

Michael leaned against the doorjamb and gazed over Leif's room. The rumpled bed, the box of squealing, wiggling puppies vying for breakfast as Lucky settled into her box. Clothes strung here and there. A Nerf basketball hoop mounted on the closet door.

Michael stumbled to the bed and sank to the edge. He started to swipe at the tears, but gave up and into his need to let go of the deep fear, the panic of almost losing his son. He'd done everything he could to protect Leif. His instinct to run outside and save the boat had nothing to do with neglect. He'd hoped to stop the predator before he entered the house.

Weary from all the emotions of the past few hours, he stood and left Leif's room. He had to face the day. The doors needed to be repaired, the fire in the furnace built up, and he had to return to the hospital.

He found a sheet of plywood in the garage and a roll of plastic. Right now, he'd remove the broken door and cover the opening to seal in the heat. Tomorrow, he'd take the door to the glass company for repairs. One step at a time.

Stay busy to keep from losing his mind.

Stirring the coals in the furnace, he added wood and opened the drafts. He wanted the house to be toasty warm before he brought Leif home so he lit the fireplaces in the living room and his bedroom.

By some fool luck, the water pipes hadn't frozen. Luck. Yeah, he'd been granted an abundance of it over the past twenty-four hours, but he'd be lying if he really attributed everything to luck. He was blessed, and he'd better get his act together and relieve Liana from the hell she had to be going through.

Over a mug of steaming coffee, he settled into a kitchen chair with a pair of tweezers and a bottle of hydrogen peroxide. He couldn't take care of anyone if his feet became infected.

Leif, Brittany and Liana; they all needed him.

Michael swabbed his feet with peroxide and flinched when the bubbling disinfectant stung. When all visual glass was removed, he rubbed his hand over his jaw. The five o'clock shadow had turned into a five in the morning beard. He needed to spruce up before he returned to the hospital.

After he stoked all the fires and fed Lucky, he stripped and stepped into his oversized slate tiled shower. The steaming spray washed over him and soothed his aching muscles and tender feet. He wished the water could wash away the huge issues filling his life.

Shaved and dressed, he slipped a pair of soft wool socks over his sore feet and put on a pair of running shoes. No cowboy boots today.

Pouring a second cup of coffee, Michael gripped his mug and wandered into the living room. He stopped in front of the floor to ceiling windows overlooking the lake and his boat dock. Yeah, one more thing to check out. Leif had been first in his mind all night, but with Leif safe at the hospital, Michael could secure all signs of Frank's attack before Leif came home.

He pulled on a jacket, and ambled through the heavily frosted grass to the dock. At least this time he had shoes on. The flare burns were minimal and could be fixed with a little fiberglass patch. Michael gripped the edge of the boat and panted with anxiety. Puffs of vapor formed in the cold air.

"My God, I almost lost him." Emotion overflowed and sent him to his knees. He rested his forehead on the edge of the boat and let the tears and anguish escape the knot in his chest.

The fire, the attack on Leif. It'd all been a hellish scene he never wanted to repeat. He blew out a deep breath and forced himself to mentally tabulate everything he should take care of before Leif came home. Work would keep him sane.

First thing on the list was to call Trinity. She'd have his hide if he didn't fill her in. Should he call Meredith? Yeah, it wouldn't be fair to leave her out. Despite her poor judgment, Meredith was the mother of his children and should be kept in the loop. "Oh, and Liana. I have to talk to her."

Last night when she'd called to check on Leif, her voice had been sad and filled with the same anguish torturing him. She already loved Leif. What had driven him to snap at her? Her presence could have given him strength instead of going it alone.

How had she stood ten years with Frank Nash? She'd unselfishly stayed in an unhappy marriage to provide her daughter with two parents and a secure home. What must Brittany think of Frank, and now of Michael for pushing them away?

Liana's confession about the guy she'd almost slept with had flummoxed him. Her near mistake didn't compare with Meredith's escapades, but he'd flashed back to the hurt of finding out his wife had had numerous affairs while he worked to provide for his family.

Now what? Should he check on Leif, then go to Liana's? Brittany's ballet recital was tonight. He'd promised he and Leif would attend. Of course they'd understand when they didn't show up. His first concern had to be taking care of his son.

****

When Michael entered Leif's hospital room, his son was sitting up in bed with a clean white bandage around his head, and a half-eaten plate of eggs and bacon on his tray.

"You look much better."

"I am," Leif said between bites. He slathered strawberry jam over his toast. "Hey, the food's not bad here, but can I go home?"

Michael cocked his head toward the door. "I met your doctor at the nurse's station. He said he'll release you if you promise to take it easy. He wants to see you in a week. Sooner, if you get dizzy or nauseous."

"I can't wait to wear my own clothes and see Lucky. How are she and the pups doing?"

"They're fine. Lucky will be happy to see you too."

The sparkle in his son's eyes lifted a weight from his heart.

Michael left the room to complete the discharge paperwork while Leif finished his breakfast. When Michael returned, a male nurse was trying to help Leif dress, but Leif insisted he could dress himself.

The sight of his son's rally after such a serious injury humbled him with deep gratitude. Two attributes he'd thought he already had, but didn't compare with the blessing of being given another chance to enjoy Leif's last two years at home, then college and whatever his future held. He rubbed his chest and took a deep breath. He refused to shed more tears. It all could have ended so differently. It made him realize he couldn't control every aspect of life.

No more than Liana could.

He'd been an arrogant ass to lecture her about the long hours at work, how much time Brittany spent home alone or at Shari's. She'd had her reasons and he shouldn't have judged her. Liana couldn't be a better mother or more responsible person. She'd been hard enough on herself and he'd piled on the guilt when he left her that night.

Man, he owed her an apology—more than one—and he owed her the truth about his feelings.

"Dad?"

"Yeah, son, I'm here. Ready to go home?"

****

A brief, but well-loved chapter in her life had closed.

Liana took one more look at her reflection. To keep Brittany from moping all day, she'd taken her shopping for a new outfit to wear after the recital tonight.

At Brittany's urging, she'd also bought a new outfit for herself. Slipping into the deep chocolate brown calf-length wool skirt, she topped it with an antique gold cashmere sweater over a matching silk camisole. She smoothed her hands over the form-fitting outfit before she pulled on the pièce de résistance: a pair of dark brown, tooled leather boots. They were fashionable, but had grip soles so she wouldn't slip and slide on the ice anymore.

She loved her new outfit. Without the sizable monthly alimony payments, she could occasionally relax and buy something for herself. Occasionally. She didn't intend to lose focus and jeopardize her budding design business.

"Mom, you look like someone on a magazine cover!" Brittany stood in the doorway of Liana's room. She looked so grown up and sophisticated, Liana's heart ached with pride.

"Thank you, honey. You look gorgeous. Are you about ready to go?"

"Almost. Is my eye makeup dark enough for the stage lights?"

Liana helped her daughter dramatize her cosmetics

for the performance of The Nutcracker. Because of her grace and talent, Brittany had earned the part of Maria, the lead dancer.

Now, if Liana could shake the melancholy dogging her every step.

She'd wanted Frank to back off. Release her alimony obligation. She hadn't wanted him to turn into a maniac.

She hadn't spoken to Michael since the call from the hospital parking lot. She couldn't blame him for being upset, even disappointed. Several times over the day, she'd wanted to call and check on Leif, but decided to back off and give them space.

It would take a long, long time for her to shake the deep sadness her ex had caused the people she cared about.

Liana dropped Brittany off at the stage door and parked in front of the school. The auditorium milled with parents and friends. She searched the crowd and spotted Richard, Shari and Cash several rows from the stage. Edging around the guests standing in the aisle, she made her way to the seat the Collinses had saved.

Her heart twanged. Brittany had invited Michael and Leif. Of course, they wouldn't come. Leif needed rest, and Michael couldn't leave him alone.

She nibbled at her bottom lip and blinked against the pesky tears. Having the Saxon men in their lives had been so sweet, but too much had happened for Michael and Leif to forgive her.

Shari hugged her. "Damn Frank for doing this to you. The man's mentally disturbed."

"I can't argue with that. I suppose he'll be held and tried in Kalispell since he committed the crime here."

She blew out a big breath. "I just wanted him to drop the alimony and be honest with Brittany."

"I know, sweetie. After the reception tonight, let's sit down with a glass of wine and talk."

The lights flashed from dim to bright, signaling the guests to be seated.

Liana settled in her chair. "Sounds good. I need a diversion."

The lights dimmed and the curtains parted. The crowd erupted into applause as Brittany toed her way onto the stage.

Liana's heart filled and overflowed with pride for her daughter. She patted her cheeks to stem the dratted tears she couldn't seem to stop. Frank really blew it. He could have been here watching the beautiful young lady he'd helped raise instead of sitting in the county jail.

Liana pushed Frank from her mind and allowed herself to be swept up in the story. The trials of the past days seemed to bring a new maturity to Brittany and her dance. Her face was delicate and wan, her brown eyes huge.

The troupe glided onto either side of the stage and the curtains closed to signal intermission. The lights went up. Liana sniffed.

"Wow, she's really good." Cash stood and stretched. "I planned to snooze through the performance, but Brittany was amazing."

Richard slapped his son on the back. "Never admit you sleep when you're at the ballet. The ladies don't like it."

"Cash, what about your sister? Didn't Meagan look good too?" Shari tugged her son's ear.

"Yeah, she's great."

Shari and Liana looked at each other and chuckled. Liana's heart lightened a shade. She glanced at the other audience members. By now some of them might have heard about Frank's antics. Her business and standing in the community could be hurt, but she had no desire to uproot Brittany again. They'd weather the storm.

The audience milled toward the refreshment bar for the pastries and drinks the drama club had provided.

Shari looped her arm through Liana's. "Let's go check out the goodies."

"I thought we were eating dessert at your house." Liana nudged her friend.

"We are, but we can nibble in the meantime. It's the holidays!"

Halfway through the crowd, Liana's eyes met deep amber ones and her heart fluttered. "Michael." His name escaped her lips on a sigh.

"I'm surprised he made it! Did you know?" Shari whispered close to Liana's ear.

"Brittany invited them last night before they left our house. After what happened, I thought he'd be home with Leif."

"Well, it looks like Leif's with him."

Leif stepped out of the crowd and stood next to his dad, a crocheted beanie cap on his head. He looked handsome in his dress clothes, but his face was pale and drawn.

Michael looked devastatingly handsome in a stark white dress shirt, and black western cut pants that fit him like a glove.

Yearning plowed through her and stole her breath. She moved toward him as if he reeled her in. A couple feet away, she breathed in his spicy scent.

"Liana."

His voice made her throat close and her eyes smart. She fought the urge to run away. She had to be a big girl and face the verdict.

"Michael."

His probing gaze made her tremble. Did he wonder what he'd ever seen in her? Unable to deal with more pain and loss, she turned to his son. "Leif, it's so good to see you. Should you be out already? How's your head feeling?"

Leif shrugged then narrowed his eye in a grimace. "Yikes, guess I shouldn't do that for a while." His full lips turned up in a grin. "I'm fine, Liana. Wow, Brittany looks awesome up there! So does Meagan."

"That's what Cash just said." Shari laid her hand on Leif's shoulder. "I'm glad to see you up and around, Leif. We've all been so worried about you."

Leif smirked. "I wanted to watch Brittany dance so I could do a review."

The adults chuckled.

"I'm sure she'll appreciate it." Liana wanted to cry over what a great little family she and Michael could have shared.

She glanced at him, wishing they didn't have to converse as if they were casual friends instead of former lovers. "If Leif feels well enough, you should hang around after the performance and say hello to Brittany. It'd mean a lot to her."

"I'd like that." Michael's eyes didn't waver for an instant. The gold-flecked amber irises reminded Liana of the times they'd been close. Very close.

"Better than that." Shari looped her arm around

Liana's waist. "You should come to my house after the recital. We're having a little reception for the girls. Shouldn't they, Li?"

"Of course, if Leif's up to it."

Leif smiled at Shari. "I'd like to go. Dad, how about you?"

"We'll see. I don't want you to get too tired."

"I won't."

The lights flickered.

"Oops, guess we won't check out the refreshments."

Shari's voice held a bubbly note that didn't fool Liana. She'd dragged her through the crowd because she'd seen Michael and Leif and wanted to make sure Liana did too.

The twinge of a headache tightened Liana's left eye. She halfheartedly smiled at the Saxons. "See you later?"

"Yeah, see you later."

Michael couldn't take his eyes off Liana's softly swaying backside as she walked down the aisle with Shari. She'd been shopping. Somehow through the crisis she'd shopped for winter boots and succeeded in looking fashionable, warm and sexy.

"If you let her go, Dad, you're not as intelligent as I always thought you were."

Michael flinched and turned on his boot heels to stare at his son. "What? What's that supposed to mean?"

"Just what I said, but we'll have to talk later. Come on, let's find our seats before they turn off the lights."

Michael followed his son toward the back of the auditorium. He'd ached to see Liana again and now the ache went deeper. This thing with Frank and how Michael had reacted, had driven a wedge between them, an awkwardness. He'd thought about her and the situation so many times during the day he'd nearly driven himself crazy.

The rest of the performance was entertaining and impressive. Both Brittany and Meagan danced like professionals. Of course, Brittany excelled in Michael's opinion. He smiled. Okay, he was prejudice. Brittany had become like another daughter in a very short time.

He wanted her to be his daughter, which meant making things right with her mother. A heightened awareness filled him when he and Leif left the auditorium after they congratulated Brittany, and drove to the Collins's. Liana would be there. Tonight could determine how their story ended.

Shari met them at the door, graciously took their coats, and motioned them into the living room. A crowd filled the large house.

Taller than many of the other guests, Michael scanned the room until his gaze met Richard's, who lifted his chin and made his way toward them. "Hey, glad you made it." Richard shook Michael's hand and clamped his other hand on Leif's shoulder. "Up for some cookies or cake?"

"I think I can handle some." Leif grinned and followed Richard to the dining room.

Shari had gone all out on a mouthwatering spread. Michael beelined to the big coffeepot. He could use a tall mug of caffeine to keep him going for another hour or so. His bed beckoned him, but he needed to stay and make Brittany happy. Who was he kidding? Brittany wasn't the only person on his mind. He needed to talk to Liana, touch her, breath in her floral scent.

On the other hand, he'd been up for the better part of forty-eight hours and suffered from an extreme case of brain fog. Tonight might not be the logical time to decide his future. He edged through the milling guests, smiling and nodding like he hadn't just lived through the most hellish time of his life. His breakup and divorce with Meredith didn't compare with the emotions he'd experienced with his son sprawled unconscious on the floor. Not even when Meredith called from Oklahoma City to announce Leif had been arrested for minor possession of a controlled substance.

Teenage rebellion he could deal with, but not the loss of one of his children.

"How are you holding up?"

Liana's voice drifted through his thoughts.

He glanced down. She'd slipped to his side without his notice. "Like a zombie. Have a cup of coffee with me?"

"Sounds like a good idea." Her lips quivered with a small smile. Her eyes were moist, and strained. She'd been crying and probably hadn't gotten any more sleep than he had.

His protective instincts spurred him to place his hand on her back and guide her to the coffee urn. He didn't care about the looks of interest sent their way, or the inevitable gossip to follow. The incident had been in the morning paper and he would continue to follow Frank's trial.

He didn't care about complications. He loved her.

The truth hit him like an arrow through the heart. He loved Liana Campbell enough to face down any kind of scandal. He'd be at her side during whatever happened with Frank—if she let him.

"Sugar?"

Michael blinked. "What?"

"Would you like some sugar?" Liana held up the sugar bowl and a silver spoon.

Heat flared through his exhausted body and refueled his mind. "I'd love some."

Her checks flushed and her breasts lifted against the curve hugging gold sweater. The need to kiss her— right here, right now—nearly drove him over the edge of propriety.

"Think we could go for a drive?"

Her eyes widened. "Now?"

"Yeah. Now."

"This is Brittany's party as well as Meagan's. Not to mention, Leif's probably tired."

Michael added a heaping spoonful of sugar to his coffee. "You're right. I'm not thinking straight."

Liana inched closer and her scent filled his head like an aphrodisiac. "I want to be alone with you too." Her voice turned soft, intimate.

Parts of him woke up with full force, but not to just have her with him tonight, but every night for the rest of their lives. "There's something I have to tell you."

"I hope it's not all talk."

He stifled a groan. "Don't do that to me in a crowd, Campbell." He fought the urge to sweep her into his arms and carry her out the door like in an old John Wayne movie. "I want more than talk, sweetheart, but as you pointed out, tonight is about the kids. We're committed to stay with the kids."

"Yes, the kids are exhausted. We can't leave Leif alone after the trauma he's been though, and Brittany's been jumpy and emotional all day."

He sipped the hot, fragrant coffee and willed the caffeine to travel straight to his blood stream. "Okay...I don't think I can wait until tomorrow to say what I need to say."

"Me either," she whispered.

His body twanged like a guitar string. He wanted to make love to Liana and sleep in her arms. Together, they'd heal from the nightmare her ex had caused. They'd face everything together. The hours of mental anguish, and his son's blunt remark about his lack of intelligence if he let Liana go, had cleared things up for him. He couldn't pass up the love of his life.

He wrapped his fingers around the thick white mug and edged closer to her. "Talk to me, because I can't go through another night without knowing we'll make it through this." He brushed his lips over her hair. "At the very least."

"Shari, great party."

Liana's greeting penetrated his daze. Michael blinked, stepped away from her and smiled at their hostess. She smiled back, but one dark brow rose in a look her kids probably dreaded.

"Yeah, well, I didn't come over here for compliments. I think you should let Brittany stay with Meagan tonight so you can go to Michael's and put Leif to bed. The kid's weaving on his feet with exhaustion, and his dad's about ready to jump your bones. In my dining room."

Michael's cheeks heated. "You're very perceptive."

"Very observant, anyway. So, what do you think? When the guests leave, I can run Brittany home for her overnight bag. We'll feed Oscar, unless you want to. Honestly, apart from giving you two some time alone,"—she cupped her hand around her mouth—"a change of scene could be good for Brittany. Meagan's been very upset and would love it if Brittany stayed. Besides,"—Shari laid her hand on Liana's arm— "Brittany loves Michael. You two are the center of her stability now. Having you together will help her through the days to come."

Michael resisted the strong urge to hug Shari. He glanced at Liana, something he couldn't get enough of. "What do you think? Are you all right with going to my house?"

Her shoulders rose and fell on a sigh. "Thank you, Shari. You're always there for me, old friend."

"Hey, enough of the old stuff. It's my pleasure to help. Think you can hang out for a while? Brittany and Meagan asked if they could formally thank everyone for coming."

"Yes, of course we'll stay." Liana swiped at a tear and hugged Shari.

Michael's heart overflowed with a powerful emotion he wasn't sure he'd ever experienced. He was forty years old and his life had just become complete.

****

While Liana went home to pack Brittany's overnight bag, feed Oscar and grab her own essentials, Michael drove Leif home and settled him into bed. His son might be sixteen, but he'd been through a life-altering trauma and needed to be pampered.

"Don't worry about me, Dad. I'm just tired. I'm glad you and Liana are trying to move past the Frank nightmare. I like her. A lot."

Michael squeezed Leif's shoulder and backed out of the bedroom. It felt damn good to have his son home and on the mend.

He built up the fire in the stone fireplace, rolled back on his heels and flinched when he hit a sore spot on his still tender feet.

He hoped Liana liked his house. He loved every square foot of rustic charm, but what would Liana think of all the wood and stone? Being a designer, she might prefer her house. Did he want to change his entire life style in order to make their relationship work?

Lucky meandered out of Leif's room and stared up at him. Her tongue hung out one side of her mouth.

"Are those pups wearing you out?" Before they knew it, the pups would be running around and needing homes.

The doorbell rang. Lucky softly ruffed.

"It's okay, girl. It's your old friend, Liana." Michael's sore feet were beginning to talk to him, but he hurried to the door. He swung it open and feasted his eyes on the woman who had occupied a good share of his thoughts and actions over the past few months. "Come in." He swept his arm out, and bowed over it. "Welcome to the Saxon home."

Liana stepped into the slate foyer a smile brightening her tired eyes. "Lucky! It's so good to see you, girl. How are the kids?"

"The kids are asleep in Leif's room."

Liana hugged Lucky, straightened and gazed around the dining room and through the arched doorway into the kitchen. "I never thought I'd get here."

"Me either." He shifted from one foot to the other.

What did she think? Acting like Lucky, he followed her into the living room. She stopped in front of the fire and held her hands toward the warmth. "It's beautiful, Michael." She looked over one shoulder and the other, her gaze held on the plywood over the broken door. She let out a huge sigh, visibly shook off the melancholy and smiled at him. "Of course I didn't expect anything less. I've seen your work. I knew your house would be special."

"You know all about me, do you?" Relieved she liked his house and didn't mention the evidence of Frank's break in, Michael moved to her side and brushed his fingers over her hair. His body went rock hard, but this time he let it. They were alone in his house. Leif was asleep and not about to interrupt them.

Michael had never brought a woman home, didn't think it was proper with a teenage boy in residence, but Liana was different. She wasn't a one-night stand. She was the woman he wanted to spend the rest of his life with.

Liana moved closer. Michael's amber eyes flashed brown and gold in the firelight and drew her toward him.

When Shari offered the solution for them to get together tonight, she'd nearly jumped up and down and cheered, but they weren't in the clear yet. Big issues still stood in their way.

"The past twenty-four hours have been terrible." She risked rejection and wrapped her arms around his waist. She leaned back to stare into his beautiful eyes. "Besides the horrendous worry about Leif and Brittany, I couldn't imagine another night spent wondering what you thought of me, and if you'd ever want to be with me again."

He ran his palms up and down her back, cupped her bottom and pulled her against him. "I've gone through the same hell, Liana. You and I no sooner had issues to work through when Frank appeared and hurt Leif. Sometime today, I realized I can't blame you for Frank's actions."

"I'm relieved to hear that because I have no control over Frank. At the same time, he would never have done—what he did—if you weren't connected with me. This morning, Brittany confessed she told Frank about you. She really likes you and thought Frank would understand. She had no idea how deep his possessiveness and bitterness ran."

"Of course she didn't. Brittany and I've clicked since day one. I don't hold either of you responsible for Frank's vengeance. Not anymore. I just thank God Leif's okay."

"Me too, Michael. He's such a good boy."

Michael chuckled. "Don't let him hear you say that. He's sure he's a man. I can't wait for you to meet Trinity. She and her brother call each other often, so she knows all about you and Brittany."

"Oh really?" She looped her arms around the back of his neck and pulled his mouth down to hers. "We'd better be quiet so we don't give them something more to talk about."

"I think we've said enough. The rest can wait until later. Right now I need you in my arms." He rubbed his hard ridge against her softness and feathered kisses up and down the side of her neck.

She moaned and her mind whirled with pent up passion. She forked her fingers through his hair.

"Where's your room?"

In answer to her question, Michael swept her into his arms and carried her through an arched doorway to a hall with two doors. "Is Leif's room next to yours?"

"One is to my office and this,"—he shifted her weight while he leaned down and opened the door to the right—"is my bedroom." He flipped a switch. Several lamps sent a warm golden glow over the room.

"Michael, it's beautiful." Liana cranked her head to take in the private space of the man she loved. The king-sized bed dominated one end of the large room with a dark, carved chestnut headboard and footboard, and a gold and brown paisley bedspread. The night stands were massive, the lamps, burnished bronze.

On the opposite wall, a crackling fire in the stone fireplace promised many cozy nights. Two club chairs flanked the hearth. He gently let her slide down his body and her feet sank into the thick wool area rug on the plank floor.

She wandered to the French doors. "I can't wait to see the view."

He slipped his arms around her middle. "Not too masculine for you?"

"Not at all. I love the Mediterranean flair."

Michael chuckled. "You can't resist studying the decor." He laved her ear with his tongue and pulled her bottom against his hardness.

Liana moaned and wiggled against him. "Sorry, it's second nature to check out a new room." She turned in his arms. "You're what I really want to study tonight."

Being with Michael was so different from being with Jack or Frank. Foremost, she was crazy in love with him. She was also more mature and knew what she wanted. They came together on a much deeper level than she'd ever imagined possible. Michael was an amazing person, inside and out.

She fumbled with the button on his slacks. "You're not making this easy," she murmured against his lips, thrilled when his mouth tilted into a smile.

"Why's that?"

"Part of you is making itself so known it's hard to get your pants off."

"Let me help." He reached between them and pushed his slacks over his hips, "Damn, my boots. Okay, let's get undressed so we can do what we want."

Liana's heart fluttered with love and excitement. She gazed at him the entire time they undressed, and marveled at his broad shoulders and muscled chest. The night they'd shared in her bedroom had been the first and hurried. She hadn't taken the time to study him in all his glory.

She laid her clothing over the back of a club chair; the new boots placed side by side. She was excited and nervous. They'd made love before, but this time was different. This time, they'd survived a near tragedy.

Turning toward the bed, her breath caught.

Wedged on one elbow, Michael lay at an angle and the lamplight glistened off his bronzed skin. She slowly walked toward him, and allowed her eyes to devour his handsome face and sculptured body. He might be forty, but he looked far from middle-aged.

She savored every second. She'd waited too long for the night of her dreams to hurry through it. Bracing one knee on the edge of the bed, Liana crawled onto the high mattress and inched toward him on hands and knees, loving the way his hot amber eyes fixated on her bare breasts.

He cupped her ribcage and pulled her on top of him. Heated skin to heated skin, they came together. Every external thought and concern vanished with the feel and scent of this ruggedly handsome, and oh, so masculine man.

His hands and lips were everywhere and stirred every nerve ending to new brilliance. Liana straddled him.

"Wait, baby. This time I'm using a condom." He reached toward the nightstand and picked up a gold packet. "You want to do it?"

The fire in his eyes sent goosebumps over Liana's body. She opened the packet and with Michael's guidance rolled it over his hard length.

"I—" She'd started to voice her concerns, but stopped.

"What, baby?"

Why mention that it'd be another few weeks before she'd know if their first time had produced a child? "Nothing. We can talk later. Right now, I just want to feel."

She braced her hands on either side of his broad shoulders and slid her hot, wet body over his. She rode him until he rolled her onto her back and pushed them into ecstasy.

Sometime later, bright moonlight woke Liana. She stretched against Michael's warm and very naked body and sprinkled his chest and neck with kisses. "Am I dreaming?" he murmured, his voice rough with sleep and lovemaking.

Liana nuzzled his throat. "If this is a dream, I hope to never wake."

Michael tilted her chin with his index finger, and gazed into her eyes. "Making love to you is as natural as breathing. I want to spend the rest of my life with you, Liana. I can't think about a future without you."

Liana trailed her fingers down his chest and circled his belly button before she continued the journey. She'd wanted to have this conversation, but after all that had happened, it scared her.

"I can't think when you do that," Michael mumbled.

"Maybe I don't want to think." She moved her hand from her point of interest and snuggled into the covers.

"I'm proposing to you, Liana. I won't live together without marriage. I realize,"—he tapped the tip of her nose—"there are things we haven't talked about. Important things."

"You know more about me than I've ever exposed to anyone."

Damn, why did reality have to rear its sometimes-ugly head? They'd been wrapped in a cocoon of lovemaking, the moonlight streaming through the windows.

Why did they have to get serious tonight?

"The future and how we blend our lives. Where we live, if you continue to work as much as you do. Basic stuff."

Liana rolled to her back, sat up and wrapped her arms around her knees. She stared across the room at the blue flame in the fireplace. "I have to support my daughter, Michael. I won't enter into a relationship to be taken care of. We've had this conversation. I worked long hours to ensure a secure future for Brittany despite the alimony payments. Now that's changed, but I still have to work. Not as much on a regular basis, but there will be times when I'll be home late for dinner, or have to work on the weekend."

Michael pushed off the pillow and sat beside her. "Hey, I didn't mean to sound like I want you to change who you are. I love who you are, but I want to spend more time with you. We'll be a team, blend our lives, our children, our homes. I don't care if I sleep in your bed or you sleep in mine, we'll work that all out."

Liana angled to face him. "It sounds like heaven to me, Michael, but can you handle it if I have to juggle my real estate clients until my design business takes off?"

"How about if I stretch my plans out next to your plans?" He ran his thumb over her lips, and leaned forward to claim her mouth with his. "How about we both accept we're individuals and won't always be thrilled with each other, but we'll still love each other and make compromises?"

She smiled against his lips. "You paint a very tempting picture." She trailed her fingertips down his chest and over his thigh, lightly scoring him with her nails.

"Damn, lady, you make it hard to focus. Are we agreed we can work out whatever comes our way to keep our marriage solvent? Neither of us wants our kids hurt over another broken family."

"I agree wholeheartedly." Liana changed her mind about not talking right now. She loved to sit in the middle of the tousled bed with a naked Michael.

The firelight cast a soft glow over the room while they discussed the things that made them tick. She could talk to Michael and never fear he'd be angry or walk away.

"I want you to work on your design business and enjoy life. We're a team, right?"

She couldn't move. If she did, the image he'd just drawn might dissolve into a million shimmering lights.

"Liana? Are you listening?"

She drew in a deep breath and blinked against tears of joy. "Yes, I'm listening. You've described the life I've always wanted. With you, I think it just might be possible." She met his gaze.

"I'm glad." His eyes went dark. "So, does that mean you'll marry me?"

Liana trailed her fingers back up his thigh, hesitating when she reached his belly. "Of course I want to marry you. More than anything."

Michael gently pressed her to the pillows and covered her with his strong body. "Good. Because I can't think straight with you in my bed. We'll finish the rest of the discussion later."

Liana giggled and happiness bubbled through her with an effervescence she'd never imagined. She was confident they'd work out their differences because they'd both experienced bad relationships and recognized the real thing.

"Yes, we'll talk later about how lucky we are." She nuzzled his throat. Her nerve endings tingled with his every touch.

"Baby, I'm convinced we're way more than lucky. Providence brought us together that day and love and dedication will keep us together."

"Providence and Lucky the stray dog, you mean." Liana smiled. "As for dedication? Never doubt how much I love you. I'm dedicated to spending at least the next fifty years with you."

There'd never be a question in her mind...she'd been waiting for Michael for too long to ever let him go.

A word about the author...

A North Idaho native, Tesa Devlyn loves exploring the world, but has a soft spot for the Northwest United States. Hewn by a rich history of determined settlers, Devlyn has found the modern Northwest to be filled with giving, caring, and inspiring people.

Please visit Tesa's facebook page at:
facebook/tesa.devlyn1